CARLA KELLY'S

Christmas COLLECTION

CARLA KELLY'S

Christmas COLLECTION

CARLA KELLY

SWEETWATER BOOKS
AN IMPRINT OF CEDAR FORT, INC.
SPRINGVILLE, UTAH

ISBN 13: 978-1-4621-1227-2

Published by Sweetwater Books, an imprint of Cedar Fort, Inc.
2373 W. 700 S., Springville, UT 84663
Distributed by Cedar Fort, Inc., www.cedarfort.com
Originally published by Signet-Penguin/Putnam in four anthologies.

LIBRARY OF CONGRESS CATALOGING-IN-PUBLICATION DATA

Kelly, Carla.
  Carla Kelly's Christmas collection : four stories filled with romance and Christmas cheer / by Carla Kelly.
    pages cm
  ISBN 978-1-4621-1227-2 (mass market : acid-free paper)
  1. Christmas stories. 2. Regency fiction. 3. Love stories. I. Title.
PS3561.E3928C37 2013
813'.54--dc23

                              2013017815

Cover design by Angela D. Olsen
Cover design © 2013 by Lyle Mortimer
Edited and typeset by Melissa J. Caldwell

Printed in the United States of America

10 9 8 7 6 5 4 3 2 1

ONTENTS

THE CHRISTMAS ORNAMENT

*I*t happened over tea in October 1815, in London, with an old friend who required few conversational preliminaries beyond the observation that Napoleon was at long last taking a sea voyage to St. Helena, and that the weather was unusually pleasant for fall.

"Excellent tart, by the way, Lord Waverly!" Sir Waldo Hannaford said, eyeing the table again. "Prune centers?"

"Yes, indeed, Sir Waldo," the older man replied. "Did ye ever think a purgative could be so tasty?"

Sir Waldo didn't, of course. There was a time when he would have eyed the tarts with a fair amount of suspicion. But he was older now and willing to indulge in something that might smooth out the effect of too much dinner last night at his daughter Louisa's house. He ate another and then settled himself before the fire, sharing the footstool with his older neighbor from Woodcote, Lord Waverly of Enderfield.

"Gilbert, I have something to ask you," he began after a long moment's thought.

"Ask away, Waldo. The only thing I have ever held back from you is the location of my favorite trout stream in Scotland." It was a joke of long standing between the two, and they both chuckled and settled back into the comfort they were born to.

"Gilbert, I have a daughter," Sir Waldo announced at last.

"I believe you have three," the marquis replied, a smile playing on his lips.

"Indeed, I have. One is married and lives here in London, as you well know, and the other followed her lord to Inverness, where, incidentally, he has an excellent trout stream on his estate."

Lord Waverly clapped his hands and then rested them on his comfortable expanse of waistcoat. "Good for you! And there is little Olivia, if I am not mistaken."

"Indeed there is, my friend, except that little Olivia grew up."

Lord Waverly looked at him over his spectacles, his eyes bright. "Did she do that too? Children have that knack, haven't they?"

Sir Waldo nodded, pleased at his friend's good nature. "She is eighteen this month, and preparing for a come-out."

"Heaven help us! Eighteen! I remember when Jemmy aided and abetted in pulling out two of her baby teeth. Eighteen, you say? A come-out?"

"That is the plan, except that Lady Hannaford and I are not so certain that a come-out is quite the thing for Olivia." He leaned forward to explain himself better. "Martha is determined that Olivia should marry within the district because she cannot bear to see her last chick fly from the nest." He looked down at his hands, wondering how to say this. "I am not so certain that Olivia would be happy with what she would find here on the Marriage Mart, anyway."

"Picky?'" Lord Waverly asked.

"No. Rather too intelligent for her own good," Sir Waldo stated, crossing his fingers that such an admission would not lower him in his neighbor's esteem. He wasn't sure.

Lord Waverly frowned and contemplated the sweets again. "I have one of those," he said.

"A prune tart?" Sir Waldo asked, following the direction of his host's gaze.

"No, no! A son too smart for his own good." He scowled at the dessert tray and motioned for the footman to remove it. "You cannot guess what he is studying now."

Sir Waldo couldn't. He had endured a year's incarceration at Magdalen College until his father was kind enough to die and provide a ready-made excuse to return home to run the estate. He had never found scholarship to his taste. "No, I cannot imagine," he said.

"He watches people move!"

"No!"

"Yes! He sketches all their motions and tries to figure out ways for them to do their tasks more efficiently." Lord Waverly made a face and moved closer. "He even attends autopsies here at London Hospital to study muscles."

"No!"

"The double firsts were bad enough, but Jemmy knows so much now that I have a hard time talking to him. He is done at All Souls, and he actually helps students who write down every pearl of wisdom that issues from his overheated mind! I call it ungentlemanly, and so I tell him, but he just laughs . . ." he lowered his voice, ". . . and ruffles my hair. They all take liberties," he concluded.

A gloomy silence settled over the sitting room; a log dropped in the fireplace. "Is he attached to a female?" Sir Waldo asked, his voice more tentative, considering his friend's obvious irritation.

"Goodness, no! He is twenty-eight, and I despair—positively despair—of grandchildren." This was obviously a sore topic with Lord Waverly, because it propelled him out of his chair to pace the room. "Since he has a fortune in his own right from his dear mama, I cannot compel him to find a wife by threatening to hang onto his quarterly allowance."

He stopped in front of Sir Waldo, his hands out, the picture of frustration. "And even if he had only a small stipend, he is so frugal he would make do all year and then probably invest the residue!" He put down his hands. "I'll wager that half our friends would wish for problems like this from the fruit of their loins," he sighed. "Truth to tell, there is a sweetness to his nature that always quells me when I think I will pick a fight with him. So would he be your perfect son-in-law?" Lord Waverly sat down heavily in his chair and stared into the fire.

"I believe he would be." Sir Waldo pulled his chair closer to his old friend. "I want someone who will be kind to Olivia, keep her in the vicinity, and not mind if she reads books."

"That would be James," Lord Waverly agreed. "Such a union might even produce grandchildren eventually." He was silent a moment, staring into the fire, and then looked at his old friend. "He is also mortally shy. How do you propose to bring this about?"

"I'm going to ask him," Sir Waldo said. "You know I am not a fancy speaker. I'll put it to him straight out."

"You're going to propose to my son?" Lord Waverly could not help smiling.

"Hmm. I suppose I am," Sir Waldo agreed, struck by the thought. He picked up his glass. "What would you say to an engagement by Christmas?" Without a word, his friend picked up his own glass, and they drank together.

It was one thing to laugh about a proposal with an old friend, Sir Waldo discovered, but quite another to actually put the suggestion into motion. Even the harvest scenery between London and Oxford failed to rouse his interest as he contemplated the next step. *My older daughters would call me the rankest meddler*, he thought as he stared out the window. *They would point out how well they did on the Marriage Mart and assure me and their mama that Olivia would find a man on her own.*

But will she? he thought, far from the first time. Even the vicar, who was not given to either reflection or observation, noted once that Olivia "looks at me as though I don't quite measure up." *I should never had indulged her whim for scholarship*, Sir Waldo told himself, again not for the first time. *Who would have known she would outshine everyone in the family, with the possible exception of her oldest brother, Charles? She is too smart for her own good. And probably at the mercy of fortune-hunters, considering her uncritical disposition. That causes me worry*, he thought.

Thank goodness that at least she was not difficult to look at, although she was no beauty, he knew. Still, even there, Olivia was a true original. She had the correct posture and loveliness of her mother and sisters, but she was only a dab of a thing. "I hope James Enders has not grown too much since last I saw him," he said to his reflection in the carriage window. "He could be intimidating to a chit like Olivia."

He knew Olivia's hair was hopeless—red like his own, though darker, but with the added defect of curling like paper corkscrews that pop from a magician's box when the lid is removed. It wasn't a matter of taming the wild mop but rather forcing it into submission. *Olivia does not help the matter much*, he reminded himself, *not when she drags it all on top of her head into a silly topknot. Well, not precisely silly*, he reconsidered, smiling at the thought. *I call it fetching, in a funny kind of way, even if her mama despairs. She is interesting to look at*, he concluded, *possibly even memorable. But a beauty? Alas, no.*

He sat back, smiling at the thought of his daughter, thinking of her quick step, her outright laugh, and her absorption in books. "It is this way, I should tell you, James Enders," he rehearsed in the carriage as the Oxford spires appeared on the horizon and the land began to slope toward the River Isis. "An estate agent once told me that even the most oddly arranged house can find a buyer. It just takes the one person who happens to be the right buyer."

Even his admitted lack of scholarship never quite prepared Sir Waldo for Oxford. Whatever his inward turmoil, he took the time to admire the loveliness of Magdalen Tower, smile at the architectural eccentricity of the Radcliffe Camera, and listen as Great Tom tolled the hour from The House. *Olivia should be here*, he mused and then chuckled at the impossibility. In his own year at Magdalen, he had passed All Souls numerous times, and never without a sense of awe, knowing that it housed the brightest among them—those who were finished with undergraduate years and embarked upon more study, a thing Sir Waldo could never imagine. He addressed the porter at All Souls and asked him to locate Lord Crandall.

"Ye timed it right, sir," the man informed him. "We are almost at Evensong, so the tutorials are over. I'll have him here directly, if you wish to wait in the foyer."

Sir Waldo did not wish to wait there, not when the quad beckoned with its trees of fall colors. *Christmas is coming*, he thought, looking at the late afternoon sky. *I wonder what my dear wife will tell me that she wants me to surprise her with on Christmas morning? I shall have to ask her soon*, he mused. The day was cool, but the sun had warmed the stones in the quad. Flowers close to the warmth of the wall still bloomed. He heard footsteps and looked up to see Lord Crandall approaching. He was content to stand slightly in the shadow of the corridor and watch the man come closer.

James Enders—Viscount Lord Crandall from one of the family's various honors—wore his black scholar's robe, which the wind picked up and made him seem larger than life for a moment. Sir Waldo smiled to notice that Lord Crandall's hair, dark like his own father's years ago, looked no tidier than Olivia's. *Hair must be a nuisance to the brightest among us*, he could only conclude. Louisa's and Mary's hair was always in place, and not even a loving father could overlook their lack of book-wit.

He had not seen Lord Crandall since the death of his second son, Timothy, seven years before, killed in the retreat from Corunna and buried with all military honor in the Hannaford vault. James, an undergraduate at New College then, had attended the obsequies, his face serious, his eyes troubled. *And I never invited him back*, Sir Waldo thought with a pang. *I was always afraid to see him again, because he was so closely allied with Tim. I may not have been fair to any of us. I wonder, first of all, if I owe him an apology?*

James was even taller than before, with that purposeful stride of all Enders men. *Not a lolly-gagger in the bunch*, Sir Waldo thought as he gazed with something close to fondness on his dead son's friend. *Big hands, big feet, and a wide mouth*, he observed. *The Almighty was generous in all ways to that particular twig on the branch of the human family. None of them handsome, but they do have hair.*

And then he was standing in front of Sir Waldo, his hand extended. Wordlessly, Sir Waldo came forward and found himself caught in a bear hug of an embrace, something he had not anticipated but which he found gratifying in the extreme. And then what would the young man do but take his hand and kiss it? Sir Waldo felt tears start in his eyes. *What is it about you Enders?* he asked himself as he allowed his hand to be kissed and then held. Such a gesture would seem strange indeed from another, but from James it seemed so fitting as to make him grateful he had come here, no matter the outcome.

"You have been too long away, Jemmy," he said simply. "Or I have."

"No matter," the viscount replied. "There's hardly a rip in the world that can't be mended. Come inside with me, and I'll send my man for beer and cheese."

Soon Sir Waldo was seated, warm and comfortable in what must be Lord Crandall's favorite chair—all rump-sprung and soft—while his host sat cross-legged on a shabby rug in front of the fire, toasting cheese.

"I suppose I should serve you something better than cheese and beer," he said, turning the fork with a certain flair that told Sir Waldo volumes about his young friend's dining habits. "I like it, though, and suppose that others should too." He deposited the cheese on a plate next to a slice of toast and handed it to Sir Waldo. "And excuse me, sir, but Madeira is for old men."

Sir Waldo took the plate, relishing the fragrance of the cheese. "This is the perfect antidote to last night's dinner," he said. It was good, he decided, and as plain and ordinary-seeming as the man sitting on the floor.

"You've been dining in London, I'll wager," James said. "Visiting Louisa?"

"Indeed, yes," he said. "I have left Lady Hannaford there." He lowered his voice. "Louisa has just been through a confinement and finds her mother's presence to be a comfort, even if this is our fifth grandchild. A son again, Louisa's third."

"Congratulations, sir," James said. He forked another

wedge of cheese onto Sir Waldo's plate and nodded for his man to pour the beer. He turned his attention to the fireplace again. "And the rest of your family? What do you hear from Charles?"

"Still in Paris, and hoping—along with all Europe, I believe—that this Second Treaty of Paris will put an end to French trouble."

He fell silent then, thinking of his second son, dead at Coruna, who would be alive yet if Napoleon had not ventured where he was not wanted. To his gratification, James seemed to understand his silence. He leaned back and touched Sir Waldo's leg, giving it a little shake. The gesture was as intimate as his earlier kiss, and Sir Waldo's heart was full. *This is the only man for my beloved Olivia,* he told himself.

"I miss Tim," James said simply. "I am twenty-eight, dear sir, and I look in the mirror and see lines and wrinkles that were not there a year ago. But Tim is forever twenty-one and young."

"So he is," Sir Waldo managed to say. He took a deep drink from the mug in his hand. *I cannot fault his ale,* he thought. *He may live like a student still, but he knows his victuals.*

"We have all been too long from each other," James said after a bite of cheese and a quaff of his own. "I did not come around because I did not wish to give you added pain."

Straightforward like all the Enders, eh? Sir Waldo thought. *You say what you think—rather like Olivia—and somehow, it is the right thing.*

"There was a time," he began, but could not continue. They ate in silence then, raising their glasses in tribute to the one who was not there. In his own book of life, Sir Waldo felt a page turn.

"Charles hopes to be home for Christmas," he said, handing his plate to the valet. "Louisa and her family too, if she and the baby are strong enough to travel."

"How nice for you," James said. "I suppose I will go to London and Papa, although it would be nice to see Charles." He waited then, expectant without appearing nosy, for Sir Waldo to explain his visit.

Sir Waldo hesitated. *As right as he is for Olivia, I have no business pronouncing this scheme I hatched,* he thought. *I could merely say something about wanting to see him after all these years, and it would be right enough. I could extend one of those meaningless invitations to visit us for Christmas and leave it at that.* He sighed. *And I could throw Olivia onto the Marriage Mart with all the other hopeful girls and pray that one man in ten thousand will see and understand her special qualities and even love her for them. Or I could speak.* He cleared his throat.

"Jemmy, I have a daughter," he began.

"I believe you have three, sir," James said with a smile. He raised his knees and rested his arms on them, his eyes on Sir Waldo's face. "Has Lady Hannaford ever forgiven Tim and me for assisting in the removal of Olivia's two front teeth?"

Sir Waldo laughed, and his young friend joined him. "Oh, they were due out, lad! The only thing Martha took exception to was when Tim taught Olivia to spit through the vacant space. I believe you were blameless in that."

"Actually, yes," he said, grinning. "How nice to have a pure heart for once."

How good to talk about Tim! "Jemmy, you are the antidote," he said simply. "I don't know when Tim was ever in more trouble. Olivia was six then?"

"I believe she was," James agreed. "Tim and I were

almost eighteen and should have known better. How is Olivia?"

"She is planning for a come-out this spring," Sir Waldo said. "Martha and I have been long away from London, but Louisa is all eagerness to do this thing for her little sister."

"She is eighteen," James said, more a statement than a question.

"Or as near as." Sir Waldo paused again. *I could stop here*, he reflected. *Who is to say that my darling girl will not find the best man on her own?* He frowned. *And who is to say that she will?* "Jemmy, I want to talk to you about Olivia." He glanced over his shoulder at the valet, and James nodded to the man. Sir Waldo heard the door close quietly. "I want to find her a good husband, but I have certain requirements."

Sir Waldo went to sleep that night in his own bed, a happy man, a father with a clear conscience. *I have explained to Lord Crandall my concerns for my dear daughter*, he thought, *warned him that she is often nose-deep in books, mentioned her considerable fortune in passing, not overlooked a single freckle or her unruly hair, and stressed her clear-eyed way of doing things.* He smiled in the darkness. *I have told Jemmy of his own father's wish to see him married and setting up his nursery and reminded him of the duty he owes there, and he took it without a murmur. Possibly I am trafficking on his own tenderness for Tim and the sweetness of Jemmy's own nature. The word* love *never came up, but the word* kindness *did. I am a happy man.*

He composed himself for sleep, thankful to be in his own bed but restless without Martha nearby. *I will leave it to James Enders to fill in the details. He knows his duty to his own family and my personal interests to this little sister of his great good friend.* Sir Waldo smiled into the darkness again. *One can hope for love too. Stranger things have happened.*

It took until the middle of November for James Enders to nerve himself to consider the next step in Sir Waldo's plan. When he should have been concentrating on student recitations and tutorials, his fertile brain was taxing itself with a plan of his own. He had earlier congratulated himself that, while he had agreed to actively consider little Olivia Hannaford—great gadfreys, was she old enough?—as a partner in marriage, the matter was not chipped onto an obelisk somewhere. *It will certainly take a month to visit Enderfield,* he reasoned. *If she takes my fancy, I can pursue the matter.*

How, he had no idea—not one. True, his undergraduate days had not been without occasional visits to discreet women, and there was even one term when he was certain he was besotted with an opera dancer. The occasions passed, as do all the storms of youth. He had gone to Almack's like the proper gentleman he was, bowed and danced, and carried on what light conversation he possessed, which was precious little. *These females do not wish to know of autopsies, and quivering muscles of rats, the beauty of motion, and the people who perform the world's labor,* he decided after one particularly profitless evening several years before. He would not have thought it possible for a living woman's eyes to glaze over while he talked, but after that evening, he did not doubt it again. He never returned to Almack's.

He knew he wanted a wife. Enough of his friends were walking arm in arm with pretty things that bore their name and children. Despite the concentration of hours and hours of rational scholarship, he found himself longing late at night, or at odd moments in the day, to reach for something besides another pillow or a second book off the shelf.

"I want a wife," he declared out loud.

"My lord, we all do," said his student, grinning in spite of himself.

"Forgive that, Walters. I received a wedding announcement from a friend today, and the matter was on my brain," he lied. "Now, where were we?"

"I was describing the function of the female pelvic floor," the student said.

James had the good grace to laugh. "Walters, that accounts for it! Do proceed, and I will remember my manners."

He delayed in suggesting to his father that they return to Enderfield for Christmas, partly out of stubbornness, and partly from a certain delicate shyness that he knew was part of his nature, which irritated him from time to time.

He did bring up the matter during dinner after one of his visits to London University. *I wonder if fricassee of liver was the right choice tonight,* he asked himself. *I have been wrist-deep in a hip reduction all afternoon, and this looks very like that.* He pushed away the plate. "Papa, let us go home for Christmas," he suggested.

The sentence had barely left his mouth when his father declared that it was a capital idea. "I am perfectly at liberty to go as soon as you wish, son," he said. He frowned at his own plate. "Ah, Jemmy, we have been so long away that things are probably shabby there. I wonder . . . do you think . . . do we dare impose on Sir Waldo to loan us Olivia to offer suggestions on refurbishment? If she is anything like her mother, she has some skills along those lines."

It was a wonderful suggestion, and James leaped on it. Only after he was lying in bed that night did he wonder if Sir Waldo had been discussing intimate matters with his own father. It seemed unlikely, considering his father's somewhat formal demeanor and Sir Waldo's easygoing nature. *Merely a coincidence*, he told himself. And that probably accounted for his dream of dissecting fricassee while Sir Waldo smiled benignly from a seat in the surgeon's gallery. At least he did not dream about Olivia; those dreams left him a trifle embarrassed with himself.

There is something about Sir Waldo's suggestion that is doing strange things to me, he thought the next afternoon as he walked from the Camera back to All Souls. *Is the world in a conspiracy?* Only moments ago among the books, he had chanced upon one of his brightest pupils and surprised himself by suggesting that they end the tutorial a week ahead of the Christmas holidays. He knew the lad—so intense, so eager to learn—would object, so he had not been prepared for the swiftness of his acquiescence.

"You don't mind?" James had inquired in all amazement.

"I'll bear the strain, Lord Crandall," was the reply, given in such a serious tone that James could not be sure if he was being quizzed. *Students today are certainly more subtly layered than I ever was*, he thought as he nodded and left the Camera.

He surprised himself further by his own heated argument with his valet that night as the poor man attempted to pack James's clothing for the return to Enderfield. James knew that his was a mild disposition, absentminded even, in all areas outside of his studies, and he disconcerted himself with the vehemence he directed toward his own shabby shirts and collars.

Mason, ever the soul of rectitude, was finally driven

to say in clipped tones, "My lord, if you will not go to a tailor, the result is what is laid before you!"

"You could have insisted more strenuously," James countered, but he knew his argument was weak at best. The valet only tightened his lips and maintained a stony silence that persisted throughout the remainder of the evening. *I have been more pointedly ignored only by cats*, James thought as he went to a cold bed, unencumbered by the usual solace of a warming pan. *I can only hope that Mason's miff wears off before he brings me shaving water with ice chunks in the morning.*

To his great relief, the shaving water was hot. Mason unbent long enough to inform his master that he had taken the liberty of writing to Lord Crandall's London tailor to request an audience the next afternoon.

"My lord, you are going to London anyway to retrieve your father," Mason reminded him. James thought it prudent not to argue.

Two days later, he sent Mason to Kent and his own relatives for Christmas. Having discharged any London duties, James and Lord Waverly traveled back along the same road through inland sleet, stopping ten miles shy of Oxford at the village of Woodcote.

On the advice of his father's butler, they dined at the inn while the family servants rode ahead to reconnoiter at Enderfield. "For while I suspect that the Carvers have been adequate caretakers, one cannot assume that the chimneys are drawing properly or that the beds are made," the butler warned.

They tarried long enough over dinner for the butler to work any number of miracles. When they arrived at Enderfield, long after all light was gone from the sky, fires were in the hearths, holland covers removed from the major rooms, and beds made. James strolled with his father through the gallery to gaze upon any number of Enders ancestors, a trifle dusty in their frames, but none the worse for neglect.

"It is a little shabby," Lord Waverly admitted, stopping before the portrait of his lovely wife, dead since James's days at New College.

"Mama is not shabby," James contradicted.

"No, indeed," his father agreed. "She never was." After a moment's contemplation, he set them both in motion again. "But we can certainly refurbish her house before she looks down on us from whatever celestial sphere she graces and despairs over husband and son!"

I am here to claim a wife who will turn this into a house again, James told himself as they proceeded toward the bedroom wing and slumber. *Mama would have liked that, Papa will be ecstatic, Sir Waldo suggested it, Tim would have approved, and I think it must be a good idea if everyone feels that way.* As he composed himself for sleep that night in his old chamber, James wondered if anyone had ever asked Olivia.

Over eggs and bacon the next morning, he knew that it was not a question to put to Olivia, or to any female probably. *One does one's duty,* he thought, *even if the nuts and bolts of the matter are less discussed between men and women than Watt's steam engine or Lavoisier's treatise on the properties of oxygen. And,* he reflected, *gentlewomen seem to have a knack for knowing. We assume the rightness of marriage, and if some among us need prodding ...* He took his cup and saucer and stood gazing out the French doors that would have been open in the summer, giving onto the small breakfast terrace. *In some matters, I am a slow learner.*

It was good to be home, he decided as he leaned against the doorframe. The snow had stopped and the sky was so blue that he squinted. The trees were bare of leaves now, and he could easily see Sir Waldo's property, the house substantial as Enderfield, if not quite so large. He thought of Tim and of his youth, which suddenly seemed so long ago.

He knew it was a simple matter to pay a morning call on the Hannafords, but by the time he worked up his nerve the next day, it was afternoon and really too late for such a call of courtesy. "They will think I am finagling a dinner invitation," he explained to his father.

"You used to do that," Lord Waverly pointed out.

"And Tim was my excuse, sir. I have none now, beyond a desire to see the family," he said. "Maybe tomorrow."

He never did pay a courtesy call to the Hannafords that week, choosing instead to organize his notes for lectures after the holidays were over and reread Ketchum's paper on motion. His father had a mild sore throat, so they did not attend church. By the next week, he realized that he had waited too long to make a casual visit and might as well give it up as a hopeless case and return to Oxford. *Some men are not destined to marry*, he told himself; *perhaps I am one of them.*

James wondered how to broach the matter to his father, who seemed content to regard him with a certain fondness and continue his own career in front of the fireplace, reading when he felt like it, and dozing when he did not. *Papa is glad to be here*, James thought. *He would be disappointed if I suggested that we return to London for Christmas.* James decided that he would find stationery in the book room and write Sir Waldo a letter, telling him to choose another son-in-law who was not too shy to pay an initial morning call.

He was in the hallway, heading for the book room with the firmest of intentions, when someone knocked on the door. He knew that his father had gone out earlier to walk among the shrubbery and breathe deep of the brisk air, so he hurried to open it, waving away the footman. He opened the door, and there stood Olivia Hannaford.

He knew he would be surprised the first time he saw her—if he saw her—because at their last meeting at Tim's funeral she was only eleven years old. *Time does things*, he thought as he looked upon her loveliness. He remembered her from her childhood, but even then he was not prepared for that certain something about her that he—the most eloquent of men on paper and in lecture hall—was totally unable to explain. *Sir Waldo was so right: I have never seen anyone like this*, he thought.

There she stood, not greatly taller than he recalled from their last meeting, but so different. She wore a heavy grey cloak with the hood up, but her marvelous hair threatened to spill out of its boundaries. *Wonderful, impudent hair*, he thought, entranced by the curls. She was covered completely by the cloak, but her shape was a graceful outline. Time, which had done nothing to ameliorate her hair, had managed to subdue her freckles. They were the palest marks now and completely bewitching. *What a woman this is*, he reflected.

"I wish you would ask me in," she said, "My feet are cold. Jemmy, that wreath has to go."

He smiled and motioned her forward. "Miss Hannaford, excuse my bad manners. Come in, please. What wreath?"

She stopped right in the doorway, and stared at him, then turned pointedly to look at the door directly next to him. "That one you are almost leaning upon. And please do not call me Miss Hannaford. I have always been Olivia to you, except when I was Oblivious, or Ollie, or . . . what was that other name Tim hatched?"

He thought a moment, resisting the urge to shake his head because he knew his brains would fall out and drop onto the floor at her feet. "I believe it was just plain Livy."

"You're too kind," she said with a smile of her own. "I believe it was Liver." She held out her hand to him. "Livy will do, unless you are determined to be formal." She wore gloves, of course, and as he took her hand, he wondered how human bones could feel so delicate. *I will have to take such good care of all this magnificence*, he told himself, and then said without another moment's thought, "Olivia, you have superior bones."

What just came out of my mouth? he asked himself in stupefied amazement. *Goodness, but she will think I am crazy*, he thought and then blundered on, "I mean . . . oh, hang it, I have seen a lot of bones in autopsies, but none of them ever felt like yours."

Open-mouthed in total shock or wonder (he wasn't sure which), her hand still in his, she stared at him.

"I mean . . ." he began lamely and stopped. *Shut up, James*, he thought. *And let go of the nice lady's hand. There's a good man. Step away slowly, and maybe she will think you are harmless. No quick motions. If she slaps you or faints at your feet, it will be only what you deserve.*

To his surprise, she did neither. While she did carefully remove her fingers from his grasp, she merely stepped back and shook her head.

"Mama would say you have not changed an iota, Jemmy," she told him.

"I probably have not," he agreed. "Olivia, please come in. I promise to remove the wreath."

"And I will make you another one," she said, stepping inside and looking around. "Oh, it has changed here."

I suppose it has, he thought to himself as the butler took her cloak. *We have stayed away since Mama died, and*

I fear that our neglect shows. He took a deep breath. "What would you do with the place, Livy?" he asked.

"Paint it and put on new wall-covering, and send the crocodiles packing," she said promptly, pointing to the chaise with the reptilian limbs, a remnant of an earlier remodeling—modish after Napoleon's plunge into Egypt.

"And go to the warehouses in London for new furniture?" he suggested, walking with her toward the sitting room. She shook her head.

"First, I would go into your attics and see what is there." She stopped. "Are you planning to marry and bring a viscountess here?"

He almost winced. "I suppose I am," he managed to say.

"I would not have thought you would ever leave All Souls," she said as they moved into the sitting room. "Papa tells me that you are doing great things there."

"I like to think so," he said, hoping for a touch of modesty where he felt only embarrassment and the surest conviction that she would think him strange, indeed, if he explained his study.

"What, for instance?" she asked.

"I doubt it would interest you," he replied. Lord Crandall prided himself on the sensitive side of his nature, but he winced again at the expression that came into Olivia's eyes after his bumbling statement. It was as though he had blown out a candle inside her.

"Perhaps not," she said, her voice as nicely modulated as before—but with something less in it, he thought, some overtone that seemed to bank the fire he had noticed when he opened the door on her loveliness.

To his dismay, no amount of small talk seemed to bring about any recovery. Gracefully, she accepted his offer to pour the tea when it came, and she certainly held up her end of the inconsequentials that both of them seemed to be uttering. A man more shallow would have not noticed a thing, but James knew he had blundered, and the deuce of it was he was not entirely sure how.

After she left, he took the wreath off the front door and stood for a long time gazing into the mirror in the entrance hall, wondering how it was that a man such as he should be permitted to roam free in England without a restraint around his neck. He was still standing there, heaping all sorts of abuse on himself, when his father returned from his stroll through the shrubbery.

"Did I see little Olivia walking home?" he asked.

"You did," James replied. He turned to look at his father. "Papa, what do you see when you look at me?"

His father frowned and stood a moment in contemplation. "Someone pleasant to look at, a little shabby at the elbows, perhaps, and possibly too tall for some doorways." He shrugged. "Other than that, I can see no glaring defects."

James groaned. "They don't show until I open my mouth, Papa! Do you know . . . can you imagine . . . what I said to Miss Hannaford?"

He felt no relief when Lord Waverly smiled back, the picture of patriarchal serenity.

"Oh, something inane about pretty ankles or her tiny waist? I am at a loss, son. Do enlighten me."

"I could not see her ankles; she was wearing boots," James said and felt his face grow hot. "I took her hand . . ." It was so stupid that he closed his eyes and rushed out the rest of the sentence. "And I told her that I have felt many bones from autopsies, but none as nice as hers! Shoot me now, will you?"

Lord Waverly laughed, which sank James further. "It would be a mercy killing, but I cannot think this county's coroner would overlook it." He took James's hand in his own, "Nice bones, son. And that froze her completely?"

"Well, no, it did not, now that you mention it," James said, a little surprised at his own density. "Actually, she went all quiet after she asked what I was doing at All Souls and I said it would not interest her."

A thoughtful look on his face, his father released James's hand and linked elbows with him, as though to stir him from further self-criticism at the mirror. "Did it occur to you, son, that she might be interested?"

"The thought never crossed my mind," James said frantically. "I have mentioned it to other ladies, and heaven knows they did not care."

"Perhaps Olivia does." Lord Waverly nodded to the butler. "Withers, do bring me tea, and something rather more strong for Lord Crandall." He patted the seat beside him on the sofa. "James, if she is interested in what you are studying, you are certainly at liberty to tell her. Surely it is not a secret." He leaned closer. "I would be the only man admitting it if I were to assure you that I know what a woman thinks. It is a mystery, indeed, and that is all I know, even after nearly sixty years of sharing this planet with creatures of the fair sex."

One could grow bitter with the lack of good advice I have received from this father, James thought as they went to the Hannafords' the following night for dinner. *And the deuce of it is, I tell the man I am in despair, and he just smiles.*

They could have taken the carriage, but Lord Waverly had suggested that they walk, which pleased James. He had a dislike of sitting in overheated rooms and was in no hurry to arrive at the Hannafords'. At All Souls it would be cheese and bread, biscuits with sprinkled sugar and cinnamon, and the window open just enough to make the beer lively. He sighed. Perhaps marriage would be a drawback. Be she ever so complacent, no wife would tolerate such a menu, or winter's chill in her sitting room. *I doubt she would allow me to hang my clothing on doorknobs either, even though it is such a convenience when I am late for tutorials.*

"Papa, how do I know if she is the right one?" he asked suddenly as they crossed to the side door on the Hannafords' terrace where they always entered.

"You listen with all your heart to what she says," Lord Waverly told him. He put his hand on James's shoulder and gave it a shake. "Pray you are not so scientific to overlook that kind of heart."

Pray I am not, he thought as he knocked on the door. If Olivia had been beautiful last week, with her hair wild and her cloak snowy, she was incomparable this night, James decided as he sat across from her at the table. His momentary disappointment at not being seated next to her was quickly assuaged by watching her animated good cheer, from the stuffed haddock to the almond crescents. Although she was a small woman, she ate well, with none of the finicky, die-away airs of ladies of fashion. He noticed that she did turn down the stewed pigeon, a particular favorite of his, and promptly decided that should she consent to be his wife, he would not miss it too much if it never appeared on their dinner table.

He carried on as brisk a conversation as was his nature, which allowed him ample time to admire Olivia Hannaford some more. Her hair was but partly tamed, a halo of dark bronze ringlets that bobbed when she laughed. *I wonder how she brushes that mop,* he thought. *I wonder if she would let me try.* The thought so unnerved him that he performed a juggling act with the brussel sprouts, which nearly saw the entire bowl slide into Lady Hannaford's lap when he passed it to her. James knew he should be making brilliant conversation, but nothing witty sprang into his brain, that brain so extravagantly admired at All Souls, and even—if he could believe the chancellor—at London Hospital, now.

Conversation wasn't essential, anyway. From dinners past, he knew that Lady Hannaford could be relied upon to furnish all the words he lacked. She did not disappoint him, at least, until the pudding, when the subject of Charles in Paris surfaced.

"Lord Crandall, it is the drollest thing possible, but what do you think Charles is bringing with him from Paris?" she asked him.

If he remembered Charles—and he did—there was no danger that whatever the Hannaford's eldest child was bearing home would be in bad taste. "Brandy for your cellar, mum?" he suggested, aware that Olivia was watching her mother, a frown on her face.

To his discomfort, Lady Hannaford laughed. "No, indeed, James!" she declared, touching his arm, "although Livy declares she will lock herself in the cellar!"

"Mother," Olivia said, and there was no mistaking the distress in her eyes. She said no more, and James thought that wise of her, considering that Lady Hannaford never turned loose of a good tale, once launched upon it.

"Charles is bringing home a fellow diplomatist with the whole intent of finding Livy's approval! I knew you would be amused!" He was not, but he managed a weak smile at his hostess. He made some inane comment, but it was forgotten the moment it left his lips.

She continued, "Peter Winston, Lord D'Urst. Perhaps you know him? I believe he was at some college or other at Oxford."

Only by serious discipline did James keep from groaning out loud. *Peter Winston?* he asked himself. *Peter Winston? Oh, why not just blend Apollo for looks, Croesus for wealth, and Solomon for his brain box?*

"Yes, I know him," he said, hoping that his tone of resignation would be taken for a certain languid sangfroid. "He was two years my senior at New College. He is coming for Christmas?" He hoped he did not sound too forlorn.

"The very man. Charles tells us that Lord D'Urst has expressed a real interest in Livy and all from seeing her miniature that Charles carries about with him," Lady Hannaford said. "Imagine that!"

He chose not to imagine anything; the reality of Peter Winston was daunting enough. "I had thought him to be married long since," he said. *Too many single gentlemen roaming loose in England are a menace to society,* he thought. "Wasn't he engaged before? Indeed, I am almost certain of it."

"So Charles wrote us, but apparently Lord D'Urst called it off because . . ." Lady Hannaford leaned closer to him, "the lady was insufficiently intelligent! Claims he wants a wife with brains." She beamed across the table at her daughter. "Between you and me . . ." *And the vicar, two old maids, Sir Waldo, my father, and your aunt at the table,* he thought glumly, ". . . we will be saving the expense of a come-out for Livy in the spring!" Lady Hannaford concluded in triumph. She blew a kiss to her daughter as the footman removed her plate. "And here I feared that your brains would be a detriment, my little love. How silly I am!"

He could not dispute her silliness and felt only gratitude when she turned to the vicar to continue her conversation with him. *I wonder why Sir Waldo went to all that trouble of securing my consent to pursue Olivia,* he asked himself as he stared down with considerable distaste at the blanc mange before him. He could have saved himself the trouble, apparently.

He put that very question to his host when they strolled to the sitting room an hour later after brandy—which gave him a headache. The other men had gone ahead, and it gave James some wintry solace to realize that Sir Waldo wanted to speak to him. He slowed his steps.

"Jemmy, I had no idea this was afoot," he said, his voice low. "Probably the fault is mine. I must have lamented one letter too often about my fears for Olivia."

"And Charles is never slow," James finished for him when he fell silent.

"You're not going to give up even before you begin, are you?" Sir Waldo asked, his eyes anxious.

It is not a matter of giving up, he wanted to tell the man. *I know Lord D'Urst and I could never measure up. It certainly isn't too late to return to London, where Papa and I have spent every Christmas since Mama died.* "Sir Waldo, he is an excellent man, and I know none of you will be disappointed," he said, hoping it would be explanation enough. "Olivia cannot help but be impressed."

Sir Waldo was silent a moment, watching slowly with his chin sunk onto his chest. "You are the one, laddie," he insisted as the butler opened the door to the sitting room. "I just know you are. Say you won't give up yet. And for goodness sake, begin!" Sir Waldo spoke in a whisper, but James could not overlook his intensity. *And I have always known you as such an easy-going fellow,* he thought in wonder.

"I will," he said, the words surprised right out of him.

"Tonight," Sir Waldo said, and to James's ears, it was not a question.

"Very well."

Resolution, he told himself, but still he hesitated in the doorway. He could see that his father had been captured for hard duty at the whist table with Lady Hannaford and her maiden aunts. Olivia had seated herself close to the fire, her embroidery stand in front of her. James did not think she was aware of him, but as he watched her, he smiled to see her slide a footstool toward the chair next to her. *If ever a man needed an invitation*, he thought.

Taking his courage in hand, he sat down beside her and propped up his feet. He hoped he looked more relaxed than he felt, but after only a few moments of sitting beside Olivia Hannaford, he began to feel burdens he had been hitherto unaware of roll from his broad shoulders.

This is odd, he told himself, risking a glance in her direction. She wasn't doing anything in particular to put him at ease, just leaning forward slightly, her attention on her handiwork. She hummed under her breath. He took a deep breath, and then a smaller, more discreet one as he enjoyed the faintest fragrance of almond. She had a slight smile on her face. *There is just something about you*, he decided, and then he opened his mouth before he thought.

"Miss Hannaford, you smell remarkably like a biscuit." He cringed inwardly, but the fear quickly passed when she pushed the needle in the linen and leaned just a little in his direction.

"You have found me out, my lord," she whispered. "I spent too long below stairs before dinner. Extract of almond covers a multitude of sins, I have discovered." To his utter delight, she smiled at him. "Perhaps I could recommend it to you after autopsies."

He laughed softly—not wishing to attract anyone's attention—put at ease by her commonsense air. "I might just go to the apothecary's for a bottle of my own." He cleared his throat. "Let me apologize for my artless declarations of last week. I am only grateful that you did not summon the constable to have me bound, trussed, and admitted to the nearest lunatic asylum."

"Oh, no," she assured him. She resumed her work at the frame. "You and Tim hatched enough schemes that I would be a silly sister indeed if I allowed comments about autopsies to throw me over." She put down the needle again and looked at her hands. "Just tell me that you did not mean that my digits are bony."

"No, Olivia. I should have said bonnie instead of bony." *Well, that was good,* he told himself when she laughed, colored up so prettily, and returned her attention to her embroidery. *In another twelve or fifteen years I might even be clever around women. Why, by then, Olivia and Pete Winston will have been married a dozen years at least and have three or four children. I wonder if I could hire a Sicilian to kill the man? Or one of Napoleon's out-of-work imperial guards?* The thought, so absurd, made him smile.

He stretched out farther in the chair and put his hands behind his head, content to gaze into the flames and breathe deep of almond extract from the Hannaford kitchen as it wonderfully scented Olivia's hands and neck.

"And now you are smiling," she began.

"I was thinking of homicide this time," he said. To his relief, Olivia only laughed. He glanced at Sir Waldo, seated beside the vicar, who was using his Sunday gestures, but saying something about "bits of bone and muscle," and "just wait till spring at Newmarket." *It cannot be a sermon,* James realized. *The man is far too animated to be discussing something from Holy Writ. Perhaps if he preached from the starting gates, we would be more entertained of a Sabbath.*

As James watched his host, Sir Waldo made a shooing motion with his hands, as though to hurry him along.

"Resolve," James said.

"Beg pardon?" Olivia asked, her eyes still on her work.

Had he spoken out loud? "Resolve, my dear, resolve," he stammered, buying a moment. "I am resolved to do something about shabby appearances and out-of-date furnishings."

She looked at him, narrowing her eyes as though she were actually contemplating his person. "I do not think your coat is so old, Lord Crandall."

"I mean the house, Olivia," he told her, even as he resolved to seek out his tailor when he returned to Oxford. "Mama's crocodile chaise still leers at us from the sitting room, and the draperies have more dust on them than the pyramids."

"Oh, dear! That was a fashion several years ago, wasn't it?" she asked.

"Dust is always fashionable in my chamber at All Souls," he joked. To his distress or delight—he wasn't sure which—she jabbed the needle into the fabric and pushed away the hoop this time.

"Sir, I mean the crocodile chaise!" she declared, speaking with some emphasis, even as she kept her voice low. "You mean this, and I mean that, and we are ever at cross comments. If you do not say what you mean, how will we ever manage when . . ." She stopped and turned quite red to his greater amazement.

"When what?" he asked, more curious now than surprised at her unexpected vehemence.

"Oh, nothing!" She looked so adorably confused and off balance somehow that he surprised himself by taking her hand.

"My declaration is this then, in plain terms, Miss Olivia Hannaford." He could not continue, because she had turned quite pale at his words, and was gripping his fingers so hard that he winced. He peered closer. "Olivia, are you breathing? I wish you would."

The moment passed. She took a deep breath and relaxed her tenacious grip.

"It is this," he continued, not certain anymore. "Our house is shabby from neglect and needs the critical eye of a female. Will you come over tomorrow morning, walk through my house with me, and give me advice on what to do about it short of a bonfire?"

She seemed relieved at his question. He could almost feel her sigh.

"Of course I will do that." She pulled her fingers away and looked beyond him across the room. "Oh, my mother is either exercising her fingers from too much discard at the whist table, or she wishes me to see about tea. Do excuse me, Lord Crandall."

She rose gracefully, quite herself again, and left him there with only the scent of almond extract for company. *Women are strange*, he thought. *Thank goodness that men have no luck with subterfuge.* He sat there peacefully enough, admiring Olivia's handiwork on the embroidery hoop. She returned in a moment with tea for them both and seated herself behind the hoop.

"Nice work," he said after a sip.

"I like embroidery," she replied, her attention on the hoop again. "What a good thing that is, considering that I will have a lifetime of it."

"What, no ambition?" he teased and was astounded when she took a long look at him and then rose and left the room. Too embarrassed to look at anyone in the suddenly silent parlor, James sat staring into the flames until what seemed like four centuries later when his father tapped him on the shoulder and said that it was time to go home.

He spent a completely sleepless night, certain that she would not show up in the morning, and equally positive that he would never see her again. The thought numbed him and set him pacing about, berating himself. *All I do is apologize to her,* he thought. *Charles and Peter Winston are due to arrive any day. It is not a matter of fixing my interest with Olivia Hannaford before the competition shows up. I cannot even get beyond apology. Lord D'Urst will come as a great relief to Olivia.* Or so he reasoned at three-thirty in the morning.

Nothing had changed his opinion by breakfast, except that he had a great dread of spending one more day at Enderfield. After a long moment staring at breakfast on the sideboard, he turned on his heel and stalked to the library, where the furniture was comfortable and much more conducive to sulking. To avoid looking at the clock, he attempted to review his notes and then glance over his sketches. Easier said than done. He found himself mentally wagering how much time had passed before each glance at the clock.

By eleven o'clock, he decided that Olivia was not coming. *And who could blame her?* he berated himself. He, for one, would not. Resolutely, he turned away from the clock and tried to absorb himself in his studies. It must have worked. He was sitting at his desk, staring out the window and thinking about action and reaction, when he heard a discreet cough almost at his elbow. He jerked his head around, startled out of his contemplation, to see the butler.

"Beg pardon, my lord, but the Honorable Olivia Hannaford is here to see you. Sir, are you in?"

Oh, I am, Withers, he thought. He paused and counted to ten slowly, not wishing to give the impression of overeagerness.

"Yes, I am. You may show her into the sitting room. I will be there in a moment."

When Withers left as quiet as he had come, James clapped his hands and stared at the ceiling. *The Lord is good*, he thought, *and kind to fools this holiday season*. He spent a moment before the mirror over the fireplace and pronounced himself totally shabby, from his worn-out shirt (kept because it grew softer with each washing), to his corduroy vest (buttons long gone but a prized possession because the vest pockets held any number of erasers and pencils), to his country leathers (comfortable beyond all reason, if not stylishly tight), to his shoes (at least they matched today). *I could have combed my hair this morning*, he told his reflection. *Too bad that I did not.*

Olivia, of course, looked as neat as a pin, dressed in a plain dark wool dress of no distinction except that it reminded him of how womanly she had become since the day eleven years ago when he and Tim had pulled out her two loose teeth. *And goodness, that hair!* he thought as he stood in the door of the sitting room, admiring her. She was not watching him but was eyeing the crocodile chaise.

"Ugly, isn't it?" he said when he had had enough of gazing.

She turned around to smile at him. "Actually, my lord, it is so stupendously, marvelously horrible that I confess I like it. Give it to me for Christmas, will you?"

"Absolutely, and up to half my kingdom as well," he told her, meaning each word.

She laughed, and he felt in his heart that for some unknown reason, he was quite forgiven for his thoughtlessness of last night.

"The chaise will be enough, my lord. I will have to keep it in my room, else Mama's pug will go into spasms. Well, are you ready to begin?"

Begin what? he thought wildly. *Is this some carte blanche to pull you onto my lap and make little corkscrews* out of your hair, and maybe see where it leads? Not even the Lord is that merciful at Christmas.

"Looking at your rooms, Lord Crandall," she reminded him, which only made him realize that he must have been staring at her like a Bedlam inmate.

"Oh, yes, yes indeed," he said. "Let us attempt the west wing, Olivia. It's the newer part of the house." He held his breath, but she made no comment on his use of her first name.

To reach the wing, they crossed through the gallery with its walls of Waverlys, Enders, and Crandalls looking down, some single portraits and others surrounded by handsome wives and numerous progeny. It had never occurred to him before how fecund a family he came from, and he was glad that the woman beside him could not read his thoughts. Olivia seemed content to stop, gaze, and stroll beside him.

"Do you suppose the children played ball in here when the day was stormy?" she asked, as they stood before one portrait.

He had never thought of such a thing, which his own mother would never have allowed, even if he had possessed brothers and sisters.

"Would you permit it?" he asked.

"Of course," she answered promptly, "after I had removed vases and other breakable items. What a wonderful room for blindman's buff."

It was a pretty thought, and it made him smile thinking of Olivia playing in here with their children. *Oh, that is a reach,* he acknowledged. *Here I am thinking of reproduction, when I should be grateful she is still speaking to me this morning. And why she is still speaking to me, I do not precisely understand.*

There were ten sleeping chambers in the west wing,

and Olivia went through them all, making notes on the tablet she carried, but spending more time looking out the windows.

"Your view is so much better than ours," she told him when he joined her at the window. "Perhaps it is the slightly higher elevation."

He uttered some monosyllable. Then they continued to another room where she admired the view of bare trees and snow-covered ground, and he admired her. *If I could think of something brilliant to say, I would*, he told himself, and then spoke anyway, as though his brain had no connection to what came from his mouth.

"Olivia, I was so rude to you last night. Why did you come today?" James winced as soon as he said it, alarmed with himself. But to his unspeakable relief, Olivia seemed unfazed by his plain speaking. She sat in the chair by the window.

"I said that I would," she replied simply, "but we must get one thing straight. Just because I enjoy needlework does not mean that I have no ambition. What it means is that I am a woman."

She turned her attention to the view outside the window again, but he sensed there was more. It was his turn to speak, as clearly as though she had told him to, and he knew in his bones that what he said would be the most important words of his life. He wanted to give the matter weighty consideration, but there she was, looking at him, expecting some comment.

"Do you mind so much?" he asked instead. He quietly sighed when she smiled at him.

"Sometimes I do, Lord Crandall," she told him. "Do you remember how I cried when you and Tim left for New College?"

He had forgotten, but now he sat on the bed

recalling her distress all those years ago and how exasperated Tim was. "I seem to remember sordid, rather caustic comments from your brother about watering-pot sisters," he said and then stopped, struck by a thought so startling that he almost—but not quite—rejected it. "But you weren't crying because you were going to miss him, were you?"

Olivia shook her head, rose gracefully, and headed for the door. She turned the page on her tablet. "Two more rooms, my lord, and then I should be going. I cried because I knew I would never be allowed to go to college. I do believe this wonderful hall suffers from no more malignancy than the need for paint."

Clearly, she did not wish to disclose any more of herself to him. As he followed her into the next room, and then the one after, he knew he had been granted, for whatever reason, some tiny glimpse into her most private corner. *Papa says I should listen to what she tells me,* James thought, as they finished in the last room and she handed him her list of suggestions. She kept her own counsel as they retraced their steps through the gallery, and he thought through his conversations with her.

As she made her way toward the entrance, he knew there was nothing to keep her in the house one more moment, and he had the dismal sense that he had failed her again. *Oh, what is she telling me?* he asked in desperation.

And then he knew, as plainly as though his own personal guardian angel—which he most certainly did not believe in, thank you—had tapped him on the shoulder and slipped him a handwritten note from the Lord Himself.

"Hold on there with that cloak, Withers," he said to the butler, who was waiting in the entranceway. "Olivia, when you asked me last week just what I was doing at All Souls, you meant it, didn't you?" He knew from the way her gaze deepened that he had finally said the right thing.

"I meant it," she assured him.

He took a deep breath. "I am studying time and motion, Olivia, and how the efficient use of the latter increases the former." He was afraid to look at her, afraid that he would see polite boredom overtake her features, which up to now were animated. "The applications are of enormous importance," he took another breath and then plunged on. "I mean, in factories."

"I imagine they would be," she said with scarcely a moment's hesitation. "If time and motion equal efficiency, then efficiency equals increased revenue, does it not?"

It did, but no woman had ever mentioned it to him before. Only the sternest handle on his emotions prevented him from picking up Olivia and planting a kiss on her forehead.

"Correct, Olivia," he replied in what he hoped was a detached, professional tone. "There is a professor at Harvard College in Massachusetts, United States, who is analyzing the motions of mill girls at a textile factory in Lowell. He has written a treatise on the subject."

The next logical step was to ask her if she would care to read the paper. He hesitated, thinking of his own friends, fellow scholars at All Souls, who had laughed and turned away when offered the paper.

"It can be as dry as . . ." He stopped, humbled almost to his knees by the trust on Olivia's face. *How strange that she should look at me like that when I only want to spare her the tedium of Charles Ketchum's paper, for tedious it is at first glimpse. And here you are, loveliest of creatures, looking at me as though this matters to you.* "Would you like to read Ketchum's paper?" he asked, his voice low, not sure if he was offering her the driest bone in scholarship or a little glimpse of himself—take it or leave it—that he had never shared before.

"I would like above all to read it," she replied.

"Don't move," he ordered. He ran down the hall to the book room and snatched the paper from his desk, hurrying back, out of breath, afraid that great good sense would have taken over and she would be gone. She stood precisely where he had left her, except that she was smiling at him.

"I did not move," she assured him. He took her by the arm to prevent any possible escape and walked her to the library, where only hours before he had stewed, despaired, and cursed his own ineptitude and paced the floor.

"I think I have quite worn it out with reading," he said as he handed her the document. "Do have a seat."

She sat on the sofa, her eyes on the paper. In another moment, he could have turned in circles, barked, and scratched himself for all the attention she paid him. As he watched in amazement, Olivia drew up her legs and made herself comfortable, her eyes focused on the close-written pages before her. He had the good sense to leave her in peace.

When luncheon came, he made an effort to tempt her with food, but she shook her head and waved him away. He did leave a tray within reach, noting to his amusement that every now and then her fingers would range across the plate without her eyes leaving the paper. He could have fed her cotton wadding. He knew the paper was long and involved, and he was not surprised when she propped a pillow behind her head and settled down in more comfort with her knees drawn up. He laughed to himself and sat in a chair just out of her vision, content to watch.

He woke later that afternoon to find himself covered

with the light blanket that his father often used in the library. Olivia, sitting straight and proper now, watched him, her excitement visible even in the way she sat forward on the edge of the sofa.

"I thought you would never wake up," she said when he opened his eyes and looked around in surprise. "Oh, I covered you. Lord Crandall, you looked so tired."

That is only because I was up all night worrying about whether I would see you again, he thought, touched to his soul. Fuddled with sleep as he was, he could tell that only a lifetime's training in manners held her in check.

"Well, what do you think?" he asked, acutely aware as he looked at her that probably not many men ever asked such a question of a woman.

She leaped off the couch as though springs released her and pulled up a footstool to sit close beside him.

"Do you know what this says?" she demanded, gesturing at the paper held so tight in her grip. She colored up then, in a most adorable way. "Of course you know what it says! I am silly. Oh, my, it is all about value and work and time."

"And efficiency," he added.

She looked at the paper in her hands. "It is all so simple," she told him. "Are all great ideas so simple?"

"Most of them, I think. Someone puts forth a theory, and the rest of us just slap our foreheads and say, 'I could have done that.'"

She nodded, so serious that he almost smiled. "Do you have your own ideas about what Mr. Ketchum has written?" she asked.

No, he decided as he leaned closer to Olivia. *This woman must never be thrown into Almack's, where ladies are only ornaments. Sir Waldo, you were so right to put us together.*

"Yes, I have my own thoughts on what Ketchum has postulated. I have even begun a paper in response to his. Would you—"

"Above all things," she interrupted. "Only let me borrow it, and I will return it tomorrow."

He stood up. "It's still a work in progress. If you have any suggestions . . . ," he began and then stopped. *That is too much to ask. And yet . . .* "I will entertain any and all suggestions from you for the improvement of my paper," he told her. *I love this woman's laugh,* he thought. He held out his hand to her and helped her up from the footstool. "And now I suppose your mama will be wondering if I have abducted you. Come with me, and I will fetch my paper."

She walked with him to the book room and took the paper from him with great seriousness. "I will guard it with my life," she assured him.

"See that you do," he said, his smile concealed in the face of her solemnity. "Heaven knows there are legions of road agents between my house and yours. Probably even Mohicans, and each one desperate for that treatise."

She claimed her cloak from Withers this time and let him put it about her shoulders.

"Oh, drat," she said under her breath as James opened the door for her. She looked at him. "I suppose we must go into your attics tomorrow and look at musty old furniture when I would much rather talk about your paper."

"We could leave the crocodile chaise and the campaign beds where they are for another season," he suggested.

"We daren't, not when I have selected colors for the walls that will never match Egyptian flora and fauna." She held out her hand to him. "But we will be fast in the attics and efficient enough even for Mr. Ketchum!"

Not too fast, he thought. *One can overdo the value of*

efficiency. He took her hand. "Olivia, you are completely remarkable," he said.

"I am nothing of the sort," she said and then made a face. "Please don't laugh, but I used to wish and wish that I could be at New College with you and Tim."

Laughter was the furthest thing from his mind. "What would you have studied?" he asked, conscious that her hand was still gripped tight in his.

She stared at him. "Do you seriously wish to know?" she asked after looking around to make sure that no one eavesdropped.

"Yes, I do!"

She sighed and released his hand. "Lovely, lovely geometry," she confided almost into his ear, her voice low. "I used to do Tim's papers for him when you two attended school at the vicar's. Oh, I confess it, I have ideas about geometry."

With a shout of laughter he grabbed her by the shoulders and planted a loud smack of a kiss upon her forehead. "And here I thought I knew everything about Tim! Do you know that the vicar never could understand why he did so well on the work from home and so poorly on examinations?"

"Now you know!" With a smile, Olivia gathered her cloak tighter around her and rolled up his paper to fit into her reticule. "Tomorrow, sir!"

He knew tomorrow would not come soon enough. Over dinner that night, he confided to his father what he had done. "She promised to read my paper and offer any suggestions," he said. He shook his head as Withers came round again with the dish of stewed haricots.

"Suppose she actually has suggestions?" his father asked.

"I will take them, of course!" he declared. "You know

how atrocious my spelling is. I confess to less uniformity than is commonly allowed."

"So you do, if that is all she wishes to change," Lord Waverly muttered, with enough hesitation in his voice to make James wonder.

He did not wonder long. When he composed himself for sleep that night—and it came sooner than usual because of his little sleep the night before—his heart was pure, his mind clear of everything except his love for Olivia. *After Christmas I shall engage an estate agent to find me a house in Oxford,* was his final thought before he slept.

He was impatient for her to arrive in the morning, so eager was he to see her again. *Confess it, James,* he told himself as he stood at the window. *You crave her praise and adulation.*

He wondered at her tardiness as the clock's hands moved so slowly. *Charles and Lord D'Urst must have arrived,* he thought with a pang. *How I wish Pete Winston had been set upon by brigands between here and Paris! My, I must look like a two-year-old here at the window,* he told himself. *It is a wonder I have not mashed my face against the glass.*

And then he saw her, hurrying along the lane, with that peculiar bounce to her step that he found so endearing. He looked closer and laughed out loud. The day was warm for December, and she had not felt the need to cover her head. Her hair was as he remembered it from years past, gathered into that funny topknot that she resorted to when time and curls thwarted her. *Will it seem odd when someday soon I ask a portraitist to commit that casual look to canvas? Olivia is my Christmas ornament, my funny little mantelpiece decoration.*

While he had far too many manners to actually shove the footman aside, James opened the door for his sweet thing and found himself almost taken aback by the liveliness that seemed to careen about in the entrance hall once she was in it. *She is a life force all by herself,* he thought in wonder.

"Mama says I should be locked in my room and fed bread and water through the keyhole for going anywhere looking like this," she apologized by way of greeting. "Lord Crandall, there are mornings when this trial of mine that sits atop my head absolutely defeats me."

"I think it is charming," he told her.

She made a face at him, and only the sternest kind of discipline kept him from sweeping her into his arms for a kiss from which she—or he—would never recover.

"You used to make fun of it," she reminded him.

He put his hand to his heart as though she had stabbed him and was rewarded with that laugh he so longed to hear.

"My dear Olivia, I am a mature man now," he said. "I would never tease you."

"Then you will never be much fun." She made a pretense of trying to reclaim her cloak from the footman, who was watching the exchange with an expression close to delight.

"Well, I will only tease you now and then," he said, wondering in the deepest corner of his heart if she had already consented somehow to a lifetime of his company. *When did this happen?* he asked himself in bliss that was close cousin to reverence. *Is there something understood? Or better yet, is there something I don't understand?*

"I would have come sooner, but I wanted to finish these," she said as she held out a sheet of paper to him. "I could hardly pry them loose from Papa at breakfast, he was enjoying them so much."

As a smile spread across his face, he stared down at

the little figures Olivia had sketched. She had taken his stupid stick figures that accompanied his treatise and turned them into clever drawings. Olivia's dainty lady of pen and ink, looking remarkably like her, stooped and bent and lifted across the page, perfectly illustrating the motion he had tried to duplicate with his own crude efforts. He laughed out loud at the last figure on the page, which was turned out, hands on hips, facing him. It was Olivia herself in miniature, down to the top-knot.

"My dear, these are charming," he said. "Please say you will permit me to use them instead of my own apologies for figures."

"They are yours," she assured him. With the same enthusiasm, she handed him his paper. "Lord Crandall, I so enjoyed reading your treatise! Mr. Ketchum himself will be completely impressed. I am certain he will want you to brave an Atlantic passage and lecture at Harvard!"

He smiled rather with what he hoped looked like modesty. "I wanted to share it with you. Any corrections?" he asked. "I never could spell."

"I can't either," she confessed. With a grin that made her look like a child again, she handed him several sheets of paper, closely written. "What I did was correct your argument beginning on page ten. Right there," she said, coming closer to ruffle through the pages of the treatise in his hand. "Somehow, you lost the gist of the argument. See. Right there. You pick it up again on page twelve, but something had to be done about ten and eleven. It took me the better part of the night, but I couldn't stop until the logic was right."

Dumbfounded, he stared down at both sheaves of paper, as though they writhed and hissed at him. "There was nothing wrong with my reasoning," he said, trying to keep his voice calm.

"Not up until page ten," she told him, her eyes narrowing slightly as he watched her face. "It was the only place where you lost the thread, Lord Crandall, and I knew you would want it back."

"Oh, you did," he said. "That was a bit presumptuous of you, wasn't it?"

As irritated as he was, if he could have taken back his words and swallowed them whole, he would have. To his dismay, her eyes widened, and then she stepped back until she was no longer peering over his arm to look at the paper he held.

"You did say that I could make corrections, did you not?" she asked. "You didn't mean it?"

"I thought ... spelling ... grammar ..." He paused, confused, and waved the paper in her direction. "I didn't think you would ever ..." Words failed him, but not long enough. "This won't do, Olivia."

She stepped back, her eyes shocked, as though he had suddenly reached out and cuffed her. Sick at heart, not sure if he was angrier with her or with himself, he watched as she visibly swallowed words on the brink of speech, drew herself up a little taller, and then seemed to retreat within herself. She looked at him and then managed a smile.

"I am sorry," she said, her voice so low he almost leaned closer to hear her—except that he was angry and would not. "I should not have presumed that you meant what you said."

He felt her softly spoken words like a shot to the heart, like an indictment, a blue-covered subpoena slapped into his hand by a grinning summons-server.

"Well, I . . . ," he began. "Olivia, I . . ."

To his everlasting shame, she put her hand on his arm. There was nothing in her eyes but contrition.

"Do forgive me," she said. "You are welcome to the

drawings. You can use the other pages to start a fire in the book room, Lord Crandall. My cloak, please."

He watched in stupefaction as Olivia accepted her cloak from the footman, who stood carved in marble.

"Perhaps we can look at the attics tomorrow, my lord," she told him as she stood by the door. "Perhaps you will not be so angry with me." And she was gone. Transfixed, he stared at the closed door, then down at the papers in his hands.

"Will there be anything else, my lord?" the footman asked, his tone detached and entirely proper. To James's sensitive ears, it sounded perilously close to reproach.

"No. Go away."

"Very well, sir."

He stood in the entrance hall a full five more minutes, his mind in a perfect tumult. *How dare she presume to correct my work?* he asked himself. *I have been at this for four years, and she only just read it last night! Amazing cheek for a girl, I would say.*

It wasn't enough to think it. In a rage, he stormed down the hall to the library and threw open the door, startling his father from solace. He paced up and down, venting his displeasure, throwing his arms about, until finally he paused before the fireplace.

"I think the flames are the only fitting venue for such impudence, Papa!" he declared. "Who does she think she is? I ask you!" Breathing heavy from his indignation, he glared at his father.

"Yes, indeed," his reply came from the depths of his favorite chair. "After all, son, you have double firsts from Oxford and everyone sings your praises now at London Hospital. What presumption from a mere child. By all means, throw the wretched thing on the fire."

It was said so quietly, which was not unusual, James

knew. His father was ever the best and calmest of men. He frowned and stared at Olivia's paper, crumpled now in his fist. Slowly, he straightened the paper against his thigh, hardly aware of what he was doing.

"Son, you alone know how hard you have worked on this paper."

It was a statement, and James could only nod in agreement, glad that his father understood his position. *I knew he would see it my way,* he thought.

Lord Waverly got himself up and held out his hand for the paper. "You are certainly justified in your anger, lad, but maybe you might wish to consider one thing."

"I doubt it."

His father shrugged. "Or possibly not. I have observed Olivia Hannaford for years, Jemmy, and I always come away with one nagging suspicion."

"That she is an impertinent baggage?" James asked.

"No, actually," his father said, his tone almost apologetic. "I am probably wrong—your own irritation at her meddling will bear me out, most likely—but I have often suspected that she is even more intelligent than you are."

James sucked in his breath as his father took the pages from him and set them on the table by his chair. "Perhaps you could just look them over when you feel less miffed. Excuse me now, son. I think I will have a walk. The air is a little stale in here, wouldn't you agree?"

After the door closed quietly, James threw himself into the chair his father had vacated and stared into the flames. He closed his eyes, seeing Olivia again, her expression so hurt and then so calm, as though she was determined not to let his petulance matter to her. The thought made him wince. *I love her and want her,* he thought as his anger cooled. *She will have to learn that there are areas where I am her superior, and that is all there is to it.*

He sat in the chair for over an hour until his mind was finally at peace again. *I think she will be inclined to forgive me*, he told himself. *I mean, she did not scream and shout . . . as I have done*, he thought next and writhed inside. He reached for the paper.

"I suppose I can at least read the thing," he muttered out loud. "Olivia Hannaford, I would like to know how you think you can do this better."

He read her addition once, set it down, and then picked it up and read it again. A third reading followed, and hard upon its heels, a fourth. When he finished the pages, he closed his eyes and gently banged his head against the back of the chair. "James Enders, you are so far removed beyond a fool that there are no words to express such abysmal stupidity," he announced to the world at large. "Someone ought to use you for a bad example in cautionary tales."

He looked at the page before him, dismayed as it began to blur and swim before his eyes. "My love, you are absolutely right," he said. "I lost the argument, and you found it, corrected it, and strengthened it."

It was the last thing he wanted to do, but he stood up, walked to the fireplace, and took a long look at himself in the mirror. *James, are you so arrogant and sure of your own scholarship?* he asked himself. *You claim to be a modern man. If this is so, how could you ride so roughshod over Olivia Hannaford? You claim to be in such sympathy with her because she has been denied the education lavished so freely upon you. You are a hypocrite.*

He did not like what gazed back at him in the mirror. Without stopping for his coat, he went outside and found his father in the shrubbery beside the house. "Father, I read Olivia's addition, and it is a masterpiece. She was completely right."

His father nodded serenely but offered no advice.

"I wish you would tell me what to do," James said, the words torn from him.

"I did, son," his father replied. "It's the only advice any man needs with a woman. Weren't you listening to me, either?"

James stopped his pacing about, looked at his father, and thought a moment. "You told me to listen to what she says, didn't you? That's it?"

"That's it. The corollary ought to be obvious to you, son. Take her as seriously as you would any man. If she gives you sound advice, take it."

He was right, of course, without question. *Only now I am listening,* James thought ruefully. "Where did you learn this?" he asked.

"From your mother."

It took him the better part of the afternoon to work up the courage to go to the Hannafords' estate. He had vowed earlier that he would never apologize again to Olivia, and here he was with the biggest apology of all. He stopped several times on the short walk, struck all over again by the notion that even though he had been wickedly, perversely unkind, Olivia would probably smooth it over and accept his mumblings with far more kindness than he deserved. *I have bumbled about in her life for only two weeks now, so I know that it cannot be love on her part,* he told himself. *Of course I love her, but surely that is different. Why it should be different,* was his next thought. *I want to wed her, have children with her, and enjoy her company and that of our children,* he thought, stopping again. *And now there is this added dimension of her excellent mind, which, if I am far luckier than I deserve, she will give to me— no, share with me. I wonder if she feels that way about me?*

His heart sank as he walked up the lane to the

Hannafords' estate. All mud-spattered, a traveling coach was stopped at the entrance, luggage still strapped on top. *Pete Winston, could you not have waited another week?* he asked himself in real irritation when he recognized the coat of arms on the door. *Whatever Olivia thinks of me, she may find you far less trouble.*

The butler showed him into the sitting room, where Charles and Lord D'Urst were standing, Charles with his arm about his sister, and Sir Waldo and Lady Hannaford close by. To his everlasting relief, Olivia came forward and took his hand.

"How good of you to come, Lord Crandall," she said, as pleasant as though they had parted on the best of terms. "I knew you would be eager to see Lord D'Urst." She grinned at him in that heart-stopping way only she possessed. "And, of course, old Charlie."

Wishing Lord D'Urst someplace due east of Madagascar, he shook hands with the man and clapped old Charlie on the back, mouthing some inanity about what a pleasure it was to see them both. They carried on a stupid conversation, and then all paused to pass smiles around again.

Oh, but I am as insipid as everyone else, he thought as he took Olivia's arm. She had not left his side in the whole meaningless exchange, and this gave him some heart.

"Sir Waldo, do allow me to borrow your daughter for a moment or two."

Sir Waldo beamed at him, "Did you like her little cartoons?"

"I did, sir. They were splendid." So far, so good, he thought, except that Lord D'Urst was frowning at him and trying hard not to look at Olivia's arm linked through his. "In fact, it is that paper I wish to discuss just briefly, if you can spare her." *Make this good*, he told himself, noting that Olivia's arm gently resting in his had stiffened at his words.

"Pete, Charlie, I know you have just arrived. Do not let me keep you from the removal of your traveling cases from the carriage. Olivia, take me to the library."

Without a word she ushered him from the room. To his utter relief, no one followed them. She led him to the library, not looking at him but not pulling away from his arm, either.

"You didn't need to bring back the sorry thing," she told him when he closed the door behind them. "The fire would do."

Now or never, he thought. He pulled her into his arms and hugged her as hard as he could. With a sigh, she clasped her hands together around his back, as though she did not wish him ever to depart from the circle of their embrace. "You do forgive me," she said finally, her words muffled against his waistcoat.

He sighed and pulled her away to look into her eyes. "No, Olivia," he corrected her. "Do you forgive me? I was so entirely wrong about your corrections, and I am thoroughly ashamed of my hypocrisy."

"Done, then," she said softly.

It was the perfect moment to sweep her into his arms again and kiss her, but he was reluctant at so bold a step and merely stood looking down at her. *How do shy men ever marry and breed?* he asked himself in some despair.

Olivia solved his problem by putting her hands on his shoulders and standing on tiptoe to kiss him on the lips. He knew what to do after that, and he did it, without any demur from the object of his admiration. He would like to have done more, but the winged harpy of good manners clattered into the room and flopped down to roost on his shoulder.

"Goodness. What got into me?" he said as he released his grip.

That was not precisely true. It was Olivia who was gripping him. With what he liked to think of as reluctance, she let go of his neck.

"Do you know, James, there is one other place—on page twenty, I think—where the argument strays again," she whispered. To his ears it was an endearment of provocative proportions.

"I will look at it when I go home, my dear," he told her. "Thank you, Olivia." He wondered if it was proper to thank a woman for a kiss, but he knew that he was thanking her for forgiving him so freely.

She must have known as well. To his heart's everlasting ease, Olivia placed her hand on his chest.

"I only wanted to do what I felt was right," she said.

"You did," he assured her. He took her hand and kissed her fingers. "When you come tomorrow for the attic expedition, we will spend more time in the book room. I want to share the conclusion of the paper with you. And please call me James. Everyone else calls me Jemmy, but I want you to call me James."

She blushed quite becomingly, which made him smile. "Very well, James. I will see you tomorrow."

"Happy Christmas," he murmured after she left the room. He went to the mirror to straighten his neckcloth and allow his high color to recede.

"Olivia, do you suffer all fools gladly, or just me?" It was a good question, and it carried him down the hall and out the front door.

The sun was setting. He stood a moment in quiet contemplation on the front steps, breathing deep of winter and smelling snow on the way. As he watched, Lord D'Urst joined him.

"Nice night, isn't it, Pete?" he asked, full of charity in this most charitable of seasons.

Lord D'Urst shrugged. "I thought you and your father generally spent Christmas in London," he said, turning to admire the same sunset.

"And I thought you had gotten married a year ago," James commented.

Lord D'Urst waited a moment to reply. "So that's it?" he asked, but it was more of a statement. "Silly me. I was certain you had given your soul to All Souls." He smiled at his own witticism.

"Not entirely, it would seem," James replied, unruffled.

They remained silent another moment, and then the front door opened and Olivia joined them. "I do not know why Mama has not invited you to dinner, James," she said.

Lord D'Urst laughed. "She is afraid he will amaze us with his scholarship, and we will quite forget to eat! That's it, isn't it, Jemmy?"

Ah, the Lord D'Urst I know and love, James thought. *He can make his barbs sound funny, and no one is the wiser.* He smiled.

"I'm certain, rather, that she is dismayed at my frayed waistcoat and shirt almost out at the elbow." *There, Pete. I beat you to it.* "She fears I will put diners off their feed."

Lord D'Urst only looked him over. "I would have thought it was because your hair is uncombed." He leaned companionably close to Olivia. "Do you know, Miss Hannaford, that we in the upper form used to wager the times in one term that Jemmy would remember he had hair and comb it?"

To his dismay, Olivia put her hand to her mouth, but was unable to entirely stifle her own laughter. His spirits rose a notch when she touched his arm. "We don't mind here at Hannaford, my lord."

Take that, Pete, he thought. *I don't notice her touching your arm.* "Olivia appreciates the finer things," he said, knowing that it did not sound at all clever, but pleased because she beamed at him. They started down the steps together, Lord D'Urst taking the moment to inform Olivia that he needed to retrieve his document case from the post chaise.

"Treaty making is tedious business, my dear Miss Hannaford," he said. He sighed. "Of course, one must make sacrifices for the good of one's nation."

Well, rally and jab, James thought, knowing that he could be magnanimous. *I will yield the field tonight, Pete, but then again, she won't be accompanying you to my attic tomorrow.* He nodded to Olivia and continued down the steps with Lord D'Urst.

He thought he knew the steps well, considering the years and years that he and Tim had pounded up and down them, but to his chagrin, pain, and amazement, he took a wrong step, and then another. Quicker than a snap of the fingers, he found himself on his back, his ankle on fire, staring up at Pete Winston.

"Gadfreys, man, did you trip over your feet?" Pete was asking him.

He would liked to have answered, but all he could do was wheeze and wish for his air to return.

Olivia hurried down the steps and threw herself beside him. "James! Can you breathe?"

All he could do was shake his head and look behind her at Lord D'Urst, who was grinning now.

She helped him into a sitting position and called for the footman.

"It's my ankle," he managed to say. "I think it's broken."

"Lord D'Urst, do help the footman get him inside," Olivia pleaded.

"I have a better idea," D'Urst said. "Since my traveling carriage is right here, the footman and I can pop him into it and take him home. You'd prefer that, wouldn't you, James? I mean, just look at you!"

"You're so kind to think of that," Olivia said.

"It's nothing, my dear," Lord D'Urst replied. "Give us a hand now, lad."

Lord D'Urst helped him into the carriage, but not without crowding his ankle hard against the carriage door, which made James yelp in pain. He was almost too embarrassed to look out the window, but at least he was rewarded by the anxious look on Olivia's face when he did.

"I'll be over first thing tomorrow," she told him. "Pray your ankle is not broken!"

"We'll be over first thing," Lord D'Urst amended. "In fact, I will come along with you now, Jemmy. Miss Hannaford, he has always required looking after, but perhaps you don't know that. Buck up, Jemmy. This shouldn't slow you down beyond a month or two."

They made the short trip in silence. James shut his eyes against the pain and breathed as shallowly as he could at every jar of the carriage. Lord D'Urst reached out to steady him several times, but he only managed to shove his hand against the offending ankle.

"That is really swelling prodigiously," he said.

"Well, don't sound too happy about it," James said, gritting his teeth. He waited for the wave of pain to subside. "Why do I have the feeling that you pushed me?"

"I would never!" Lord D'Urst declared, his eyes wide. He laughed and gave James's ankle a squeeze. "Jemmy, dear boy, I would never have to resort to low tactics. You're just clumsy."

Perhaps he was. It was not a calming reflection, he decided. Lord D'Urst, all sympathy and concern to Lord

Waverly, deposited James in his chamber and left after promising to come tomorrow with Olivia Hannaford. He sweated and suffered through a visit from the surgeon, who poked and prodded and pronounced the ankle unbroken. Mr. Walton was kind enough to wipe off his face and then peer at him with the sympathy of ten.

"Lord Crandall, an actual fracture would feel better than this nasty wrench." He pointed his finger at James. "You are to stay entirely off that leg for at least two weeks. I will even insist that two footmen carry you to the commode when nature calls."

"Oh, goodness! Not that!"

Mr. Walton only smiled at his anguish. "Now, now, Lord Crandall! Your own father tells me how you long for solitude to work on dissertations. Now you will have solitude to your heart's content! Good night now, Lord Crandall. Take these powders every four hours, keep the ankle elevated and cool, and let me know if anything changes."

Nothing will change, James thought wearily as his father walked the surgeon downstairs. *I will eat my Christmas pudding with a book propped open beside me, as I usually do. Olivia will drop by until Lord D'Urst becomes more interesting. My ankle will heal eventually, and I will return to Oxford without my Christmas ornament.*

After a sleepless night that the powders did nothing to improve, he felt no better in the morning. He waved away food; the pain in his leg only added to the queasiness in his stomach. He lay in bed completely frustrated and hardly able to bear the agony of even a light coverlet on his ankle.

Olivia arrived early as she had promised, with Lord D'Urst in tow, wearing his sympathy like a pose. The portrait of boredom, he stared out the window on the falling snow while Olivia sat beside James. He was too gone with pain to say anything. *And what good would it do?* he asked himself in perfect misery. *Pete will overhear everything I try to say to this wonderful creature, and I have no clever repartee, even in the best of times, which this is definitely not.* He could only gaze at Olivia in mute appeal.

She surprised him by lifting the cover off the end of his bed to look at his wounded ankle. When she put her hand near to touch it, he flinched.

"Poor dear," she murmured. "I have not touched it, and you cannot even bear the thought."

"Jemmy, have a little heart!" Lord D'Urst admonished in a most rallying tone. If he had felt better, James would have relished the glare Olivia gave the man.

"James, you need some help," she told him.

He could not deny it. "My father has sent for Mr. Walter again."

She nodded and looked around the room. "That is what I need," she said.

He tried to follow her gaze, but he was lying flat on his back. He heard her by his desk and then Lord D'Urst laughing. She returned with his woven waste basket, empty now, and folded a towel inside it.

"I don't mean to hurt you," she told him as she carefully raised his leg, and then rested his foot and ankle inside the basket. "There now." She felt his other leg. "You're cold, but with the weight gone now, I can add a blanket or two."

"Foot of the bed," he said, shivering from the pain she had caused, even as he appreciated her care. She opened the chest and extracted two blankets, covering him and tucking them in on all sides. He closed his eyes, enjoying the warmth and the relief of pressure on his ankle.

"Now I will wait for the doctor," she said, seating herself beside him again.

"Not necessary," he managed to say. "Perfectly all right."

"See there, my dear, even Jemmy says we can leave," Lord D'Urst said. "Jemmy, does your butler have a key to the attic?"

"I am waiting for the doctor," she repeated.

"My dear Olivia! You take too much upon yourself!" Lord D'Urst protested. "Surely the surgeon knows best."

"I am not convinced," she said quietly. "You may leave if you wish, my lord; James is no trouble to me."

Yes, leave, by all means, James thought. It hurt too much to turn his head, but he could hear Pete Winston huffing off to sit in the window seat. Olivia continued to hold his hand, stroking his wrist. *I am three parts dead and she moves me*, he thought simply. *I astound myself.*

When the doctor came, she took him immediately to task, mincing no words, overriding all his protests until the man appealed to James.

"Do what she says," he told the surgeon. "I trust her."

"Over my own judgment?" exclaimed the doctor.

"Over your own judgment."

With a great sigh, the doctor mixed more powders and left the room without a word. When Olivia followed him into the hall to continue her argument, James couldn't help but think of a mother wren, fluttering and chattering at foes twenty times her size.

"She's certainly a managing little baggage," Lord D'Urst said from the window seat. "Charles never told me that about her."

"New to me too," James said.

She returned to the room and quickly prepared another dose of powders. She put her arm under his head to raise him and whispered, "This is much stronger and will put you under for a while. James, Lord D'Urst can help me locate the furniture in the attic."

He groaned, but not from pain this time. He closed his eyes and yielded himself without a murmur into the arms of Morpheus.

There he stayed, through several days that had no meaning to him. He was dimly aware of assistance to the commode from his footmen, along with his father's presence now and then. Olivia came, he thought, because at least once there was a rustling of skirts and the faintest fragrance of almond extract. And then one morning he woke to see snow falling.

He lay as still as he could, unwilling to invite the stab of pain so familiar to him now. He lay on his back and watched the snow fall, feeling at peace with his body for the first time in days. On experiment, he moved his foot slightly and was rewarded with a dull throb instead of shooting agony.

"Well, that is better," he said out loud.

"Eh?" Charles sat by his bed this time, his eyes on the book in his lap. "Are you in the land of the living again, Jemmy?"

"I could be," he said. "Give me a hand, Charlie, and help me sit up."

His friend obliged, and in a moment he was upright again, propped against the headboard with many pillows. He raised his knee slowly, anticipating the pain, and then relaxed when he discovered that pressure on his leg actually felt good now from that angle.

"I may live," he announced. He ran his hand over his chin. "Another week and I'll have a beard," he commented, pleased that he felt well enough to joke. "Charlie, did you get nominated to keep this morning's death watch?"

"Something like," he teased in turn. "We've all been drawing straws. The short straw loses and gets you." He patted James's shoulder. "Don't despair about the refurbishing you were attempting with Livy. She and Pete have been careening about the countryside from warehouse to warehouse, accumulating paint and wallpaper enough to redo Prinny's palace at Brighton."

"I'm delighted," he said with what he hoped resembled gratitude, even though he felt none.

"Knew you would be pleased, lad," Charles said. He leaned closer. "And I am pleased as well. Your accident may have turned out to be just the thing to guarantee Olivia's attachment to Lord D'Urst, a thing I have been plotting for some time now. I suspected they were suited for each other. How gratifying to have one's efforts borne out."

James sighed. Charles looked at him in some consternation. "Are you certain you are feeling better?" he asked.

"Of course I am," he lied.

"I knew you would be pleased, considering how you and Tim—God bless his memory—used to practically share Livy as a little sister." Charles stood up. "Let me summon the watch from below stairs, Jemmy. You'd probably like a trip to the necessary, and maybe a shave. Some gruel or barley water?" he joked.

Slip some strychnine in my morning broth while you're at it, James thought. "Thank you, Charlie. I appreciate your ministrations. I leave you at perfect liberty to return to Hannaford!"

"Not so fast, James!" Charles said. He tugged on the bell pull and sat down again. "Louisa showed up two nights ago—I suppose it was the day after your accident—and who should she have in tow besides children and husband?"

"I can't imagine," James said.

"Her stupid brother-in-law!" Charles declared. He made a face. "I think Papa has been telling the world of his concerns for Livy, and Louisa communicated them to Felix, who has somehow convinced himself that he will be the answer to Livy's prayers! You remember him, don't you? I'm quite happy to sit over here at Enderfield from Christmas Eve until Twelfth Night with that lunatic loose at Hannaford, don't you know."

James nodded, feeling weaker by the moment. "Certainly Felix is my favorite man milliner and Bond Street beau! Charles, could you help me to lie down again? Perhaps I am hasty in sitting up."

Charles did help, smoothing down the covers with some of that same touch that Olivia possessed. "The worst of it is watching Pete and Felix glare at each other and dog poor Livy from room to room," he said as the footman came into the room. "If she can escape, I'll send her your way."

That vague promise was his only consolation as the day wore on. *I can understand Olivia's desperation to avoid Felix at all cost,* James told himself when she did not materialize. He will make Peter seem all the more palatable. And what female would not be impressed by a diplomatist who has been everywhere from glittering St. Petersburg to backwater Washington, D.C.? He wearily waved away his father's efforts to administer more powders. *I have an entire new wardrobe on order in London, but it would never impress Olivia,* he told himself. *The moment I hang clothes on my frame, they wrinkle. Dust balls see me coming and climb aboard for the ride. I look in the mirror, and my hair tangles. And now I am too clumsy to negotiate stairs I know as well as the ones here at Enderfield. I am probably even a threat to national security.*

If he could not walk at present, James discovered how

effortless it was to spend a day pacing up and down in his mind, wondering if a cloister in the French Alps would take a Protestant, or if only felons were allowed to go to Sydney or Melbourne. His heart bruised more surely than his ankle, he knew he could not bear to be the recipient of a wedding invitation from Olivia Hannaford.

He drifted in and out of sleep as the afternoon waned, not caring much whether he lived or died. He told himself that he was cured of love, until he woke when someone lighted the branch of candles by his bed. He opened his eyes to look upon Olivia.

"James," was all she said as she took his hand and held it. After a long moment in which he was certain he was holding his breath, she brushed the hair from his forehead and leaned her cheek against his for the smallest moment. "It is so blissfully peaceful here."

"How did you manage to escape?" he asked, wishing that she would stay close to him, even as she returned to her chair.

"Felix exhausted himself playing jackstraws with my nephew David and had to lie down." She looked beyond him to some blank space on the wall. "Lord D'Urst has closeted himself with my father and mother." She sighed, and with visible effort returned her gaze to him. "He has declared himself, James. He promises me exotic locales and libraries galore and tutors."

"For geometry?" he asked, not trusting himself to say more.

She shook her head. "I mentioned geometry to him, and he laughed." Olivia was careful to avoid his eyes. "He says it is wonderful that I am so smart, but he thinks that a female should be more interested in poetry and Shakespeare. I do like them," she added hastily. "Don't think me ungrateful." She ran her finger along the stripe in the blanket. "He wants to shape my learning. He says that he wants his children to be raised by an intelligent woman. Not our children, but his children. Mama tells me that Lord D'Urst is all a woman could wish for and that it is a good offer."

"Your father? What does he think?"

She hesitated. "I cannot tell. He became so quiet when I told him of Lord D'Urst's offer. Mama says he's just melancholy because I am his youngest child. What do you think?"

"It probably is a good offer," he said after excruciating thought. He gritted his teeth and raised himself up on his elbow. "You know how much you enjoy scholarship. Here is a grand opportunity, even if it must be Shakespeare instead of Euclid." *What puny words,* he thought. *I love her beyond all measure, but what could she possibly see in me? Sir Waldo, you were wrong.*

She said nothing for a long while, returning his gaze to the distance. Her wordless indictment smote his heart. He wanted to reach for her hand, to tell her of his love and beg her patience with the foolishness of the male sex in general, and him in particular. He closed his eyes instead. When he opened them, she was on her feet and looking down at him with an expression of real sorrow.

"Lord D'Urst says he even knows of a *maison de coiffure* where they will tame my hair." She fingered a curl that had declared its independence from the bun low on her neck. "Right up until he said it, I thought I wanted that too."

To his total misery, she kissed his forehead and went to the door. "Lord D'Urst says that I am a work in progress. Do you see that when you look at me?"

"Sometimes," he said. "I must be honest."

"Do you know what I see when I think of you?" she asked suddenly, the words coming out with some force.

He shook his head, almost afraid of the intensity in her voice.

"I see a good man. Not a brain or a title or a double first. Just a good man. 'Night, James."

He cried himself to sleep, something he had not done since the death of his mother. He was sick to his soul, and the pain far exceeded the throb in his ankle. *Just what is any man after in a wife?* he asked himself. As he finally lay still, exhausted by his tears, it occurred to him that he could pinpoint the moment he fell in love with Olivia Hannaford. He closed his eyes to see the moment again, to watch her striding along the lane between the two houses, her top-knot bouncing about, the picture of energy and endless fun. It had nothing to do with her scholarship or whatever potential she represented, he decided, but only the breadth and depth of her. *Olivia just is*, he knew now, *and when she is, I am.* He roused from melancholy long enough to share dinner with his father, who ate from a tray in the sickroom.

"I trust you will not mind, son, but Lord Nuttall has invited me to play whist tonight."

"On Christmas Eve, Papa?" James asked, amused, in spite of himself.

Lord Waverly laughed. "It is the proclivity of two old widowers to entertain each other as we choose, son! I am only an estate away should any crisis strike."

It already has, James thought. "Very well, sir. Let me wish you Happy Christmas now, for I plan to be asleep before you return."

He had asked the footman to gather up his treatise from the book room and bring it to him when he heard a firm knock on the front door. When his heart leaped into his throat, he reminded himself that Olivia never knocked with such firmness. All the same, he sat up and ran his fingers through his hair. The door opened.

"Oh, it is you, Peter," he said, unable to hide his disappointment.

Dressed in his overcoat and wearing a natty beaver hat that just shrieked continental good taste, Lord D'Urst made himself at home—except that to James's eyes, he did not look comfortable. When he did not say anything, James spoke. "Are you on your way to Christmas services with the Hannafords?"

"I am, James, and that is why I have come." Lord D'Urst stared down at the floor as though expecting to see a message written on the carpet. James peered at him in some surprise. *I could almost suspect contrition*, he thought, *or at least a near relative to it.*

"Pete?"

Lord D'Urst looked up, roused from whatever reverie he had permitted himself. "I don't go to church often, Jemmy, but own to a certain squeamishness about a subject sitting somewhat sore on me." He cleared his throat. "I did push you on the steps, and I wanted to apologize." He sat on the edge of his chair, as though in a hurry to end such self-reflection. "I had no idea you would fetch such a sprain, but, Jemmy, I wanted time to court Olivia, because for some reason I cannot fathom, she seemed to favor you. I hope you'll be understanding."

James could think of nothing to say.

"She is all magnificence," Lord D'Urst continued, his eyes lively. "And so charming! When I think of what I can make of her, I am almost bereft of speech."

"What you can make of her? I do not understand."

"Jemmy, sometimes you are so simple! What man could resist to tinker with such a female?"

I could now, he thought. "Have you made her an offer?" he asked.

"Yes."

"And . . . and did she accept?"

Lord D'Urst smiled. "She said she would let me know tomorrow. I am ready for the best news." He reached into his pocket and pulled out an elegant case. "What do you think of this?" He touched the clasp and revealed a single ruby on a gold chain.

"Beautiful," James said, and he almost meant it.

"I have written a note, and I will give it to her first thing. I'll own that you are good with a phrase. What do you think of this?" he asked, handing a sheet of paper to James.

James read the little note, gulped, and read it again, his spirits rising. "My beloved, you are my Christmas ornament, my own pretty bauble. —Peter."

He let his breath out slowly. "Precisely the right words, Pete. I couldn't possibly have said it better." He returned the note, willing his hand not to shake.

"Yes, I thought it would be the right touch," Lord D'Urst said modestly. "She is a pretty bauble, isn't she?"

She is, if that is all you see, James thought. "She certainly is. I don't know that I feel full of forgiveness for this thick ankle, Pete, but I do know that you'll get what you deserve tomorrow."

"No hard feelings, Jemmy?"

"Not one."

He could hardly wait for Peter Winston to quit the room. He broke into a sweat that left him trembling, but he managed to hobble to his bookshelf and retrieve a dusty volume. He shivered in his nightshirt but sat at his desk a long moment, staring at Euclid's theorems, before he dipped his pen in the inkwell. "I am no great shakes at mathematics, Olivia," he wrote on the flyleaf. "Between us, I believe one plus one equals one. Somehow, it equals two as well. Marry me?"

He wrapped the geometry text in brown paper discarded from another book, tied it with string, and wrote in big letters on the outside, OPEN AFTER LORD D'URST'S GIFT. His heart peaceful, he summoned his footman, let the man help him to bed, and then told him to take the package to Hannaford's. He went to sleep then and dreamed of pleasant doings.

He woke early, refreshed and hungry for the first time in a week. Even his father was surprised at the prodigious breakfast he packed away.

"Now, Father, if you would help me to the window seat, I am expecting a visitor."

"Olivia?" his father asked, his expression full of concern.

"If I am supremely lucky, and I wager I will be." *What a sunny Christmas day*, he thought as he leaned back against the pillow his father had thoughtfully provided. The blanket was warm against his bare legs. He needed a shave, and he had spilt porridge on his nightshirt, but he didn't think Olivia would mind.

"If I recall Tim's habits from earlier days, you Hannafords will eat breakfast first and then open presents," he announced to the winter birds that fluttered around the suet ball outside his window. He made himself comfortable, reached for his treatise, and turned to page twenty where Olivia said he had lost the drift of the argument again.

He found the spot and was beginning a correction when he saw Lord D'Urst's traveling carriage moving at a rapid pace down the road. "Oh God, Thou art kind to sinners and foolish men on this Thy day," he prayed out loud. No matter that he understood anatomy, his heart was so high in his throat that he knew if he opened his mouth, it would flop into his hand. He swallowed mightily and then almost shuddered with delight at his next sight from the window.

Olivia hurried down the lane. She had not taken the time to do her hair, and it perched in his favorite topknot. He peered closer, noting his book clutched to her heart. He held his breath as she stopped and stared at his house for the longest time. To his everlasting joy, she began to run. With a wince and a gasp, he hobbled back to bed. In another moment he heard light steps on the stairs, and then Olivia threw open the door and practically catapulted herself into the room. Without a word, he pulled back the covers.

"Just look out for my ankle," he warned as she threw off her cloak and lay down beside him.

She kissed him, and he quit worrying about his ankle.

"Yes, I will marry you," she said when he let her up for air.

"I take it you said no to Lord D'Urst," he said, pillowing her head on his arm.

She raised up to look at him, indignant. "He had the nerve to write that I was his Christmas ornament! Can you imagine such a thing?"

He could, and did, and then tucked the words away, never to be used again. She pillowed her head on his chest. "And then I opened your package. Thank you, my love, from the bottom of my heart."

"That was what did it?" he asked, relishing the warmth of her.

She laughed and touched his face. "No! Well, it helped, but I had resolved to marry you weeks ago, James Enders."

He stared at her in surprise. "Even when I was bumbling, and erring, and apologizing around the clock?"

She nodded, burrowing herself in closer to him.

"Before that. I have a confession to make. Before you arrived, Papa took me aside and told me that he thought you would make an excellent husband. He said that you were coming home for Christmas to make me an offer and that I should accept it, as you were the best possible choice for me."

James could only gape. "Even when I was looking like your worst nightmare?"

"I own you did strain it, James," she agreed, her breath soft on his neck. She kissed his ear. "I trust my father. I always have. He told me that you would do, and I trusted him until I could see for myself that he was right."

Sir Waldo, I will be a most grateful son-in-law, he thought as his heart filled with love for his neighbor. He held Olivia close.

"You realize, of course, that it would be easier to marry Peter."

She nodded and looked at him, and he could see how serious she was. "That occurred to me as I was walking over here, love, and I had to stop and think a moment," she told him. "How simple it would be to let someone take charge of my life! But you will not do that, will you? That's a little scary, James. Are all women loved so much, or only a privileged few?"

"Your life is your own, Olivia," he whispered in her ear. "All I ask is that you share it with me and our children. I will protect you and shelter you, but before God, I will not try to change you."

There were tears in her eyes now. "And it will be the same with me. I love you." She kissed him thoroughly.

This is a better cure than powders, he told himself when he could think again. "I'm not so certain I will be up to cutting much of a dash in a wedding dance, Olivia, unless you prefer a lengthy engagement."

She shook her head. "We should wait only just long enough for the crisis to pass at my house."

"Crisis?" he asked. "I take it your mother is not too excited about this turn of events." He kissed her. "Face it, Olivia, you are marrying a shag-bag instead of an elegant diplomatist."

She turned her lively eyes on him. "Oh, the crisis is much more diverting, James. What should my nephew David do this morning but throw out spots! Louisa is certain it is chicken pox. Those tidings of great joy sent her stupid brother-in-law Felix into a dither from which I am certain he will never recover. Charles is still laughing about it." She gasped then and put her hand to her mouth. "Lord D'Urst doesn't even know about this! Should Papa write and tell him? Suppose he breaks out in spots in Paris at the treaty table?"

"Our elegant Lord D'Urst?" James said. "Such a crisis! Oh, I wish it did not hurt to laugh!"

Olivia's eyes opened wider still. "Do you suppose du Plessis or Louis the Eighteenth have had the chicken pox?" She started to laugh. "Oh my, what a Christmas gift that will be!"

It required no real imagination to pick up the thread of her thoughts. He settled himself more comfortably on his back and tightened his arm around his darling, who gratified him by resting her head upon his chest and putting her arm across him in a gesture he could only call possessive.

"Think of it, my love; the source of contagion will be traced to Lord D'Urst, and there will be diplomatic reprisals of the worst kind. He will be sent in disgrace to . . . to . . . oh! what is the dreariest capital imaginable? Perhaps Washington, D.C., where the politickers conspire and duel with one another. What do you think, lovely lady?"

She was far too silent. He glanced down at her, snuggled so peacefully within the circle of his arm, and chuckled to himself to notice how even her breathing was. *Oh, so you have also discovered what an exhausting business love can be?* he thought. He kissed the top of her head. "Olivia?"

"I was just thinking," she defended herself, her voice drowsy. "Only a ninny would sleep at a time like this."

"And what were you thinking?" He had made a pleasant discovery of his own; he never would have thought that such wondrous hair could be so soft. He kissed her head again.

"I was merely enjoying the oddest phenomenon, James," she told him. "How is it possible that when I am lying here with you, I have the feeling that no one in the world has ever experienced such wonder?"

He laughed. "Do you think this is worth a scientific study?"

He felt her laughter, even though he did not hear it. "I think not, my love," she told him, "although I do anticipate any number of excellent collaborations with you." She sighed. "James, for being no Christmas for you, and a worrisome one for me, this is the best Christmas."

How peaceful this is, he thought as his eyes started to close. *I could tell you that scientists should not deal in absolutes at this stage of the hypothesis, particularly since I have the wonderful suspicion that our Christmases will only get better each year.*

"I love you, Olivia," he said instead, and he knew with a conviction that left him almost breathless that this was an indisputable absolute.

MAKE A JOYFUL NOISE

*S*on, I own that being a Christian is onerous at times."
Like many of his mother's pronouncements, this
one was a bolt out of the blue. Peter Chard smiled behind
his napkin as he blotted the remnants of dinner from his
lips, and then did the same for his little daughter Emma.
He winked at Will, who sat next to Mama on the other
side of the table.

"How do you mean, Mama?" he asked. He draped his
arm over the back of Emma's chair so he could fiddle with
her curls. "Seems to me that Our Lord mentioned on at least
one occasion that His yoke was easy and His burden light."

"Peter, Jesus could say that because He never had to
deal with our vicar!"

Chard laughed. "Mama, some would argue that He
probably deals with the vicar more than we do! But please
explain yourself."

It was all the encouragement she needed. "Pete, I find
myself trussed as neatly as a Christmas goose and it is
only October."

"Grandmama, if you would not stop to talk to Mr.
Woodhull, but only shake his hand and walk on, you
would stay out of trouble at church," Will said as he
reached for the last apple tart.

Peter laughed again and pushed the bowl a little
closer to his son. "Mama, it seems I cannot take you

anywhere!" he teased. "And here I thought Sunday was harmless. Am I to assume that you have promised something that you are already regretting?" He pulled out his pocket watch. "We are only two hours out of church, and you are already repentant. It must be serious."

Louisa Chard, the Dowager Lady Wythe, sighed. "Oh, Pete, what a stupid thing I did! Son, I made the mistake of asking about the Christmas choir."

Will ceased chewing. Emma, as young as she was, tensed under Chard's hand. *Are my insides churning? Dare I blame it on dinner?* he asked himself.

The choir. Too little could not be said about it, and here was Mama, tempting the devil. By some awesome, cosmic twist, St. Philemon's Christmas choir was a freak of nature. During the year, a choir occasionally accompanied services with no complaint. But Christmas? He shuddered. *Are we too proud? Do we not listen to each other? Are there poor among us that we ignore too much? Does the Lord use the annual parish choir competition at Christmas to flog us for sins real and imagined?*

It seemed so. What had begun when he was a boy as a friendly competition between three small parish churches had grown into a monster. "What, Mama, did the vicar ask you to assassinate one of this year's judges, and you have second thoughts?" he quizzed.

"I would not have second thoughts!" she exclaimed and blew a kiss to her granddaughter, who regarded her with large eyes. "Emmie dear, I would never," she assured the child. "No, son. In a weak moment, I agreed to help in this year's recruitment. That is all."

Chard relaxed. "Mama, I know how much you love to gad about and drink tea. Now you are only adding recruitment to your agenda as you career about the parish boundaries."

Lady Wythe sighed again. "People will run from me," she declared as she rose from the table and signaled to the footman to do his duty.

"Papa, I am tired," Emma said as he picked her up.

"So am I, kitten. If I tell you a story, will you take a nap?"

"If I don't take a nap, I know you will, Papa!" she teased as he carried her upstairs.

Emma, love, if I were to tell you how much I like Sunday afternoon and napping with you, my friends would hoot and make rude noises, he thought as he stretched out on her little bed and let her cuddle close to him. The rain began before he was too far into a somewhat convoluted story about an Indian princess and her golden ball. The soothing sound of rain sent Emma to sleep before he had to create an ending where there was none.

Funny that I am forgetting my stories of India, he thought as he undid the top button of his breeches and eased his shoes off. *It has not been so long since I adventured there.* He seldom thought of Assaye anymore, a battle cruelly fought and hardly won. When the morning paper brought him news now of Beau Wellington in Portugal and advancing to retake Spain, he could read the accounts over porridge with detachment unthinkable six years ago in humid, bloody India—

That is what hard work does to my body, he thought as he kissed Emma's head and let her burrow in close to him in warm, heavy slumber. *I can be kinder to the Almighty than Mama,* he thought as his eyes closed. *Thank thee, dear Lord, for my children, my land, and our own good life.* He frowned. *But please, Lord, not the Christmas choir.*

When he woke, the bed was absent of Emma, as he knew it would be. He turned onto his side and raised on one elbow to watch his children sitting on the carpet, playing with Will's wooden horses and cart. *Will looks like me*, he thought with some pleasure, and not for the first time. *He will be tall and will likely stay blond too. He has Lucy's eyes*, he thought, *but not her pouty mouth, thank goodness.* Both children had his mild temperament, and he was more grateful for that than any physical blessings. *There will be no tantrums in these darlings*, he told himself. *No railings, no bitterness, no accusations where none were warranted, and no recriminations. When they go to their wife and husband someday, pray God they will go in peace and confidence.*

It was his continual prayer, and he could see it answered almost daily. He and Mama were raising beautiful, kindly children. If that meant doing so without wifely comforts, so be it. He had known few enough of those, anyway. He lay on his back and covered his eyes with his arm. *To be honest*, he thought, *I know that someday I will have to face a heavenly tribunal and receive some chastisement for the relief I felt when I learned of Lucy's death. I will take my stripes, and I will not complain. God is just, and quite possibly merciful.*

How peaceful it was to lie there and listen to his children play, knowing that tomorrow he would be in the fields again—always in the fields—seeing to the last of the harvest and attending to the thousand duties that a man of considerable property rejoiced in. Tomorrow night he would likely fall asleep before Mama was through talking to him over her solitaire table, or before Will had finished explaining his latest lesson from Mr. Brett's school. He would quickly fall asleep again in his bed. There was no wife to reach for; he was too tired, anyway.

By breakfast next morning, Mama had still not relinquished her agonies over the Christmas choir. "I can count on you, can I not?" she asked.

"Of course! What is it that our choirmaster wants us to torture this year?"

"I heard him mention something about Haydn and 'The Heavens Are Telling,'" she said.

He winced. "Perhaps our salvation lies in our simplicity?" he suggested.

Mama regarded her tea and toast somewhat moodily. "It lies in good voices, son, and you know it! Why is it that no good singers lurk within parish boundaries? I call it unfair."

"They are only hiding. You will find them, Mama," he assured her. "I have every confidence in you."

She glared at him again. "All I want is to win just once, Peter. Just once."

If you say so, Mama, he thought later as he swung his leg over his horse and settled into the saddle for another day. His route took him past St. Philemon's, and as usual, he raised his hat to Deity within and raised his eyes to the distant hill where he could see St. Anselm's—only slightly larger, but filled with singers apparently. A half turn in the saddle and a glance over his left shoulder showed him St. Peter's, a parish blessed with golden throats. He smiled, wondering, as he always did, what strange geographical quirk in property and parish boundaries had located three churches so close together. The living at St. Phil's was his to bestow, and he had been pleased with his choice. Mr. Paul Woodhull was young, earnest in his duties, and genuinely cared about his pastoral sheep. He had a little wife equally young, earnest, and caring. Too bad neither could carry a tune anywhere.

He rode toward his own fields, the sun warm on

his back and welcome in October. Soon it would be cold, and the snow would come. As Sepoy carried him up the gradual slope to his hayfield, he noticed the woman walking through the field. He smiled, wondering for the umpteenth time who she was. He had noticed her first in August's heat, when she walked with only a bonnet dangling down her back. All he could tell about her was that she was slender but not tall and possessed dark hair. Since September she had been cloaked as well as bonneted. He had mentioned her to Mama once over dinner, but Louisa Chard—she who knew all shire news—only shrugged. "Perhaps she is a relation of the Wetherbys, and you know I do not visit them," was her pointed comment.

He rode toward her once out of curiosity when she crossed his land, but she only edged away the closer he came, so he changed his mind. *If I were a lone woman, I would not choose to be harassed by a stranger on horseback*, he reasoned and gave her a wide berth. He was always mindful of her, even if he never asked anyone else who she was. He even dreamed about her once and woke up embarrassed. He vowed not to think about her again, and he seldom did, even if he saw her every day.

For no real reason, he turned to watch her as she skirted the boggy patch in the low spot on the path that had probably been there since Hadrian built his wall. She stepped over the creek that ran so cold and continued her steady pace to the top of the rise. He noticed that she was walking more slowly than in August, and then his attention was taken by his men in the hay field; he did not think of her again.

Chard worked all week on his farm at that same steady pace which had characterized his army service in India and which had earned him the nickname Lord Mark Time. It was a stupid name bestowed on him by a few fellow officers and was never used by his own men, who knew him best. He thought about it one night and considered that those officers even now lay rotting in India, having discovered in the last minute of their lives, and far too late to profit from, that steadiness usually overrules flash and dash. At any rate, it had proved to be the quality most in demand at the Kaihla ford in Assaye.

"Mama, am I stodgy?" he asked suddenly.

Lady Wythe looked up quickly from her solitaire hand. "Well, not precisely, Pete," she said finally, after rearranging some cards. "Careful, perhaps, and certainly reliable." She laid down the rest of the cards, sweeping them together to shuffle and cut again. She folded her hands in front of her. "I would call you firm of mind, but only a little set in your ways."

"Predictable?" He couldn't resist a smile at the look on her face. "Now be honest, Mama."

"You are predictable, indeed, but it doesn't follow that this is a defect," she protested.

He glanced at the mantelpiece clock. "It is nine o'clock, my dear, and my usual bedtime," he said. "Perhaps I will astound you and remain awake until midnight!"

She laughed as she rang the bell for tea. "You would astound me, indeed, for I know you have been in the saddle since after breakfast."

I am much too predictable, he thought as he stared into the fire hours later, his eyes dry from reading. Mama had given up on him two hours ago and kissed him good night, and still he sat reading, wondering what he was trying to prove, and to whom.

He paid in the morning by oversleeping, with the consequence that St. Phil's was full when he arrived. He knew that he could march down the aisle and take his patron's pew, where for centuries Marquises of Wythe had slumbered through services, but he was not so inclined. Mama sat there even now with Emma and Will, but there was a shyness about him that made him ill wish to call attention to his tardiness. Lucy used to relish her late arrival and the opportunity to peacock her way to the family box. He chose not to.

Will noticed him as he genuflected and sat in the back, and he came down the aisle to join him. Will's clothes smelled faintly of camphor, and it was a reminder, along with the hay, grain, and fruit of the vine tucked in his barns, that the season had turned. He noticed that Will's wrists were shooting out of his sleeves. His son would be nine early in the New Year. Mama would scoff at the expense, but Chard decided that it was time for Will to meet his own tailor. *I will take him to Durham, and we will both be measured*, he thought, pleased with himself.

They stood and bowed when the acolyte bore the cross down the aisle. The smell of incense rose in his nostrils, and then the little procession was past. As he sat down again, he noticed a woman, well bundled in her cloak, standing in the aisle, hesitating. He motioned to Will to move closer to him and give her room, but she chose instead to seat herself directly in front of him.

He sat back, concentrating as always on the service because he cared what Mr. Woodhull said, and he felt a genuine need to express himself in prayer. *I am so blessed*, he thought simply; *it follows that I should be grateful, even if gratitude is not stylish.* They rose for a hymn. As usual, he prepared to flinch at the unfortunate lack of musical ability among his tenants and fellow parishioners. That he did not, he owed entirely to the woman standing in front of him.

He had never heard a more beautiful voice, full-throated and rich, with a vibrato that was just enough without overpowering the simple hymn they sang.

"Oh, Papa."

He glanced down at Will, who appeared to be caught in the same musical web. He put his arm around his son, and they enjoyed the pleasure of a beautiful voice together.

He was hard put to direct his attention to the rest of the service. When he and Will returned to the pew after taking the sacrament, he tried to see who she was, but she had returned to the pew before him and knelt with her head down, as he should be doing. Instead, he knelt behind her again and watched her. Only a moment's concentration assured him that she was the woman who walked the hills. The cloak was shabby up close.

From what he could tell, she was small but sturdy. She was the happy possessor of a wealth of black hair, long and managed into a tidy mass at the back of her neck. He could see nothing remarkable about her—no ribands, no jewelry—until a baby in the pew behind him burst into sudden wails, and she turned around involuntarily. She was beautiful. Her eyes were wide and dark, her features perfectly proportioned, and her lips of tender shape. To Chard's honest delight, she smiled at either him or Will before she turned back around.

When the Mass ended, he wanted to speak to her, but he found himself hard put to think of a proper introduction. To his knowledge, she was not a tenant, so there was no connection. From the look of her cloak, clean but well worn, she was not of his social circle. While he puzzled on what to do and nodded and smiled to various friends, she escaped and his ordeal was over.

He took his time leaving the church, waiting until the last parishioner had congratulated Mr. Woodhull on his sermon. He held out his hand before the vicar could give him the little bow that always embarrassed him. The vicar shook his hand instead.

"My lord, I trust you found the sermon to your liking? I remembered your fondness for that scripture, which you commented upon at dinner last week."

Scripture? What scripture? Dinner? Bless me, I am an idiot, he thought wildly before he had the good sense to nod with what he hoped looked like wisdom. "I appreciate your thoughtfulness, Mr. Woodhull," he said, praying that the vicar would not question him about the sermon. "Tell me, sir, if you can," he ventured, "do you know who that lovely woman was sitting in front of me? She has the most extraordinary voice."

"Ah yes, a rare thing in this parish," the vicar replied with dry humor. "Has Lady Wythe commissioned you to help her find some voices for our Christmas competition?"

He was too honest to perjure himself further. "Not entirely, sir. I simply could not help but enjoy her voice. I will certainly inform my mother, of course," he added.

They were walking together toward the foyer. Chard looked up as they neared the entrance. The day had turned colder. He hoped that the beautiful woman had a ride home, wherever it was she lived.

"Who is she?"

"You can only mean Junius Wetherby's little widow."

"Junius Wetherby?" he asked in surprise. "I had no idea that rascal was married, much less dead." *And what a relief that is*, he thought without a qualm. He only remembered Junius as a care-for-nobody who gave the district a bad stink.

"And yet, it is no puzzle why they are keeping it so quiet." He looked around him again. "I gather that the Wetherbys, despairing of the church, bought the scamp a lieutenancy, which took him to Portugal." The vicar moved closer. "Apparently he met Rosie, promptly married her, and about a week later, fell out of a window while he was drunk."

Chard blinked in surprise. The vicar shook his head.

"The Wetherbys sent for his body and his effects, and Rosie showed up too, to everyone's amazement."

"Is she Portuguese?"

"No. From what I have learned of the whole business—which is precious little—she is the daughter of a Welsh color sergeant. Imagine how that sets with the Wetherbys, who probably think even captains are not sufficiently elevated!"

He had no love for the Wetherbys, but Chard winced anyway. "Trust Junius to disrupt, even from beyond the grave," he said. "Well, good day, Mr. Woodhull."

"Good day, my lord. Remind your mother of the necessity of recruiting a choir, if you will, sir. She promised, and I shall hold her to it."

They were waiting for him in the family carriage, but he indicated Sepoy tied nearby and motioned them on. The wind was picking up now, and he quickly regretted that he had not tied his horse behind the carriage and joined his mother and children inside. In his rush to not be late to church, he had forgotten his muffler, so he buttoned his overcoat as high as he could and resolved to move along quickly.

As Sepoy took him up the rocky path to home, the woman caught his eye again. Head down, she struggled across the field toward the Wetherby estate, which was still two miles distant. He stopped a moment and watched her and then continued on his way.

"She is Welsh, Mama," he said over Sunday dinner. "Perhaps that accounts for the beautiful voice. Oh, and she is a sergeant's daughter."

"She smiled at me," Will added.

"No, I think it was at me, son," Chard teased.

"No, Papa," Will said, sure of himself.

"Obviously, she has had a profound effect on both of you!" Mama declared. With a glance at her grandson, she leaned across the table. "But, Pete, really! A sergeant's daughter and a Wetherby? That is more strain than any of us can stand." She laughed. "Can you imagine how things must be at the Wetherbys'? No, I do not think we want to get embroiled in that."

"It was just a suggestion, Mama. Her voice is so pretty."

And her face, he thought later that night as he wrestled with accounts in the bookroom. It had been the most fleeting of glances, and by nightfall now, he remembered only the beauty of her eyes. He put down his pencil and rubbed his temples where the headache was beginning. *I must admit it*, he thought. *She stirs me. One glance and she stirs me. No wonder wretched Junius was a goner.* He chuckled softly. *And I do believe she did smile at Will.*

By the end of the week, the last of the hay was stacked in ricks, and he faced the fact that he must have another barn. A visit to the Corn Exchange sent him home smiling with the news that corn was up and that the year would enjoy a prosperous conclusion. The day ended less satisfactorily with the sight of Rosie Wetherby walking in the cold. From the warmth of his carriage, he reached the glum conclusion that quite possibly she was not wanted at the Wetherbys' and chose to walk away her days out of bleak necessity.

He was on the verge of mentioning something about his suspicions to Mama, but she gave him news of her own. "Son, I have succumbed to the fact that I must beg for a good soprano, even if she is a sergeant's daughter and a Wetherby," Mama said as soon as the footman served dinner and left the room. "I have written a note to the Wetherbys, stating that I will call on Monday."

"Take Will along," Emma teased.

Will, bless his calm demeanor, ignored his sister. "I would be happy to escort Grandmama," he declared, which left Emma with nothing to say.

"I will be depending on tenors and basses dropping from the sky before practice begins in two weeks," Lady Wythe said as she set down her fork in exasperation. "I so want a good Christmas choir for once, if only so my friends who reside within the parishes of Saints Anselm and Peter will not quiz me from Christmas to Lent!"

"Would you consider changing your circle of acquaintances?" Chard asked with a slight smile. "Or perhaps becoming a Muslim?"

"Certainly not! I will find singers!"

As it turned out, by nine o'clock, while she lamented in the sitting room and he read to Emma and Will in his own bed, events smiled upon Lady Wythe. Her daughter wrote a hasty, tear-splattered note to tell of chicken pox among her offspring and the dire necessity of her mother's presence immediately in Leeds. The welcome news was handed to her by postal express. The courier had scarcely left the house when she arrived at her son's bedroom, letter held triumphantly aloft.

"Pete, I am needed in Leeds!" She handed the letter to him and sat on his bed. "Now how can I possibly help Mr. Woodhull locate singers?"

He looked at her as warning bells went off in his head. "Mama, you don't imagine for one moment that this task of yours is to pass to me."

She gathered her grandchildren to her side. "Children, I cannot believe your father would fail me at this desperate moment when young lives are at stake in Leeds!"

"From chicken pox?" Will asked, always practical.

"It is scarcely fatal, Mama," Chard stated but knew

when he was defeated. "Bella needs you, I am sure. We'll manage here."

"And the choir?"

In his mind, ruin, disgrace, and another year's humiliation in the Christmas competition passed in review. "I will discharge your duty, my dear. Now get Truitt to help you pack. If I know Bella, she needs you this instant. I will escort you."

Leaving his children in the care of housekeeper, butler, and numerous doting servants, Lord Wythe took his mother south to Leeds and the open arms of his little sister, Bella. He lingered long enough to observe the ravages of chicken pox among his nieces and nephews, notice that Bella was increasing again, and visit some former brothers in arms for needed information. Equipped with it, he wrote a few letters, walked the floor one night with a particularly feverish niece, and returned at noon on Monday at peace with himself and possessed of a plan.

Mercy, but I am tired, he thought as he changed clothes, ate standing up because he was tired of sitting, and kept one eye on the clock.

"I can go with you to the Wetherbys', Papa," Will offered.

Perhaps not this first time," he replied, "but I do appreciate your interest, son." He took longer than usual with his neck cloth and wished for the first time in years that he had a valet. "How is that?" he asked finally.

"A little crooked," Will said. "Bend down, Papa." Chard did as he was advised, and Will tugged on the neck cloth. The result was much the same, but he complimented his son and let him carry his hat to the side door, where his butler handed him his overcoat again. He took the hat from Will. "I am off to hunt the wild soprano, my boy," he said, and Will laughed. "Do wish me luck."

To be fair, there really wasn't anything the matter with the Wetherbys, he decided. He knew that if someone were to ask him point blank, he would be hard-pressed to explain his dislike. But there you are: *I do not like Sir Rufus Wetherby or his family*, he thought as Sepoy stepped along with his usual sangfroid.

Chard decided that Sir Rufus was very much like a cat that had insinuated himself into their household years ago. Someone—was it Bella?—named the beast Wooster for no discernible reason. Wooster had showed up one night at the servants' entrance, hollering and importuning, and then zipped in when someone opened the door as if he had forgotten something inside.

Wooster never left, Chard remembered with a smile.

He usurped the best spot before the fireplace and always rushed to the scraps bowl before the other more polite household felines. In his rush to be first, he invariably ate too much and then threw it up, after much upheaval and noise. He would dash back to the bowl and repeat the process before the cook got disgusted and threw Wooster out. Wooster never learned. He was always there, first in line, when the door opened.

Bella loved the disgusting creature, but Papa threatened to anchor the cat in the driveway and run over it with the barouche.

That would be Sir Rufus, Chard thought. *He has to be first at the food bowl. He is merely a baronet, yet he takes what he thinks are the best spots in the Corn Exchange, or the tavern, or even at church, when it suits him to go. It must chafe him that the Wythe box is so prominently situated*, Chard thought. *I believe he would have felt right at home with Cortez or Pizarro, rushing about and claiming things in the name of Spain. Sir Rufus is oblivious to the disdain of others and thinks himself quite my equal.*

Chard owned to some discomfort over that last thought. "I wish he would not fawn and slave over me because I am a marquis and he is a baronet, Sepoy," he told his horse. "It smacks of the shop and embarrasses me. Perhaps that is why I never visit him."

The house, while large, never looked as though it belonged there. Chard gazed around him as he waited for someone to open the door. He decided that the general lack of permanence may have been partly to blame because of the painfully fake Greek temple that some misguided Wetherby had considered high art placed far too close to the front entrance. *Mushrooms*, he thought, and then had the good grace to blush and wonder perhaps if the first Lord Wythe centuries ago had been rendered insufferable by his title.

The butler ushered him in, asked his name, gulped almost audibly, and then backed out of the hallway to leave him standing there like a delivery boy at the wrong door. Chard grinned when he heard Lady Wetherby shouting, "Sir Rufus! Sir Rufus!" into some nether part of the building. *Sir Rufus?* he thought in huge delight.

So it was that he had a large smile on his face when Rosie Wetherby entered the hall. He had only enjoyed the tiniest glimpse of her beauty a week ago during Mass, but surely no Wetherby by birth ever looked so good. It was Rosie. His smile deepened.

She carried her cloak over her arm as though she were intent upon an expedition. "Oh, excuse me," she said, and to his pleasure, her voice had that pleasant lilt to it so typical of the Welsh.

"You really don't want to go outside," he said, without introducing himself.

"Oh, but I do," she returned as she raised her arms to swing the cloak around her shoulders.

He noticed then that she was pregnant, and farther along than Bella. *Oh ho, Mrs. Wetherby, so this is why you are walking slower in October than you did in August*, he thought, pleasantly stirred by the lovely sight of her, so graceful in her maternity.

"Well, keep your head down," he advised as he came to her side to open the door. "Don't go too far from the house. If it starts to sleet, the stones will be slick."

She looked at him. "You're more solicitous than every Wetherby on the place," she whispered, her eyes merry. "They just tell me not to track in mud."

He laughed, wished he had some clever reply to dash off, and stopped short, the hairs on his neck rising, when Lady Wetherby shrieked behind him, "Lord Wythe! How honored we are! For heaven's sake, Rosie, close the door before he catches a cold!"

Rosie Wetherby did as she was told. For all her bulk, Lady Wetherby managed to leap in front of him to curtsy, her sausage curls at last century's style bobbing like demented watch springs. "We are so honored, my lord! And isn't that like your clever mother to let us think she was coming!"

"She was," he replied, stepping back a pace to ward off such enthusiasm and bumping into Rosie. "Pardon me, my dear." He turned around to look at Rosie Wetherby's loveliness. "You are . . . ?"

"Rosie Wetherby," she said and held out her hand, which he shook.

"You should say, 'Mrs. Junius Wetherby, my lord,' and then curtsy!" Lady Wetherby admonished.

"Lord Wythe! We are honored!"

He looked around again, his head ringing with so much exclamation in a tight space, to see Sir Rufus advancing upon him, bowing as he came. Suddenly the hall was much too small, and all he wanted was out. He looked at the door handle with some longing, noticed Rosie's laughing eyes on him, and struggled to control the hilarity that warred with the chagrin inside him.

He held up his hands in self-defense as Sir Rufus minced closer. "My mother was called away by family business and I am merely discharging a duty for her, sir," he said, talking much too fast and feeling out of breath from the exertion of confronting more than one Wetherby at a time. As they looked at him, their expressions rapt, he grabbed Rosie by the hand and pulled her closer to him, closer than he intended, but his surprise move caught her off balance, and she leaned against him. "I need a soprano for the Christmas choir," he said.

"Rosie, my lord? That is why you have come?" Lady Wetherby asked, making no attempt to hide her disappointment.

Well, did you think I was going to ask you to dinner? he thought sourly as he helped Rosie right her soft bulk, which—truth to tell—felt so good. "That's why," he finished lamely. He almost didn't trust himself to look at Rosie Wetherby because she was making small sounds in her throat that sounded suspiciously like laughter. He did look, because he knew he had to enjoy her up close as long as he could. "We really are a dreadful choir, my dear, and we need some help."

Sir Rufus and his wife crowded closer, and on a sudden whim, Chard whipped up the hood on Rosie's cloak and opened the door. "I think Mrs. Junius Wetherby and I will discuss this outside on a short walk," he told them firmly as he closed the door practically on their noses.

He took her hand because he feared that the front

steps would be slick. They were not, but he did not relinquish her. They walked quickly down the steps, mainly because she was tugging at him to hurry. He understood a moment later when she stood behind a yew tree and laughed.

A few minutes later, he gave her his handkerchief to wipe her eyes. "Oh, I do not know what you must think of me, but I don't know when I have seen anything so funny," she said when she could speak. She looked up at him, and he wondered how anyone could be so lovely.

"They . . . they are a tad overwhelming," he agreed.

"I could tell, sir," she replied and indicated a park close to the house. "I always find myself with an urge for a long walk."

He took her firmly by the arm again, appraising her and wondering how far along she was. "I know. I often see you walking my land," he said.

She stopped. "Perhaps I should apologize for trespassing," she said.

"No need. I'm sure the doctor has told you it is good exercise."

She blushed and looked away. "I've not seen a doctor. The Wetherbys think that is a needless expense. Bother it, Lord Wythe, I am a needless expense here. There. I have said it." She continued walking. "I will be happy to sing in your choir. Promise me it will keep me from this house day and night!"

"I wish I could," he replied, not sure what to say.

Mama would tell me I have stumbled onto a real bumblebroth, he thought. Good manners dictated that he say nothing, but for once in his life he ignored it. *Put me on the same acreage with the Wetherbys and I lose all propriety.* "I . . . we . . . none of us had any idea that Junius Wetherby was married, much less deceased, Mrs. Wetherby."

He winced at his own words. *I wonder anyone lets me off my own place*, he thought as he wondered if she would reply to something so ill-mannered.

"And what are they saying?" she asked quietly. She sat down on one of the more than ugly benches designed to look like a fallen log.

He stood beside her. "That you are Rosie Morgan, a Welsh sergeant's daughter with the army in Portugal."

"That's true," she said and turned to look him straight in the eye. "But I have never earned my living on my back. My da was a good man."

"I am certain he was." It sounded stupid the minute he said it, as though he didn't believe her and was just being polite.

Rosie Wetherby must have thought so, too. She gave him a patient smile. "That is not enough for you, is it? It certainly isn't for the Wetherbys."

He gritted his teeth, realized how much he disliked being lumped with the Wetherbys, and knew she was right. A veteran of marriage, he did the wisest thing when dealing with women who were right: he said nothing and looked as contrite as possible.

"My mother was the daughter of a vicar in Bath, well educated, but perhaps not handsome enough to attract one of her own kind who never looked beyond a pretty face," Rosie explained with the air of someone who had explained this too many times. "They met at church, and Mama lost her heart." She smiled. "And her mind, too, some would say. Da thought she was beautiful."

He picked up the narrative. "Oh, dear. Were there recriminations and threats, and tears, and hasty words that no one could retract?"

She nodded. "Mama eloped with Sergeant Owen Morgan, and her father in all Christian charity told her never to return. She did not." Rosie Wetherby gave him a level look. "Yes, she married beneath her. No, it doesn't follow that she was unhappy. I do not know anyone who had a happier childhood than I did."

He was silent, thinking how kindly she had just set him down.

"The Wetherbys do not believe a word of this, naturally. Perhaps you don't, either, but it is the truth."

"So you have lived everywhere and frankly led the kind of life that I know my children would envy."

She smiled again, but without that patient, wary look. "Do you know, I suppose I have. Of course, Mama insisted on teaching me manners, niceties and airs, I suppose, but none seemed to mind that. Da taught me to sing."

"So I have noted."

"I was born in Jamaica and lived in Canada and Ceylon." She sighed. "Mama died there, and Da and I soldiered on."

"You've never lived in England?"

"Never." She shivered and looked about her at the snow falling. "I cannot seem to get warm enough."

Not in that cloak, he thought. "And then it was Portugal? And Junius Wetherby?"

"Da died there," she said simply, quickly. "Junius Wetherby was a lieutenant in his regiment—Da was color sergeant—and he offered me 'protection.'" She made a face.

Chard nodded. He knew what that meant. "No choice, eh?" he asked quietly.

"Well, let us just say I made him improve his offer until it included marriage. I have followed the drum all my life, Lord Wythe." She smiled. "I suspect I knew more about soldiering than Junius, but we'll never know."

"I hear he met with a distressing accident," Chard said when her silence lengthened.

"Aye, he did," she agreed. "Only four days after our marriage, he was drinking with his comrades and sitting in a third-story window. He leaned back to laugh at someone's joke, forgot where he was, and lost his balance. Ah, me."

The sleet began that he had been predicting ever since he left his house. Rosie Wetherby shivered and moved closer to him but made no move to rise and go inside. He looked at the house, wondering just how bad it was indoors for her to prefer sleet. "You . . . you chose England?"

"What could I do?" Her expression hardened for a moment. "I wouldn't know my grandfather the vicar if he came up and shook hands—which he would never do— and I couldn't stay with the army, of course. Junius had just enough money to get me almost here."

"Almost?" He was nearly afraid to ask.

She pulled her cloak tighter and hunched over, as though trying in some unconscious, involuntary way to keep her unborn child dry. "It got me as far as Durham."

"But that is twenty-five miles away," he exclaimed, caught up in her story. "What did you do?"

"I walked, sir!" she replied, making no effort to hide the amusement in her eyes. "I told you I had followed the infantry from my birth."

"Yes, but—"

She laid her hand on his arm briefly, lightly. "Lord Wythe, it was summer, and at least there are no snipers between Durham and here!"

He laughed along with her. "I'm an idiot," he apologized.

"No, you're not," she replied. "I hardly need tell you that I came as a complete surprise to the Wetherbys."

He closed his eyes, tried to imagine the scene, and discovered that he could not.

Rosie must have been watching his face. "Yes, it was every bit that bad!" she assured him and made a face of her own. "And what do I discover but that Junius was a third son and someone who did not figure very high, even in Wetherby estimation."

"Yes, he has . . . had two older brothers," Chard said.

". . . where he told me he was only child and heir," she continued. She looked back at the house again. "Mrs. Wetherby grudges me every bite I eat and counts the silverware every time I leave the dining room. I know she does not believe a word I have said. It's much more pleasant to walk outside, Lord Wythe, even in weather like this."

She was silent for a moment as the sleet pounded down. *It cannot be good for you to sit out here,* he thought, wanting to edge himself even closer and offer what puny protection she could derive from his body. *Should I put my arm around her?* he asked himself, and decided that he should not.

"You would like me in the choir?" she asked, reminding him of his purpose.

"Indeed I would! Will and I—Will is my son—sat behind you at Mass two weeks ago and were quite captivated by your voice."

"Will." Without any self-consciousness, she scrutinized his face, and then he saw a smile of recognition in her eyes. "Yes, you were right behind me. His smile is like yours."

"Yes, I suppose it is." He hesitated and then plunged ahead. "He's been telling his sister Emma for two weeks now that you smiled at him and not me. He was quite taken with you."

She laughed. "I like children." She touched his arm again. "Tell me about this choir, my lord."

"It is without question the worst choir in all the

district," he said promptly. "Possibly in the entire British Isles. Every year our three neighboring parishes meet at one or the other's church before Midnight Mass. We were each supposed to sing a hymn or a carol, but the whole thing has gotten rather elaborate and become a competition." He stood up suddenly and pulled her to her feet. "Mrs. Wetherby, it is too cold to sit here! Shall we at least walk?"

He tucked his arm firmly through hers, and she offered no objection. She let him lead her down a line of overgrown shrubs that had the virtue of masking the house. His arm, with hers tucked close, rested ever so slightly on her ample belly.

"We have little talent, but some of us—my mother among them—feel a real need to win just once."

"You don't care one way or the other?"

He surprised himself by shaking his head. "Not really. The fun for me is just to sing with Will, even if we are not very good."

"Then Will is lucky," she said. She looked at him, and through the freezing rain that made her cheeks so pale, he could see little spots of color. She rested her other hand lightly on her belly. "As you can tell, I will be as big as a house by Christmas."

He smiled at her frankness, thinking of Lucy, who hid away during her confinement with Will. *I suppose she did not want the neighbors to think what we were doing to make a baby,* he reflected with some amusement. "No matter. You are not tall, and we can hide you behind some altos." He cleared his throat. "I plan to continue my recruitment."

"In the neighborhood?" she asked. "My lord, you said this parish is short on good voices."

"Ah, well, I am recruiting rather farther afield than

my mother intended," he admitted. "She was supposed to keep this appointment with you today, but her grandchildren in Leeds have chicken pox, and she is there."

"So you have taken charge?"

"Why, yes, I have. You are my first project." He led her toward the house. "And if you should come down with a sore throat, I will be disturbed, as choir practice begins on Tuesday next. Let me take you indoors, Mrs. Wetherby."

She offered no objection, but he had to tug her along.

Even then she stood a moment at the front steps, her eyes bleak. "Do you know, I think they are trying to figure out how to turn me away, my lord," she murmured as though it were merely an interesting complication. "It is a good thing that Christmas is only two months away. Perhaps the charity of the season will overtake them. Good day, Lord Wythe."

He nodded good-bye—because he could do nothing more—mounted his cold horse, and took his leave. He looked back once to see Rosie still standing in the doorway as though she intended to bolt back into the cold and snow once he was out of sight. *Don't, Rosie*, he pled silently. *Stay inside where it is warm, even if the inmates are unfriendly.*

"I have a soprano," he announced over dinner. The news was received with reservation from Will and interest from Emma.

"Papa, she is only one soprano," his ever-practical son reminded him.

"True, Will. That is indisputable. You must look at this like a brigade major."

"Which you were, Papa," Will said with pride.

He winked at his son and took Emma upon his lap there at the dinner table. "It is like this, son," he began, lining up three small bowls that even now the footman was attempting to fill with pudding. "If you put your best soldier between your two greenest recruits, what happens?"

Will looked at the three bowls. "Oh, I see," he said and looked at Peter with a frown. "Mrs. Wetherby is going to teach the other sopranos to shoot, spit, and swear?"

Emma laughed. Peter hugged his daughter to his shoulder so Will could not see his huge grin. "My dear Will, she will teach them to sing and give them her confidence. And whoever told you about shooting, spitting, and swearing?"

"Why, you, Papa," Will said with a grin of his own. "But is she going to be enough?"

"I am depending on more," he replied.

"From where, Papa?" Emmie asked as she ate her dessert.

"Oh, here and there," he said, knowing that his vague answer would never satisfy Emma. "From . . . from the Great North Road, my dear."

"Papa, that is far-fetched," she told him and turned her attention to the pudding.

The house was quiet after he heard their prayers and tucked them in their beds. He stood a long while watching them as he always did, whether he was dog-tired from harvest or weary from the irregularity of lambing in the raw Northumberland spring. Emma had been nearly a year old by the time he returned from India after the six-month-old news of Lucy's death in childbirth. And there was Will then, almost four, and big-eyed with the sight of him in his sun-faded, patched uniform—a stranger from another planet. He had spent many nights in the nursery, reacquainting himself with his son and meeting his daughter. Now that Lucy was gone, resigning his commission was the easiest thing he ever did. He knew he would find enough challenge in Northumberland's dales to keep him there, barring a French invasion.

As he stood there that night, grateful in his love for his children, he was teased with another thought, one that had not crossed his mind in more years than he could name. *I want a wife*, he thought.

The thought stayed with him as he checked all the doors, sent his old butler protesting off to bed, and sat down in the library, prepared to stare at the flames until they turned into coals. He spent more time at the window, watching the first snowfall of winter lay itself down in a thick blanket. When he finally lay down to sleep in the quiet house, he was at peace with himself. *This was a good day*, he thought. *I wonder what tomorrow will bring?*

Tomorrow brought a valet by the name of Owen Llewellyn, with a note from Colonel James Rhys of the Welsh Fusiliers, who knew a good joke when he heard one. "You may return him if you wish," the note read, "but if he suits, keep him." After a rather querulous paragraph about the vicissitudes of waging peace in the wilds of Kent, Colonel Rhys wrote farewell and wished to be remembered respectfully, etc., etc., to the Dowager Lady Wythe.

Chard examined his new valet, noting his dark Welsh eyes and slight build. There remained only one question, and he asked it. "Tenor or bass?"

"Tenor, sir!" the valet responded with a snap-to and clicking of heels. He burst into "Men of Harlech," which even brought Chard's old butler wheezing up the stairs to stand transfixed by the bookroom door until the recital ended.

"Admirable, Llewellyn," Chard said when the man finished, still standing at attention. "You will be a remarkable valet. Just keep my clothes clean, make sure my shaving water is hot, and . . . Llewellyn, are you paying close attention?"

"Yes, sir!"

"Under no circumstances are you to go outside without a muffler around your neck."

"No, sir!"

As it turned out, he was too busy that day to worry much about Rosie Wetherby. He found himself welcoming a new under-bailiff, one Dafydd Williams from Cardiff, who by coincidence or divine intervention sang bass. It gave him not a qualm to see young Williams safely bestowed into respectable quarters and to hear the glad tidings of great joy that Williams was recently married to his lovely Meg of Llanduff near Cardiff.

"And does she . . . ?"

"Alto, my lord."

"Send for her at once."

In fact, he would have gone to his mattress a happy man, except that Emma was cross through dinner, refused her favorite baked apple with cream dessert, and was feverish by bedtime. He knew it was more than a crochet when Emma, most independent of his children, let him hold her on his lap until she fell into fitful slumber. He was not at all surprised when she came to his bed in the middle of the night, crying and clutching her throat. He kissed her, pulled her in close, and dozed and woke with her the rest of the night.

Dr. Barker called it catarrh and ordered bed rest and warm liquids. "I see this so often when the season turns to winter," he said with a hand on Chard's shoulder. "I expect Emma will be grumpy and melancholy in equal parts. Give her these fever powders every four hours. Do you have someone to watch her?"

He didn't, actually. He knew better than to bother Mama, busy with chicken pox in Leeds. The housekeeper had left only yesterday morning to visit her ailing sister in Durham, and she had burdened the maids with a long list of assignments. His old bailiff's wife was nursing lumbago, and the lovely Meg from Llanduff was not expected yet.

Will sat with his sister that morning while Chard worked in the bookroom with his bailiff, completing plans for the new barn and settling housing arrangements for the construction crew he expected any day. By noon, Will was worried and Emma in tears.

"Papa, she does not even argue with me," Will said over luncheon. "I mean, I told her that I could beat her to flinders at jackstraws, and she just nodded!"

"This is serious, indeed."

He had a plan. In fact, as he stood at Emma's window, he realized that this was only one of many plans he had been scheming ever since Mama shouldered him with the choir. It had occurred to him last night, and nothing since then had convinced him that it was a silly idea. Quite the contrary: the more he thought about it, the better it sounded. He told his footman to summon the carriage.

The Wetherby estate was shrouded in fog as he drove up, and he liked it that way. The unspeakably stupid Greek temple was invisible, and the house itself, with its superabundance of trim and dormers, was mercifully indistinct.

Lady Wetherby insisted on plying him with éclairs and macaroons in her sitting room, even though he really wanted hot coffee. She listened to his recitation—practiced in the carriage on the drive over—and shook her head.

"Rosie is really quite common," she said, leaning closer and licking the chocolate from the éclairs off her fingers. "I should wonder that you don't worry it will rub off."

"I will take that chance, ma'am," he replied, focusing his attention on a hideous vase of peacock feathers as Lady Wetherby dabbed at the crumbs on her chest. "I need her help with Emma for a few days, if you think you can spare her."

"As to that, of course," Lady Wetherby said. "Truth to tell, I was wondering what to do with her this week." To his dismay, she edged even closer. "My darling Claude's fiancée is coming for a visit, and I do not want her to have to rub shoulders with someone from such a low class as Rosie!" She shuddered, and her greasy curls shook. "She tells a story about being wellborn, and her manners are pretty enough, but I cannot believe any of it. I wonder what Junius was thinking?"

Junius never thought much that I recall, Chard reflected to himself. *Serves him right for getting drunk and falling out a window. If I had been but four days married to Rosie, I wouldn't have been sucking on sour mash with my comrades.*

"Well, madam?" he asked finally, hoping to put enough curl in two words to remind her—somewhere below the level of her dim awareness—that he was a marquis.

It must have worked. She rose, curtsied until he feared for her corset stays, and left the room. In remarkably short order, Rosie Wetherby appeared in the doorway, satchel in hand, her cloak over her arm.

He rose quickly, pleased all over again at the sight of her. "So you will help me, Mrs. Wetherby?" he asked simply.

"You know I will," Rosie replied. She dabbed her hand across her eyes, and he noticed as he came closer to help her with her cloak that there were tears in them.

"Are you all right?" he asked, speaking close to her ear as he put her cloak around her slender shoulders.

"Never better," she assured him. "I told Lady Wetherby I would return when you no longer needed me."

He knew that he would embarrass her if he uttered the first reply that rose to his active brain, but he was beginning to surprise himself with the fertility of his imagination. "It shouldn't be above a week. On behalf of my child, I do appreciate your help."

Lady Wetherby returned, all smiles, to see them out of the house. More particularly, she patted his arm, ignored her daughter-in-law, and made so much of him that he wanted to snatch Rosie in his arms and run screaming from the house. As it was, he closed the door on Lady Wetherby before she was entirely finished speaking, took a firm grasp on Rosie because the steps were icy, and escorted her carefully to his conveyance.

"I really don't have very good balance these days," she confessed as he helped her into the carriage. "Do you know, Lord Wythe, sometimes I look in the mirror and wonder where Rosie Morgan has got to."

"Would you change things?" he asked, berating himself silently that he had never managed to learn the art of small talk.

"Some things," she admitted. She rested her hand on her belly. "Not all. But that's the way life is, isn't it? I learned that in the regiment, and it was a good school."

He nodded, made sure of the warming pan at her feet, and tucked a blanket around her. She smiled her thanks at him and then looked out the window. He noticed that she dabbed at her eyes once or twice in the short drive, but he knew he had not earned the liberty to ask her how he could help.

"Emma is six," he said finally, as the carriage turned into his estate. "She is independent, outspoken, and rather thinks she commands her brother and me."

"Does she?" Rosie asked.

"Oh, probably," he agreed, noting again that he was not embarrassed to show his complaisance to Rosie Wetherby. "I would do anything for her." He touched her arm. "If she knows that, at least she has the grace not to hold it over me like a sword."

"Lord Wythe, do you not have a wife?" she asked finally.

He was surprised that Lady Wetherby—she who could spread stories like farmers spread manure—had not unrolled his whole genealogy before her. *I wonder if they even talk, except when that harpy berates her daughter-in-law and tells her how common she is.*

"She died when Emma was born. I was serving in India. I returned home and resigned my commission." He stopped, dissatisfied with how brusque he sounded. He was silent as the carriage rolled to a stop. He contrasted the welcome of his home—large to be sure, and gray like the Wetherbys'—with the estate he had come from and found it wanting in no way.

The footman was there in the drive to help Rosie from the carriage, but Chard assumed that responsibility, letting her lean for a moment against his shoulder as she got her balance. She gripped his hand and relaxed when she saw that the walk was shoveled and no ice was on the steps. He felt a twinge of pride as she looked about her, a smile on her face.

"I like the white trim," she said and looked up at him, her eyes bright. "Tell me, sir, does the stone turn pink when the sun sets?"

"More of a lavender," he replied as he helped her up the steps. "You should see it in the spring when the flowers are up in the window boxes." *And when the lawn is green and seems to roll right down to the stream, and the lambs* are stiff-legged and bonking about, and the orchard is a dazzle of apple blossoms. "I love it here." *What a clunchy thing to say,* he berated himself, but she smiled at him, and there was nothing but kindness in her brown eyes.

He took her right upstairs to Emma's room. Will sat there, his chin on his palm, watching his sister. Emma opened her eyes when she heard him enter the room.

Rosie did not know his children, but she did not hang back in the doorway. She came forward right beside him, first to stop at Will's chair. "You must be Will. How lucky Emma is to have a brother who will watch her."

Will leaped to his feet, and Chard had to turn away to hide his smile. *Oh, Rosie, think of the conquests you have made,* he thought.

"Wou—would you like this seat?" Will asked.

She smiled at him but shook her head and turned to Emma. "Not now, my dear, but thank you. I rather think I will sit with Emma."

"Emma, this is Mrs. Wetherby," he said softly as Rosie settled herself on the bed. "She's here as long as you need her."

To his amazement, independent Emma heaved a sigh and reached for Rosie, who gathered her close. "My throat hurts," she whispered and then burst into tears.

Chard blinked and felt his face redden with embarrassment. "Mrs. Wetherby, you must think we are unfeeling brutes here," he said. "Truly, we have seen to her care."

She glanced at him over her shoulder as she smoothed Emmie's tangled hair. "Never mind that, sir. Sometimes a little lady just needs a mother." She wiped Emmie's face with the damp cloth that Will handed her. "And what a fine brother she has! My dear, could you go downstairs and talk your cook out of a half-cup of treacle, some mint, and a spoon? Emmie, with Will's help, your throat will be better in two shakes. My lord, please hand me the hair-brush over there. Nothing does a body better than a good hair brushing."

They both did as she said. When he closed the door quietly, Emmie's eyes were closed and Rosie was brushing her hair and humming to her.

"Papa, she's good," Will said as they went downstairs together. "Did Mama do things like that?"

Probably not, he thought. Lucy had told him on several occasions how much she disliked the sickroom, and mewling, puking babies. "Of course she did," he lied. "You're just too young to remember." He touched his son's shoulder. "You're going to discharge your duty with the cook? Good." He rested his hand on Will's head for a brief moment. "Just think, son; maybe you could come down with something too."

Will grinned at him. "Or you, Papa."

How tempting that would be, he thought later that afternoon when he let himself into Emma's room. Dressed in a fresh nightgown, his daughter slept. The room smelled of lavender and clean sheets. Rosie sat in the chair with her feet resting on the bed, an open book on what remained of her lap, her eyes closed, too. She opened them, even though he was sure he had not made any noise.

"I'm sorry," he whispered. "I did not mean to wake you."

She sat up, her neat hair coming out of its pins, and to his mind, incredibly appealing. "I should be awake, my lord," she whispered back. "You will think me none too attentive."

He sat carefully on the bed so as not to disturb his daughter but also not to miss a single opportunity to admire Rosie Wetherby.

"I . . . Will and I are convinced that you really must be an angel."

She put her hand over her mouth so she would not laugh out loud, but her eyes were merry. "I doubt that in my present condition I could fly too well, sir!" she looked at her charge. "She is better, isn't she? You have a lovely daughter. Does she look like her mother?"

"Like Lucy? No," he replied, amused by his own thoughts. "She is her own person." He admired Emma's serenity after a night of restless sleep. *Hers and mine*, he thought, suddenly tired.

He was aware that Rosie Wetherby was watching him with that same look she had earlier trained on Emma. "I am fine!" he protested to her unspoken question. "Just a little tired."

"And you were likely up all night with Emma, weren't you?" she asked. "I hope you are not planning to sit up with her tonight, my lord."

"Well, yes, actually."

"No," she said. "I am going to be sharing Emma's room, and whatever she needs I can give her. I have already spoken to the footman, and he is arranging a cot for me."

"That is truly too much trouble for you," he said, but it sounded weak to his own ears.

"It is no trouble," she replied. "I cannot tell you what a relief it is to be useful to someone. Thank you for asking me, my lord."

The pleasure truly is mine, he thought as he nodded to her, took another look at Emma, and left the room. *There is something so restful about Rosie Wetherby*, he decided as he went slowly down the stairs to the bookroom. It may have been her condition that made her so. He liked the deliberate way she did things, from brushing Emma's hair to touching Will's shoulder when he brought her what she needed from Cook. *She seems to be studying our comfort*, he thought, *and what a pleasant thing that is. I wish she would touch me*, he thought suddenly. He blushed and set his mind firmly on the ledgers on his desk.

Father in heaven, please take me away from these, he thought later as the afternoon waned. He made a face and closed the ledger, adding it to the stack on the desk. *My barns are full, my stocks are high, and I could probably buy Paris if I wanted it. Why the restlessness?* "Lord, grant me a diversion from stodgy prosperity," he said, and he looked out the window and smiled.

They were coming. It could only be his construction crew for the new barn, hired by his old one-armed colonel, retired now in Wales. *One, two, three, four,* he counted as he stood by the window, *and they have brought all their tools.* He glanced at his desk, with its drawing of the barn he needed, and then the copy of Franz Josef Haydn's "The Heavens Are Telling" lying next to it. "But more to the point," he said out loud as he took a tug at his neck cloth and looked for his coat, "can these builders sing?"

They could and did, he discovered, and with the same enthusiasm that his new valet had shown. It was starting to snow again, and the temperature was dropping even as he stood there in the driveway, hands in his pockets as the men gathered around. To his unutterable joy, they looked at each other, someone hummed a note, and they sang "While Shepherds Watched Their Flocks by Night." The song rang with all the fervor that he remembered from the Welsh Fusiliers in India, singing in spite of—or perhaps because of—the worst conditions.

How is it that the Welsh can even make the closing notes hang in the air as though they sing in a cathedral? He sighed with pleasure. One of the men stepped forward, didn't quite bow (which pleased Chard even more), and introduced himself as Daniel ap Jones, late sergeant of the Fusiliers and a graduate, like himself, of the hard school of Assaye. "I outrank them others, sir," he said, indicating the other singers. "Your old friend in Swansea indicated that you might like that song, considering that it's a local favorite."

"Aye, it is, Jones. Think on," he replied, lapsing gracefully into the color of local speech. He looked down the lane again as another conveyance approached, and then back at Jones, a question in his eyes.

"Our wives," Jones said. "The colonel thought you could use them too."

"I am in heaven, Jones," he replied simply. "And do they sing as divinely as you?"

The men looked at each other. "All except Lloyd's wife, sir," Jones explained, the remorse deep in his voice. The other builders chuckled and nudged the one who must be Lloyd. "He married Gracie Biddle from Devon, and she can't even carry a note to the corner and back."

"Ah, lad! Me auld lady can cook!"

Lord bless the military, he thought. The whole unloading of wives, children, household goods, and tools was accomplished with a certain precision that made him proud, even though he was six years removed from the army. "Just long enough, I suppose, for me to forget what a tedious, nasty business it really was," he said to Rosie that night, his feet propped on Emma's bed as he relaxed in a chair he drew up close.

Rosie nodded. "Glorious once in a while on parade."

She sat next to Emma on the bed, her fingers light on the child's hair. "Did you ever fight with the Fusiliers, my lord?"

He nodded. "I commanded an excellent brigade, my dear, but I was always glad when the Fusiliers were close by." He looked at his daughter, who rested, dreamy-eyed and at peace with herself, against Rosie's round belly. "And now, my dearest Emma, you have been tended, coddled, fed, read to, and entertained for the better part of the day by someone much kinder and softer than your father. Let me recommend sleep to you now."

Rosie smiled at him, and he could only smile back, because she was irresistible. "Emma assures me that you are kindness itself, my lord," she teased.

He bent over to kiss his daughter, but stopped when he noticed how round her eyes had become. She was looking at Rosie, a question in her eyes.

"The little one always gets lively in the evenings, Emma," the woman explained, resting her hand on her belly. "Only think how busy I will be when she . . . or he . . . is born."

Emma let out a sigh, her eyes still filled with amazement as she pressed her ear against Rosie. Before he could stop her, she grabbed his hand and placed it against Rosie's side. "Papa! Can you imagine anything half so wonderful?"

He could not. As embarrassed as he was, Chard knew Emma would be upset if he snatched his hand away. Trusting that Rosie would not smite him for his most ragged of manners, he kept his hand where Emma held it, touched by the tumult within. He remembered better times with Lucy, when she had wrapped her arms around him as they lay in bed and he had felt the steady kicking of their unborn son against his back. "It is wonderful, Emma," he agreed, sorry that his voice was not more steady. He took his hand slowly away, too shy to look at the Welsh woman.

"Did I do that too?" Emma asked him in hushed tones.

"I'm certain you did, love," he assured her.

She sat up. "But you don't know?"

"I wasn't there. I was in India." *Oh, that is hardly going to satisfy her,* he thought, *not this daughter who questions everything.* He held his breath, exasperated with himself.

Emma frowned at him, and he knew he was trapped into more explanation than he wanted to begin, especially under the amused glance of Rosie Wetherby. "Then how . . ." Emma paused, her frown deepening. "Grandma told me—"

To his relief, Rosie came to his rescue. "My dear, do you think your questions can keep until your grandma returns?"

Emma nestled next to Rosie again. "Do you mean that my father does not know the answers?" she asked softly.

Peter laughed. "No, you scamp! It is merely that this is a subject not to be discussed lightly."

"I promise I won't tell Will," Emma whispered. "I only want to know how babies get in and how they get out. That is not so much to ask."

"No, it is not," he agreed, reminding himself that if he had wanted an easy path, he could still be in the army— with Wellington now in Spain—and far away from questions that made him sweat more than combat.

"Do you know, Emma, I can answer those very questions," Rosie said finally. "That is, if your father will allow me."

Quite possibly I will kneel at your feet and worship the ground that you glide over, he thought. "Mrs. Wetherby, you're on," he said without allowing her a millisecond to change her mind. He kissed his daughter. "Good night, my dear."

Emma kept her arms around his neck. "Papa, you could stay and listen too. Perhaps you will learn something."

He laughed and kissed her again. *I probably would,*

he thought as he stood in the doorway and watched the two of them with their heads together. *How odd, Mrs. Wetherby, how odd. I do not know you well, but I trust you. Your mother-in-law claims that you are common, but I call you uncommon.*

Uncommonly fine, he considered as he relaxed in the next bedchamber, listening to Will read his geography and paying no attention to his description of the land of Serendip. True, he had been no farther from his holdings than Leeds in the past six years, but he knew he had never seen finer brown eyes anywhere. Her lips were full and seemed as generous as her nature. True, it would take a man with a greater imagination than he possessed to divine what a figure she really had.

"Is that how it is, Papa?"

"I'm afraid so, son," he replied with a shake of his head. *I am undone over a woman seven months gone with child who is the daughter of a Welsh color sergeant, and worse and worse, the widow of a scamp with cheese where his brains should have been.* "There's no explaining it."

He looked up to see Will frowning at him over the top of his geography. "Papa, all I wanted to know was whether the water is truly that blue in Colombo's harbor."

Chard blinked. "Son, I had my mind elsewhere."

"Next door, Papa?" Will asked, and Chard started again. *Am I so transparent?*

"Well, yes, actually," he managed.

Will closed the book and came to him where he sat.

Chard made room for him. "Papa, I am worried about Emma too, but I think that Rosie—"

"Mrs. Wetherby," his father corrected him automatically.

"She wanted me to call her Rosie," Will said. "Rosie

can manage Emma, so you needn't worry and get all blank in the face."

And blank in the head, he thought. "Son, it is time for bed."

"Papa?"

"Hmm?"

"Do you think Rosie would wait for me to grow up so I could marry her? That's what I would most like to do."

Chard smiled at his son. "I think you should not place too large a wager on the matter. Come now, and climb into bed."

Will did as he was told. "Maybe someone like Rosie then?" he amended after Chard kissed him good night.

There is no one like Rosie, Chard thought as he closed the door and went quietly downstairs.

She was waiting for him in the sitting room before the fireplace, where the butler had directed her, ready to pour tea. He seldom drank tea in the evening, because he hated to get up in the middle of the night to deal with its consequences, but he took a cup from Rosie and then made sure she had the most comfortable chair, with a pillow behind her back.

"I trust now that Emma is armed with enough information to make her dangerous at family gatherings?" he joked as Rosie relaxed into the chair. He pushed a low stool under her feet when she raised them. "Do I dare take her anywhere?"

The woman sipped the tea appreciatively and leaned back. "Of course! I assured her that everything I told her was privileged information and that she was not to divulge it to any of her friends. Or Will, she assured me." She laughed and leaned forward to touch his wrist as he sat close to her. "She is so bright."

He cleared his throat. "It . . . it doesn't embarrass you to talk about such things?"

She thought a moment and then shook her head. "Children like to know what is going on, sir. It's only life."

"So it is," he said. He was silent then, looking into the fire and feeling no need to talk. It was enough to sit with Rosie.

He was working up to some conversation when his bailiff came into the room with idle nonsense about grain storage that apparently could not wait until morning. With real reluctance, he offered his apologies to Rosie, set Cook's good biscuits closer to her elbow, and followed his bailiff to the bookroom, hating every step of the way.

He knew she would be gone to bed when he returned, so he almost did not go into the sitting room again when his bailiff was through. *I should at least ring for my footman so he can remove the tea,* he thought as he hesitated at the door.

The room was dark, the fire settling into a glow of coals that reminded him of Christmas. *I wonder where I will find my Yule log this year?* he thought idly. *And I am certain that it will take me all of the next month to figure out a way to invite Rosie Wetherby to celebrate the season with us without all her deplorable in-laws sniffing at her heels.*

He went to throw himself down in his chair again, but there was Rosie where he had left her, only asleep this time, her head pillowed against the chair wing, her feet tucked under her. Without a word, he sat himself on the stool where her feet had been, relishing the sight of her.

"'Rosie? Rosie?" He called her name quietly, and she did not waken. *Oh, too bad,* he thought with real pleasure as he carefully picked her up and went to the stairs. She was hardly a weight at all as he climbed the stairs with his Christmas soprano. She settled against his arm as though she belonged there, and he was hard put to lay her down, even when he stood over her cot.

He put her down with great reluctance, pleased at the boneless way she slept. This was not a woman to thrash about or walk the floor for no reason, growing more irritable by the moment and berating him because this was Northumberland and not London. With a sigh, Rosie Wetherby succumbed to the mattress, made it her own, and offered no objection when he removed her shoes.

Her stockings were clean but darned many times.

He picked up one of the shoes he had set down and looked at the run-down heel and the sole thin from walking. He knew he was in no position to offer her anything, and he could think of no subterfuge that would trick her into accepting even a pair of cotton stockings from him. *This is a season of giving, and as a widower, I cannot give her clothing. It would only appear forward or suggestive of mischief*, he thought.

He blew out the candle on the nightstand and turned to go. Some impulse turned him around again—him, the least impulsive of men. He knelt beside the bed and rested his hand on her belly again. The baby inside was sleeping now for all he knew. With a smile, he pressed steadily on Rosie's side until the little one moved away from his hand and kicked back, to his delight. He lightened the pressure of his hand and tensed all over when Rosie murmured something and covered his hand with her own. *I do not dare move*, he thought in panic. The baby continued to kick, and in another moment, Rosie's hand was heavy as she returned to deeper sleep.

He waited another moment beside the bed until her breathing was regular again, but even then he was not inclined to leave the room. He sat for a while in the chair, content to watch them both, until he realized with a guilty pang that his valet—the tenor—was probably waiting up for him. *At least Owen Llewellyn is not the sort to wring his hands and grieve if I am late,* he thought as he left the room quietly. *And I did tell him never to wait up for me.*

To his relief, Llewellyn was asleep in his little corner of the dressing room. He had laid out Chard's nightshirt and robe, and the fire was just high enough for comfort. In a moment, Chard was in bed, if vaguely disappointed with his solitude. *Emma will not want me tonight,* he thought, his hands behind his head as he stared at the ceiling. Will seldom gets up in the night. At least his feet were not cold; Llewellyn had thoughtfully placed a warming pan in his bed.

Soon Christmas will be upon us, he thought, closing his eyes and enjoying the warmth. *Mama will ask me what I would like for a present, and I will never be able to think of anything, as usual. We will probably go to Bella's, provided her little criminals are over the chicken pox. Brother-in-law Matthew will carve the goose, and Bella will look at me in that soft way of hers. She will assure me that it would be no trouble to find me an agreeable widow, or a maiden lady who would be relieved to splice herself to a farmer with a pedigree (however little he bothered about it), considerable wealth, and two children.*

"There is no reason for a woman of fashion or sense to marry you!" she had raged at him during his recent visit to deposit Mama. "I have always thought you handsome, but you will insist upon wearing your clothes until they are fit for nothing but the rag bag, and it must have been months since someone with skill cut your hair."

He grinned in the dark, remembering how his mild comment that at least he did not stink and never scratched in public had only served to propel her irritation to undreamed-of heights. He knew they should both be embarrassed, because Mama had to intervene, as she had been doing for more than thirty years, but Lord forgive him, it was still fun to tease his little sister Belly.

His thoughts changed direction. He turned over on his side and looked out the window. He had forgotten to close the draperies, but then, he seldom closed them. The stars were as bright as the coming of winter could make them. He thought then of Haydn and his choir, all bedded down for the night and ready to begin building him a barn tomorrow. This would be a choir competition that no one forgot. It was his last thought before the sky brightened with dawn.

Even though he and Will hurried through breakfast with Emma and Rosie, the Welsh carpenters were already hard at work when they arrived at the building site. *Bless me! They are singing*, Chard thought as they approached the farmyard. *I am in heaven.* He and Will just stood and listened, arm in arm, admiring the crispness of the notes in the cold morning.

"Why are they so good, Papa?" Will asked, his voice hushed and reverent as the carpenters, to the rhythm of hammers and saws, sang a hymn they were both familiar with.

"Some say it is merely because they are from Wales," Chard replied.

"Emma would call that a silly reason," Will said after a moment's thought.

"What would you say?"

His son smiled. "I would say it didn't matter, as long as they sing so well."

Chard nodded. *No question that you are my son*, he thought, pleased with himself. *I suppose it irritates Emmie, but some things just can't be explained.*

They helped where they could that morning, but it was soon obvious to Chard that his old friend in Wales had chosen this crew for both singing and building capacities. He was glad enough to retreat inside after sharing lunch with his crew in the shelter of the cow barn close by. Will shivered with cold, even though Chard knew he would never admit it.

"Will, perhaps we should rescue Mrs. Wetherby from Emma for an hour or two. You wouldn't mind entertaining your sister, would you?" he asked, careful to overlook Will's chattering teeth.

"If you think they won't miss us here, Papa," he said.

Chard shook his head. "They can spare us, lad." They arrived upstairs to find the doctor with Emma, thumping her for soundness, while Rosie sat in the window seat, relaxed and yet watchful at the same time. *I have seen cats guard their kittens like that*, Chard thought with amusement. He joined her in the window seat.

"I suppose I must hope that he declares Emma sound of wind and limb," she whispered to him finally.

"You 'suppose'?" Chard asked, surprised.

She nodded, not taking her eyes from the doctor.

"You will not need me anymore when he declares her fit."

He could say nothing to that because she was right.

Now that is a dreadful turn of events, he thought and thrashed himself mentally for not considering the eventuality. *I am a butterfly, living for the moment*, he told himself in disgust. *While I would never wish Emma ill, it is too bad Rosie is such a proficient nurse.*

"Excellent, excellent, Lord Wythe!" the doctor declared as he straightened up. "Another day and Emma will be sound as a roast. Right, my dear?" he beamed at her, as Emma glared back and tugged at her nightgown.

He walked the doctor downstairs, only half-listening

to his story of neighborhood illnesses, and all the while thinking, *Tomorrow I will have to return Rosie to those deplorable Wetherbys. Lady Wetherby will never spend a penny to take Rosie to the silk warehouse for even a pair of stockings, much less a cloak that isn't full of holes. I wonder if Rosie even has a single nightgown or nappie for the baby.* The thought upset him as nothing else could. He remembered all the care and attention he had lavished on Lucy when she was waiting Will's arrival: her clothes, the special food, a cradle specially made, and more nightgowns, sacques, and receiving blankets than Will could ever use.

"Doctor, when you return tomorrow, would you ask Mrs. Wetherby if she would like to talk to you about her approaching confinement?" he asked as they stood together by the front door. "I am also quite willing to take on the charge for that event, because she has been so helpful to me here. I will let that be my gift of thanks."

"I suppose this means that the Wetherbys are doing nothing for her?" the doctor asked. He must not have expected an answer, because he hurried on. "We've been hearing things in the village." He allowed the footman to help him into his coat. "Ah, me. Of course I will speak to her tomorrow." He sighed again. "Things must have been at a pretty pass for her in Portugal if she thought marrying Junius Wetherby would improve her situation."

"From what she has told me, her hand was forced. She is surely not the first to contract a disastrous alliance under a fog of optimism," Chard heard himself saying. *Where did that come from?* he asked himself.

After his return from India, Chard had resolved that he would not think about Lucy and what had gone before, but as he sat in the tub that afternoon, chin on his knees, he found that he could not help it. There was no point now in asking himself why he had ever agreed to the wedding. He had not needed her money; there was no land of any value that came with her; his parents (not hers) were under no obligation. He had met her at an assembly ball in Durham, but he had met other young ladies there before. True, she was a pleasure to look at, and the daughter of a well-connected family, but that was all.

I would never have pursued the affair on my own, he decided as he soaped himself and let Owen Llewellyn pour warm water over him. *My family has always known me to be shy, and bless their hearts, they thought to help. The thing is, why did I ever let them talk me into it? And more to the point, am I still so pliable?*

He thought he was not. No farmer was more resistant to panic than he, especially in the Corn Exchange, when the buyers were more irritating than fleas, calling bids. He had the instinct to know when the bid would go no higher and waited until then.

He had stood firm at Assaye when he wanted to scream and run and dig a hole somewhere and drop himself in it. In a voice as calm as though he had asked someone to pass the bread at table, he had gone from man to man, encouraging, prompting, standing tall as shot and shell whizzed around him at the Kaitna ford. What was it about Lucy Monroe that he had been unable to cry off when he knew he wanted to? Why was he so unable?

I should never have listened to all my friends and relations telling me what a prize I was getting in Lucy Monroe, he thought as he wrapped himself in his robe and sat looking out the window. *What little conversation we had before marriage showed her to be a shallow, vain little thing. I should have withdrawn my offer, taken my lumps, and left the field.*

He winced and felt his shoulders grow cold, even though the room was well heated. *Instead, I married her and discovered quickly that my wife was no fun. She was fueled by no love, like, or even lust, and saw no more to me than a title for herself and the promise of London, in which I sadly disappointed her. She hated every minute of her confinement with Will and never wanted me near her again. Almost never.*

His lips set in firm lines, Chard dressed quickly, shaved, and tidied up after himself before he remembered that he had a valet to do all that now. *The sad thing is,* he told himself as he went downstairs to dinner, *I like women. And now there is nothing.* He paused on the bottom step. *I am too much an honorable man to go near a doxy, even though none of the longings have left me. I work hard because I need to be tired every night. I am afraid to make another attempt. When left to my own devices, I am a coward. Shame on me.*

He was grateful that he did not have to make conversation on the way to choir practice. His carriage was filled with the Welsh women, and the men came after in the gig and on horseback. Rosie Wetherby sat next to him, her eyes bright with the pleasure of being with her father's countrywomen. He glanced at Rosie, who was crammed so tightly against him that he could feel her baby kick. It should have flattered him that she was so loath to leave his house tomorrow, but it only sank him deeper, knowing there was nothing he could do to stop it.

St. Philemon's was brightly lit, and he was gratified to see so many carriages, gigs, and blanketed horses there. He drew his singers around him for a moment of strategy before they went inside. "I know you will do your best," he said simply, and then laughed and shook his head as some of the veterans of Wellington's army grinned at him. "Lads! I know what you are thinking! Although I must sound like every officer who has ever exhorted you on the field of battle, believe me, this is more important than Agincourt and Blenheim combined!"

He enjoyed their laughter, and continued, to their amusement, in his brigade major voice. "If we do not have a good choir, my mother will be sorely disappointed. I will have to sneak into a back pew at St. Phil's every Sunday morning, and the vicar will preach deadly sermons from Leviticus or Revelation to take his revenge upon me. Do your best. England may not care much, but I do."

The steps were icy, so he turned instinctively to look for Rosie. He found her at his side, grasped her by the elbow, and helped her indoors without saying a word.

Once inside, he looked at her. "That was silly, wasn't it?" he said.

She shook her head. "Lord Wythe, do you know what your singers are already saying about you?"

"I can't imagine." And he couldn't. While he had admired the Fusiliers in India, he had never commanded them. "Well, maybe I can," he amended, as he walked with her to the choir seats at the front of the chapel. "I am Lord Mark Time, eh?"

He could tell he had surprised her with that nickname. "Oh, no!" she exclaimed. "Mostly they are excited to be working for you, because they remember you from India." She leaned closer. "Were you really a legend there?"

It was his turn to stare. "Not that I know of," he replied honestly. "They must have me confused with someone else."

"No, they don't," she replied. "Men like that don't confuse their heroes."

"I never imagined—" he began.

"You probably never did," she said.

He looked at her. "I'm not the quickest man on the planet."

"Yes, you are," she said. "What you also are is humble, and I think it must be so rare that no one recognizes it."

She touched his arm. "For your children's sake, please never change."

He stared at her. No one had ever spoken to him like that before, and her words fell on him like warm rain. He had no idea what to say and was relieved when the choirmaster asked them to take their seats. His face still blazing with embarrassment, Chard settled her between two of the weakest sopranos and took his place with the basses. His under-bailiff made room for him, leaning close to whisper, "Sir, thank you for sending for Meg."

He shrugged off any reply, his eyes on the choirmaster. "Really, my lord, you'll like Meg's voice," Dafydd Williams assured him. "I think she can be made useful around the estate too, sir."

Startled, Chard glanced at his under-bailiff and then looked down at the music the bass on the other side was handing him. *I wonder, Williams, if you would believe me if I told you that I wasn't thinking about your wife's voice when I sent for her?* he thought. *I wanted you to have Meg close, and that was all.*

"Doesn't matter about the estate, Williams," he whispered back, even as the choirmaster—no respecter of marquises—glared at him. "You have a nice little cottage. Just let her keep it for you." He laughed and then put his hand over his mouth when the choirmaster started in his direction. "Consider it an early Christmas present."

The St. Philomen's Christmas choir waited a few minutes more to allow two latecomers to seat themselves, and Chard looked over his contribution of singers, noting with a brigade major's strategic eye how wisely they had spaced themselves among the uninitiated. *I appear to have three sopranos, two altos, three tenors, and three basses,* he observed.

With half an ear, he listened to the choirmaster's

usual greeting, which contained, as it did every year, equal parts of resignation and exhortation, mingled with sufficient rue to dampen even the celestial enthusiasm of a multitude of the Heavenly host. *I must suggest to Mr. Woodhull after Christmas that it is time to replace our choirmaster,* he thought, and then he smiled at the idea of approaching his vicar, who would not recognize a tune even if it bit his bottom. *He will wonder why I am so inclined but offer no resistance. Ah, well. This is one of the few occasions in life when being a marquis and the holder of Woodhull's living will carry the day,* he told himself.

The choirmaster cleared his throat, and everyone looked up expectantly. "My dears, let us not tackle the Haydn immediately but warm up first on a hymn." He turned to the organist. "May I suggest 'The Mighty Power of God Unfolding'? A note please, sir, if you will."

It was a rousing, familiar hymn, and everyone knew it. The sound of incredible, perfect harmony exploded in the church, booming from wall to wall with all the majesty the hymnist must have intended but which had never before been even remotely achieved at St. Phil's. By the end of the first stanza, the choirmaster was gripping the lectern, his knuckles white. At the completion of the chorus, he waved the choir to a halt and staggered to a seat.

A soprano and a tenor from the front row reached him first, fanning him with Haydn, while an alto loosened his neck cloth. He sat for a long moment under their ministrations and then waved them back to their seats with a hand that shook. The doctor, who only dreamed that he was a bass, took his pulse and then helped him to his feet. He guided him back to the lectern, and the choirmaster clamped his hands firmly again, a changed man.

It was still a moment before he could speak. "My

dears, the strangest thing happened," he said finally, sounding like a different man. "I dreamed that you were singing, and in tune. How singular." He looked down at the music before him, but to Chard's view, he was not actually seeing anything. "I am certain it was a trick of hearing. Let us tempt fate again and try a mellower hymn. 'Lambs Sweetly Feeding,' if you will be so kind, my dears."

The soft beginning was no more difficult than the magnificent spiritual call to arms that had preceded it. As led by the Welsh singers, each note was sustained, melodic, and softer than dew on the hillside. Chard did not sing, preferring to listen to those around him and enjoy their special national gift. He noticed that others of the choir were doing the same thing. The Welsh singers could not have been more oblivious. They sang with the fervor peculiar to their race, fervor he had remembered all these years and thousands of miles from dry Indian washes and the scorch of a sun that burned up everything but song.

The hymn ended, the choirmaster closing it with all the feeling and artistry of a man half his age. "This is a miracle," he declared. "My dears, do let us examine the Haydn before us." He leaned forward to confide in them. "I admit I was wondering if we would have the capacity for this selection. Wasn't I the silly one?"

They sang for more than an hour, the choirmaster in such a state of bliss that his wife had to tug at his arm finally. When that effort proved fruitless, she dragged his watch from his coat pocket, opened it, and waved it under his nose like smelling salts. "Very well, if we must," he grumbled.

We must, thought Chard. He glanced at Rosie, who was starting to droop. In another moment, they were dismissed, and he was at Rosie's side. Without a word, he helped her into her cloak and assisted her from the church. She was quiet on the ride home, and he could think of nothing to say. It was enough to sit next to her. Before they turned into the lane before Wythe, she leaned against him, asleep.

Sitting there in the dark carriage, with the other women silent and sleepy around him too, he realized with a pang how much he missed the conversation of women at night. True, Lucy had not been the warmest of females, but early in their marriage he had enjoyed her inconsequential chatter about the events of the day, told in their entire minutia from her point of view. It was always different from his, and it charmed him somehow to know that women were different creatures entirely. *I miss that,* he thought as the carriage came to a stop and Rosie woke up. She apologized for crowding him, but he only smiled and helped her down.

Will was asleep when they checked on him. To Chard's eyes, his son was sleeping peacefully, but Rosie had to tug up the blanket higher and smooth his hair before she would leave the room. *This must be what mothers do,* he thought as he watched her bend down awkwardly to kiss him. *I am sure Lucy never did.*

Gracie Biddle Jones, who could not carry a tune, had volunteered to sit with Emma. When they came in the room, she said good night quickly and left the room. Rosie felt Emma's forehead and nodded in satisfaction. She turned and held out her hand to him. "Good night, my lord." He had no excuse to stay, so he went to his own room, knowing somehow that he would be awake all night.

When the doctor arrived in the morning, he went first to Rosie as he had promised, spending some time with her in another room separate from Emma. He came out to assure Chard that Mrs. Wetherby was strong as a little French pony and right as a trivet.

"Doctor, all similes aside, will she do?" Chard asked point blank as he walked with him to Emma's room.

The doctor laughed and clamped his hand on Chard's shoulder. "Someone would think it was your baby, laddie, and not poor Junius Wetherby's!" he exclaimed. "She's fine, and she knows to send for me when her time comes." He frowned then. "Can't trust the Wetherbys with so much sense."

The doctor passed sentence next in Emmie's room and doomed Rosie Wetherby to expulsion by his cheery news that Emma "simply couldn't be more fine, and aren't we all happy about that?"

No one was. Will dragged around with a long face as Rosie carried her small bundle downstairs. Emma was a thundercloud, refusing to be placated with his promise of a ride on horseback with him as soon as she was a little better. And Chard knew he had not felt so dreary since that long voyage from India when he had paced the deck and wondered what he would do.

The day was fine enough, so he took the gig. As they rode along, Rosie turned her face up to the sun. "I do not suppose there will be many more fine days like this." She looked at him. "Does winter come early and stay long here?"

"Aye," he said simply, berating himself that he had no conversation. If he possessed any glibness, he could at least tell her how much he appreciated her help; and if he had enough nerve—not the battlefield kind but the sitting-room sort—he could confess in an offhand, insouciant sort of way that she had certainly inspired him into thinking about looking for a wife. As it was, he was silent and miserable.

"My lord, is there a workhouse hereabout?" Rosie asked suddenly.

Her question dumbfounded him, and he nearly dropped the reins. "A what?" he asked.

"A workhouse," she repeated, softer this time, as though she hated to say it again. She looked at him, as if trying to decide if she could really speak. The words came from her mouth as if pulled with tongs. "Lady Wetherby says that will be my fate."

"She must be joking," he finally said when he could speak. "Come to think of it, she has always been overly dramatic." The Wetherby house was in sight, and he slowed the horse without thinking. "Surely you misunderstood her." He turned his attention to the horse, unsure of what to do in the face of such a question. "I am certain you did, Mrs. Wetherby. Pay it no mind," he added hastily.

She was a long time silent, and he knew somehow that he had failed her. "I probably misunderstood her," she said, her voice low, her eyes down. "And here we are now." Rosie held out her hand to him. "I can get out by myself, my lord. No need to trouble yourself."

He protested, but she was out of the gig before he had time to get down. She retrieved her bundle from the back and gave a small curtsy. "My lord, make sure Emmie stays indoors for a few days, and tell Will . . ." Her voice trailed off, and she could not look at him. "Well, just tell him good-bye." Then she was gone inside.

He rode home knowing he had failed her somehow, and it bothered him through what remained of the day and into dinner. Weary with everything, he pushed away his favorite Yorkshire pudding, which only brought consternation to the footman's face and Cook upstairs in tears. His evening was spent in tense kitchen diplomacy that left him with a headache, an inclination to chew nails, and the thought that if he were married, his wife could handle the domestic turmoil that now fell to his lot.

I am making a muddle of my life, he thought as he went to bed. *My daughter still pouts because Rosie is gone, my son mopes about, and I am a coward where women are concerned. What was it that Rosie meant by her remark about a workhouse?*

He saw her in the morning as he rode toward the new barn. She walked slowly on a distant hill, leaning into a stiff wind. "Rosie, go inside," he muttered to Sepoy. "Surely it is not that bad at the Wetherbys."

Because he made a point from then on to ride a different way to the barn, he did not see her again until the next choir practice. He had arranged for Dafydd Williams and his lovely Meg—here now, and truly a beauty—to pick up Rosie for practice.

He wondered all day what he would say to her, but that night she came to him and spared him the trouble of a first move. She held out two folded pieces of paper. "My lord, if you don't mind, I wanted to write to Will and Emma and want to spare the expense of the penny post."

He pocketed the letters. "I'll be happy to see that they get your letters. You can probably depend upon prompt replies." He hesitated. "They miss you, Mrs. Wetherby."

To his chagrin, tears welled in her eyes. She struggled to control them, and he flogged himself because he did not have the courage to take her hand or say something—anything. She was about to speak to him when the choirmaster rapped on the lectern for their attention.

Halfway through the Haydn, Peter Chard admitted to himself that it was not beyond the realm of possibility that Rosie Wetherby loved his children nearly as much as he did. When the choirmaster finished by easing them through favorite passages from Handel's Messiah, it came to Chard that he loved Rosie Wetherby, daughter of a Welsh sergeant and a foolish, wellborn lass, widow to the most worthless Wetherby on the planet, and mother soon of that man's child. *I am a fool where women are concerned*, he concluded simply.

He thought about Rosie constantly through November and into December. Letters came and went regularly between Rosie and his children, delivered during choir practice. He hated himself for it, but he read Will's letters from Rosie after his son went to bed. Emma had secreted hers someplace where he could not find them. He had occasion to thank God that Will possessed a less suspicious nature.

They were funny, well-written letters, telling about things she saw on her walks, mentioning last week's Northern Lights, and describing events from Portugal, the West Indies, and Canada where she had adventured with the army when she was young and in her father's care. Chard wrote her several letters of his own, which he never mailed.

He pinned his hopes on Christmas coming soon. The choir was fine beyond words, and there was no way they could ever lose the competition this year. *Life will return to normal*, he told himself, even though he knew that was the biggest lie he had ever perpetuated. Well, the second biggest. *I must talk to her*, he told himself over and over on the day of the last practice.

Snow was falling, and Dafydd and Meg were late with Rosie. There was only time for them to slide into their seats before the choirmaster's downbeat. Chard sang with his eye on Rosie. Even in the dim church light, he could tell that she was more pale than usual. When he caught her eye once, there was such a look of utter hopelessness on her face that he could only stare and wonder.

The choirmaster kept them long after the hour for the practice to end. "This is our final rehearsal, my dears," he reminded them. He leaned forward in conspiratorial fashion. "I have heard rumors that our efforts have not gone unnoticed at St. Peter's and St. Anselm's." He permitted himself the luxury of a chuckle. "I have even heard that they are worried."

I am worried, Chard thought, with another look at Rosie. When the choirmaster released them, Chard rose to go to her, only to be collared by Mrs. Barker, the doctor's wife, who chose that moment, of all the moments in the cosmos, to thank him for his clever idea of finding all those Welsh singers. She went on and on as he watched Dafydd help Meg and Rosie into their cloaks.

"Excuse me, Mrs. Barker," he said finally. He hurried down the aisle and outside, holding out the letters from his children as Williams lifted Rosie into the gig. "Mrs. Wetherby, these are for you," he said, handing them to her.

Williams took his seat in the gig, made sure the blanket was snug around Meg, and then looked at Chard expectantly. Rosie opened her mouth to speak and then closed it again. She tried to smile and handed him letters for his children. "Good-bye, sir," she said as Williams spoke to the horse.

To the best of his memory, she had never said good-bye to him. Usually it was, "Next week then, sir?" The thought troubled him all the way home.

The next morning, he remembered the letters and went to the bookroom for them. There were three instead of two. With fingers that shook, he opened the one addressed to him, read it, and then called for his carriage. He ignored the startled looks of his butler and downstairs maid as he ran down the hall, pulling on his overcoat as he went, and not even bothering to stop for his hat. "Spring 'um," was all he said to his coachman after giving the direction of the Wetherby estate.

Halfway there, he became aware that Rosie's letter was still crumpled in his fist. He smoothed it out and read the words again. Not that he had forgotten them from the first reading—he knew they were burned in his brain forever. "They are turning me out, sir, because they do not want me around when their precious Claude marries his high stickler from Durham. I am not sure precisely what their plan is, but Lady Wetherby has made it quite plain that I am not part of the family circle. She swears she has proof that my baby is not Junius's, but she does not produce it. I am sorry that I could not accommodate you and sing in the Christmas choir, but they have assured me that I will be gone by then. Please accept my kindest regards for your good health and fortune. Remember me to your children."

He didn't bother to raise the stupid gargoyle knocker on the Wetherby's front door but barged into the house, shouting for Rosie. Lady Wetherby, teacup in hand, came from the breakfast room followed by Claude, looking more oafish than usual.

"Where is Rosie?" he demanded, grabbing Claude by his shirtfront and backing him up against the wall, where he began to cry and plead for his mother. Chard shook Claude like a terrier shakes a rat and repeated his question six inches from the sobbing man's face.

Lady Wetherby's shrieks of "Murder! Murder!" brought Sir Rufus from his bookroom. As Chard slammed Claude against the wall again and Lady Wetherby screamed, Sir Rufus leaped back inside the bookroom and locked the door. *Well, I like that*, Chard thought as he gave Claude a final shake and let go of him.

A door opened upstairs. Chard looked up to the first-floor landing and then took the stairs two at a time to stand by Rosie Wetherby. "I need some help," she said simply. "If you could—"

"Get your cloak," he interrupted.

Without another word, she did as he said. He followed her into her room, one quick glance telling him about the paucity of Rosie's life with the Wetherbys. There was no fire in the grate, no carpet on the floor—nothing of any color besides the pictures Emma had been drawing and sending each week. He was almost surprised to see that they had allowed her a bed.

"Is there anything you want to take with you?" he asked, furious with himself for his lack of courage in love.

"N-no," she stammered, "just my bonnet."

"No baby clothes, nothing of your own?" He wished his voice was not rising, but it was.

She shook her head and took a step away from him.

"I have nothing."

"Come then." He took her by the hand and helped her down the stairs, taking them slowly because she could not move fast and trying to calm himself because he knew he was frightening her.

The door Sir Rufus had retreated behind was still closed, but he gave it a good kick as they passed it. He stopped in front of Lady Wetherby and narrowed his eyes. "You people are deplorable," he said, all his fury focused now in those few words.

Lady Wetherby glared back. "Dear Lucy must be spinning in her tomb. I am amazed what lengths you will go to for a soprano," she sneered.

"You don't know me," he replied.

Rosie burst into tears in the carriage, and he had the good sense to hold her close. When she wiped her eyes finally with his handkerchief and blew her nose, he held her away from him a little and took a deep breath.

"Mrs. Wetherby—Rosie, if you please—would you mind terribly if we took a bolt over the border and spliced ourselves?"

He could not overlook the surprise in her eyes. "You can't be serious, my lord," she said.

"Never more so, Rosie. I can't have my best soprano vanishing a week before we sing," he teased. *This won't do*, he thought as he saw the confusion in her beautiful eyes, red now with weeping. "I love you, Rose. Won't you marry me?"

She nodded and then blew her nose again.

As man and wife, they returned from Scotland quite late that night, both considerably shocked by what they had done. *Well, I am shocked*, Chard reasoned as they rode in silence. *I had no idea I was so impulsive.* He glanced at Rosie's profile, calm now after a storm of tears before and after the brief ceremony. *And you, my love?*

The house was dark, which suited him. He helped Rosie upstairs to his own room, found one of his nightshirts for her, turned down the coverlet on the side of the bed that would be hers, and went downstairs to write to his mother. When he came to bed, Rosie was asleep. She made no protest when he gathered as much of her close as he could and went to sleep. He couldn't remember a better night's rest.

In the morning, Will and Emma were pop-eyed, astounded, and then silent for the space of a few seconds when they heard the news. Then Emma burst into tears and threw herself into Rosie's arms, which only set off his wife again. Will leaned against him. "Papa, why do they do that? I'm happy, but it doesn't follow that I want to cry."

"Oh, Will," was all Chard could manage. Let him find out someday on his own time how skittish pregnant women were.

In answer to his letter, Mama was home in jig time to gasp and scold and storm and rage about the sitting room while he listened, his hands behind his head, his long legs stretched out in front of him, content. The sight of him so relaxed seemed to set her off further, but he could not help himself. He had never felt better. Rosie was upstairs in his—their bed, because Dr. Barker said she needed rest. Already her complexion was pinking up again, and her eyes had that familiar sparkle.

"Son, you have not heard a word I have said!" Louisa Chard concluded. She had not even removed her traveling coat and was only now stripping off her gloves.

"I have," he replied. "Let me see: the entire village thinks I have run mad in my attempt to retain my best soprano. And my favorite: Lord Wythe is cuckoo, probably the result of inbreeding among England's better houses." He gave his mother a sunny smile. "Was that the gist?"

Mama gave him a look that would melt glass. "You have made us a laughingstock. You are giving the protection of your name, position, and honors to a common soldier's daughter who is bearing a child of this shire's most notorious scoundrel!"

He smiled. "That's it, Mama." He straightened up then. "Mama, I am a farmer. Time passes pretty regularly here. I'll continue farming, Will and Emma will thrive, the new little one will fit right in, and we'll be happy. I hope you can adjust, Mama. If not, there is the dower house, or Bella."

Mama left that afternoon after another row when he asked her to remain to at least hear the choir he had got together, "At your command, I might add." She chose instead to return to Bella's for a good sulk, and it bothered him less than he would have thought.

Rosie came downstairs a day later, her serenity restored. She didn't say much to any of them, and he did not press her. Every now and then, he would catch her just watching him. *You are wondering what kind of a queer fish you have caught, aren't you, my dear?* he thought. There was a question in her eyes, but until she found the courage to ask it, he would not intrude on what remained of her pride and dignity.

Christmas Eve brought a skiff of snow in the morning. The house smelled of candied fruit, rum sauce, and cinnamon. Chard and Will spent the afternoon finding baby clothes in the storeroom. They took their findings to Rosie, who was resting again. He knew she would cry at the sight of all those clothes, and she did, sobbing into another of his handkerchiefs as she folded and unfolded the mound of nightgowns and blankets.

He helped her dress that night for the competition, buttoning up the back of her dress, pausing to kiss her neck before the last few buttons. She looked around in surprise and then smiled at him. "I know I am a trial." She took his hand where it rested on her shoulder. "I do need to ask you something, Peter. It's a favor. No, no, it is not that—" She stopped. "It's something I need to know."

"Do I really love you, or have I done this to secure a soprano?" he asked softly.

She gasped, turned around, and took his face in both hands. "No! I do not doubt that you love me," she said with sudden ferocity that made him go weak inside. "I've always known that. It is something else." She raised herself to kiss his lips, standing sideways to accomplish this because of her bulk.

His arms were around her, his face in her hair. He wanted to kiss her again, but Emma bounded into their room and tugged at his shirt. "Papa, Will says we have to hurry." She grinned up at Rosie. "Do you like to kiss my father?"

"Very much, my dear," Rosie replied promptly. She released him and sat on the bed. "Emmie, if you will help me with my shoes, that will give your father time to tuck in his shirttail and slap a little color back into his face."

They rode to St. Anselm's, the most distant of the three churches, but the largest. He was pleased to see the nice fit of the kid gloves he had bought Rosie that morning. She rested her hand in his, gripping it tight at intervals.

"Nervous?" he asked.

She nodded. "Can we talk tonight?" she asked as the carriage stopped and the children clambered out. "I still have a question. Please."

Suddenly he knew what it was she needed to know, and he also knew that he had a great secret for her too. *We will certainly have to trust each other,* he thought. He felt a rush of love for her that left him almost reeling. "Of course," he whispered back as he rose to help her from the carriage.

At the entrance to the church, she stopped suddenly and leaned against him for a long moment. "Afraid?" he asked.

She nodded but said nothing. People stared at them as they came into the church, but he did not care. His life and happiness were no one's business but his own. He knew his neighbors; in time, they would come to know and appreciate his wife.

He was about to sit down with the rest of St. Phil's choir when his old bailiff, who never came to church, shouldered his way through the crowd. "My lord! My lord!" he was shouting, as the church fell silent. "Your barn! It's on fire!"

Without a word, the Welshmen in the choir rose at

once and followed him out of the church. In minutes they were on their way across fields to Wythe and the distant barn. *Let it be a little thing*, he pleaded as they rode toward the high, thin plume that grew more black and dense as they approached.

To his intense relief, the new barn was intact. "Look here, sir, just beyond," one of the men shouted. "It is the old cow barn!"

So it was. The old structure that had probably been a tool shed since the Bishop of Durham's days was blazing away, the roof gone, the stones so hot they popped. He motioned them all to stand back and then looked around to discover that everything he had stored there—old tools, extra pails, spare rope, harness needing repair—was lined up neatly on the grass.

He smiled. It didn't take a genius . . . "I think that St. Phil's marvelous, majestic choir has been diddled by an Anglican arsonist," he said. "Someone from St. Anselm's or St. Pete's has thoughtfully selected my most expendable, distant outbuilding to burn, after removing anything of value inside."

Dafydd Williams shook his head. "I don't know, sir, but what you Northumberlanders aren't more trouble than all those Mahrattas at Assaye," he murmured.

Someone started to laugh. "How did the Welsh get a name for being troublemakers, sir?" someone else asked.

Chard looked around him, in perfect charity with his wonderful choir. "Ah, well, maybe next year. Come, lads. Since they so thoughtfully left us the pails, let us extinguish this little diversion. Let us sing, too, while we're at it."

Smoky and soot-covered, they returned to St. Anselm's long after both the competition and services were over. Another Christmas had come. It only remained to collect his wife and children and go home. "Mr. Wood-hull," he said to his vicar who waited inside the church, "it was only a small blaze and not my new barn. Merry Christmas!"

"Don't you want to know what happened?" the vicar asked as Chard looked around for his wife.

"Eh?"

Mr. Woodhull gripped his arm, completely forget-ting his place. "My lord, we won!"

"That's not possible," Chard said. "Almost the whole men's section was with me. And may I suggest that you advise the vicars of our neighboring parishes to preach an occasional sermon on repentance!"

"We won," the vicar repeated. "When it looked like you would not return in time, the choirmaster suggested that we turn to the Messiah. You know, that selection you had been using as a warming exercise?"

He nodded. The vicar smiled. "And when Mrs. Weth—Lady Wythe sang that part, 'And gently lead those who are with young,' there was not a dry eye in the building."

As the words sank in, he stared at the vicar. "But . . . but who sang the other parts? The Welsh men were gone!"

"We had the Welshwomen, of course, and let us say that either our Lord chose to smile on us for one night, or perhaps—just perhaps—our choir has been learning from masters. Congratulations, my lord."

"I'm delighted," Chard said, suddenly tired and in need of his own bed and Rosie to keep him warm. "Where's my wife?"

It was the vicar's turn to stare. "I thought you came from Wythe."

"No. We came right here from the upper pasture. What's wrong?"

Mr. Woodhull took his arm and started him for the door. "When Lady Wythe finished singing, she asked to be taken right home. Lord Wythe, I do believe you had better hurry there. It may be that our Lord is sharing His birthday with someone else."

He set records getting to Wythe, his mind a perfect turmoil. She had been so quiet all day, and she kept gripping his hand at intervals on the ride to St. Anselm's. *I remain an idiot,* he told himself in exasperation. *She was in labor and I didn't even know it. What a dolt Rosie has yoked herself to! Obviously she hasn't a clue in the world how to choose a husband. I had better be her last one, or no telling what trouble she will get into.*

Emma and Will were both asleep on the sofa in the upstairs hall, and he passed them quietly. The doctor stood on the landing, as well as two of the Welsh women.

"Didn't you say January?" he asked the doctor. "I distinctly remember January."

The women laughed. "They come when they're ready. She has a daughter," one of them said as he opened the door.

He went inside on tiptoe, taking off his smoky overcoat and washing his hands and face before coming to the bed where Rosie lay with her little one. He sat beside them, staring at the pretty morsel cradled so carefully in her arms. She was as beautiful as her mother, with the same dark hair.

"Rosie, she's a wonder," he whispered.

Her eyes were closed, but he knew she was awake.

Too tired to open her eyes, he thought. *And I was putting out a stupid fire.* "I wish I could have been here, Rosie," he said simply. "It won't happen again like this. You had to know the baby was coming. Why didn't you tell me?"

She opened her eyes, and his heart melted with the

expression in them. *You're going to love me, even if I am stupid and stodgy and unimaginative, aren't you?* he thought.

With an effort, she moved her hand from the baby to cover his hand. "I don't think you really cared if we won or not, did you?"

He shook his head and kissed her. "You know it never really mattered. Did it matter to you?"

She nodded. "Singing matters. I had to be there."

He got up, took off his shoes, and lay down on her other side. "I think you cut it a little close, love."

She nodded again. She turned her head to look at her baby. "I have something I should have asked you sooner."

He put a finger to her lips and raised up on his elbow so he could watch her expression. "Let me spill my budget first. If I am not mistaken, it will answer your question." He cleared his throat, wondering just how far back to go. *Begin at the beginning,* he told himself. "After Will was born, Lucy didn't want anything more to do with me."

"She was an idiot," Rosie murmured, her eyes closed again.

"Well, yes, but that's neither here nor there. I was in Ireland with the regiment, and we were headed to India. I was summoned home."

"Summoned?"

"Yes, and it did surprise me, because I was pretty sure from things I had heard that Lucy was grazing in other pastures."

Rosie opened her eyes wide and stared at him. "Did you know the man?"

"Yes, indeed. Someone rather high-placed in the government. You'd know the name, but I can be a gentleman. Lucy obviously wanted me to share her bed, but I chose not to and left the next morning for India as I had planned."

He paused and waited, knowing that Rosie was quick. "Emma?" she gasped.

". . . is another man's child. I had been summoned home to Lucy's bed to do my conjugal duty and avoid a scandal. I knew it from the moment I heard of Lucy's death in childbirth. Letters are so slow to India, my love."

Rosie was silent, taking in what he was saying. She pulled her own daughter closer, and as he watched, the tears slid from her eyes to puddle in her hair still damp from the sweat of childbirth. He let her cry, knowing that he had answered her question.

"During that terrible voyage home, I thought about what I would do. Everyone thought Emma was mine, but I knew different. I could have created a dreadful scene. It might even have toppled a government I am not too fond of."

"But you could not," Rosie said, burrowing closer to him. "That would have destroyed Emma."

He felt his own tears rising this time. "Rosie, I looked down at that innocent baby, and I could not do it. Emma may not be bone of my bone like Will, but she is my daughter." He patted her hip. "And that, wife, is my great secret. I trust you to keep it. I'll never fail your—our daughter, either. She is already mine, because she is yours."

Instead of answering him, she handed him her baby, and it was all the response he needed. He sat up, holding his new daughter as Rosie rested her head against him.

"Depend on me," he whispered as he kissed the little one. "Depend on me."

AN OBJECT OF CHARITY

Captain Michael Lynch never made a practice of leaning on the quarterdeck railing of the *Admirable*, but it hardly seemed to matter now. The crew—what was left of them—eyed him from a respectful distance, but he knew with a lift to his trounced-upon heart that not one of them would give less than his utmost, even as he had.

His glance shifted to that spot on the deck that had glared so brightly only last month with the blood of David Partlow, his first mate. One of his crew, when not patching oakum here and there to keep the *Admirable* afloat or manning the pumps, had scrubbed that spot white again until all trace was gone. Still he stared at the spot, because now it was whiter than the rest of the deck.

What bad luck, he thought again. Curse the French who had sailed to meet the *Admirable* and other frigates of the blockade fleet, gun ports open and blazing a challenge rare in them, but brought about by an unexpected shift in the wind. Most of all, curse the luck that fired the frigate *Celerity* and sent her lurching out of control into the *Admirable*.

And maybe even curse Partlow for rushing to the rail with a grappling hook just in time for the *Celerity*'s deck carronade, heated by the flames, to burst all over him.

Another *Celerity* gun belched fire then, and another, point blank at his own beautiful *Admirable*, one ball

141

carrying off his sailing master and the other shattering the mainmast at its juncture with the deck. "And they call that friendly fire," he murmured, leaning on the railing still as the *Admirable* inched past able ships in Portsmouth harbor.

There would be an inquiry, a matter of course when one ship had nearly destroyed another. He knew the Lords of the Admiralty would listen to all the testimony and exonerate him, but this time there would be no *Admirable* to return to. It would be in dry dock for three months at least, and he would be sentenced to the shore on half pay. The lords might offer him another ship, but he didn't want any ship but the *Admirable*.

Lynch was mindful of the wind roaring from the north, wavering a point or two and then settling into a steady blow. He couldn't fathom three months without the wind in his face, even this raw December wind.

At some exclamation of dismay from one of the crew, he looked up to see the dry dock dead ahead. *I can't stand it*, he thought. He didn't mind the half pay. Even now as he leaned so melancholy on the rail, his prize money from years and years of capture and salvage was compounding itself on 'Change. If he chose, he could retire to a country estate and live in comfort on the interest alone; his wants were few.

The scow towing his ship backed its sails and slowed as it approached the dry dock. In another minute a launch nestled itself alongside. His bosun, arm in a sling but defying anyone but himself to do this duty, stood ready to pipe him off the *Admirable*. His trunk, hat case, and parcel of books were already being transferred to the launch. The bosun even forgot himself enough to lower the pipe and suggest that is was "better to leave now, sor."

"Curse your impertinence, Mays!" Lynch growled in

protest. "It's not really like leaving a grave before the dirt is piled on, now, is it?"

But it was. He could see the sympathy in his bosun's eyes, and all the understandings they had shared through the years without actually calling attention to them.

"You'll be back, Captain," the bosun said, as if to nudge him along. "The *Admirable* will be as good as new."

And maybe it will be a young man's ship then as it once was mine, he thought, stirring himself from the rail. *I have conned the* Admirable *for fifteen years, from the India Wars to Boney's Berlin and Milan decrees that blockade Europe. I am not above thirty-six, but I feel sixty, at least, and an infirm sixty at that.* With a nod to his bosun, he allowed himself to be piped over the side.

Determined not to look back at the wounded *Admirable*, he followed his few belongings to Mrs. Brattle's rooming house, where he always stayed between voyages. He handed a coin to the one-armed tar, who earned his daily mattress and sausages by trundling goods about town in his rented cart. It was almost Christmas, so he added another coin, enough to give the man a day off, but not enough to embarrass him; he knew these old sailors.

And there was Mrs. Brattle, welcoming him as always. He could see the sympathy in her eyes—amazing how fast bad news circulated around Portsmouth. He dared her to say anything, and to his relief, she did not, beyond the communication that his extra trunk was stowed in the storeroom and he could have his usual quarters.

"Do you know how long you will be staying this time, sir?" she asked, motioning to the 'tween-stairs maid behind them to lay a fire.

He could have told her three months, until the *Admirable* was refitted, but he didn't. "I'm not entirely sure, Mrs.

Brattle," he heard himself saying for some unaccountable reason.

She stood where she was, watching the maid with a critical but not unkindly eye. When the girl finished, she nodded her approval and looked at him. "It'll be stew then, Captain," she said as she handed him his key.

He didn't want stew; he didn't want anything but to lie down and turn his face to the wall. He hadn't cried since India, so it didn't enter his mind, but he was amazed at his own discomposure. "Fine, Mrs. Brattle," he told her. He supposed he would have to eat so she would not fret.

He knew the rooms well—the sitting room large enough for sofa, chairs, and table; the walls decorated here and there with improving samplers done by Mrs. Brattle's dutiful daughters, all of them now long married. His eyes always went first to the popular "England expects every man to do his duty," that, since Trafalgar, had sprouted on more walls than he cared to think about. *I have done my duty*, he told himself.

He stared a long while at the stew, delivered steaming hot an hour later and accompanied by brown bread and tea sugared the way he liked it. Through the years and various changes in his rank, he had thought of seeking more exalted lodgings, but the fact was, he did not take much notice of his surroundings on land. Nor did he wish to abandon a place where the landlady knew how he liked his tea.

Even to placate Mrs. Brattle, he could not eat that evening. He was prepared for a fight when she returned for his tray, but he must have looked forbidding enough, or tired enough, so that she made no more comment than that she hoped he would sleep better than he ate. Personally, he did not hold out much confidence for her wish; he never slept well.

The level of his exhaustion must have been higher than he thought, because he slept finally as the day came. He had a vague recollection of Mrs. Brattle in his room, and then silence. He woke at noon with a fuzzy brain. Breakfast and then a rambling walk in a direction that did not include the dry dock cleared his head. He had the city to himself, possibly because Portsmouth did not lend itself much to touring visitors, but more likely because it was raining. He didn't care; it suited his mood.

When he came back to his lodgings, he felt better and in a frame of mind to apologize to Mrs. Brattle for his mopes. He looked in the public sitting room and decided the matter would keep. She appeared to be engaged in earnest conversation with a boy and girl who looked even more travel weary than he had yesterday.

He thought they must be Scots. The girl—no, a second look suggested a young woman somewhere in her twenties rather than a girl—wore a plaid muffler draped around her head and neck over her traveling cloak. He listened to the soft murmur of her voice with its lilt and burr, not because he was prone to eavesdropping, but because he liked the cadence of Scottish conversation and its inevitable reminder of his first mate.

As he watched, the boy moved closer to the woman, and she grasped his shoulder in a protective gesture. The boy's arm went around her waist, and she held it there with her other hand. The intimacy of the gesture rendered him oddly uncomfortable, as though he intruded. *This is silly*, he scolded himself. *I am in a public parlor in a lodging house.*

Never mind, he thought, and went upstairs. He added coal to the fire and put on his slippers, prepared for a late afternoon of reading the *Navy Chronicle* and dozing. Some of his fellow officers were getting up a whist table at the Spithead, and he would join them there after dinner.

He had read through the promotions list and started on the treatise debating the merits of the newest canister casing when Mrs. Brattle knocked on his door. She had a way of knocking and clearing her throat at the same time that made her entrances obvious. "Come, Mrs. Brattle," he said, laying aside the *Chronicle*, which was, he confessed, starting to bore him.

When she opened the door, he could see others behind her, but she closed the door upon them and hurried to his chair. "Sir, it is the saddest thing," she began, her voice low with emotion. "The niece and nephew of poor Mr. Partlow have come all the way from Fort William in the Highlands to find him! The harbormaster directed them here to you."

"Have you told them?" he asked quietly as he rose.

She shook her head. "Oh, sir, I know you're far better at that than I ever would be. I mean, haven't you written letters to lots of sailors' families, sir?"

"Indeed, Mrs. Brattle. I am something of an expert on the matter," he said, regretting the irony in his voice but knowing his landlady well enough to be sure that she would not notice it. *What I do not relish are these face-to-face interviews*, he thought, *especially my Number One's relatives, curse the luck.*

"May I show them in, or should I send them back to the harbormaster?" she asked. She leaned closer and allowed herself the liberty of adding that while they were genteel, they were Scots. "Foreigners," she explained, noticing the mystified look that he knew was on his face.

He knew that before she said it. David Partlow had come from generations of hard-working Highlanders, and he never minded admitting it. "Sturdy folk," he had said once. "The best I know."

"Show them in, Mrs. Brattle," he said. She opened the door, ushered in the two travelers, and then shut the door quickly behind her. He turned to his guests and nodded. "I am Captain Lynch of the *Admirable*," he said.

The young woman dropped a graceful curtsey, which had the odd effect of making him feel old. He did not want to feel old, he decided, as he looked at her.

She held out her hand to him, and he was rewarded with a firm handshake. "I am Sally Partlow, and this is my brother Thomas," she said.

"May I take your cloak?" he asked, not so much remembering his manners with women—because he had none—but eager to see what shape she possessed. *I have been too long at sea*, he thought, mildly amused with himself.

Silently, her eyes troubled, she unwound the long plaid shawl and pulled it from her hair. He had thought her hair was ordinary brown like his, but it was the deepest, darkest red he had ever seen—beautiful hair, worn prettily in a bun at the nape of her neck.

He indicated the chair he had vacated, and she sat down. "It is bad news, isn't it?" she asked without any preamble. "When we asked the harbormaster, he whispered to someone and gave me directions to this place, and the woman downstairs whispered with you. Tell me direct."

"Your uncle is dead," he told her, the bald words yanked right out of his mouth by her forthrightness. "We had a terrible accident on the blockade. He was killed, and my ship was nearly destroyed."

She winced and briefly narrowed her eyes at his words, but she returned his gaze with no loss of composure, rather like a woman used to bad news.

"Your uncle didn't suffer," he added quickly, struck by the lameness of his words as soon as he spoke them. He was rewarded with more of the same measured regard.

"Do you write that to all the kin of your dead?" she asked, not accusing him, but more out of curiosity, or so it seemed to him. *"All the kin of your dead,"* he thought, struck by the aptness of the phrase and the grand way it rolled off her Scottish tongue.

"I suppose I do write it," he said, after a moment's thought. "In David's case, I believe it is true." He hesitated and then plunged ahead, encouraged by her level gaze. "He was attempting to push off the *Admirable* with a grappling hook, and a carronade exploded directly in front of him. He . . . he couldn't have known what hit him."

To his surprise, Sally Partlow leaned forward and quickly touched his hand. *She knows what he meant to me,* he thought, grateful for her concern.

"I'm sorry for you," she said. "Uncle Partlow mentioned you often in his letters."

"He did?" It had never before occurred to him that he could be a subject in anyone's letters, or even that anyone thought him memorable.

"Certainly, sir," she replied. "He often said what a fair-minded commander you were, and how your crew—and he included himself—would follow you anywhere."

These must be sentiments that men do not confide in each other, he decided as he listened to her. Of course, he had wondered why the same crew remained in his service year after year, but he had always put it down to fondness for the *Admirable. Could it be there was more?* The matter had never crossed his mind before.

"You are all kindness, Miss Partlow," he managed to say, but not without embarrassment. "I'm sorry to give you this news—and here you must have thought to bring him

Christmas greetings and perhaps take him home with you."

The brother and sister looked at each other. "It is rather more than that, Captain," Thomas Partlow said.

"Oh, Tom, let us not concern him," Sally said. "We should leave now."

"What, Thomas?" he asked the young boy. "David Partlow will always be my concern."

"Uncle Partlow was named our guardian several years ago," he said.

"I do remember that, Thomas," Lynch said. "He showed me the letter. Something about in the event of your father's death, I believe. Ah yes, we were blockading the quadrant around La Nazaire then, same as now."

"Sir, our father died two weeks ago," Thomas explained. "Almost with his last breath, he told us that Uncle Partlow would look after us." The room was silent. Lynch could tell that Miss Partlow was embarrassed. He frowned. These were his lodgings; perhaps the Partlows expected him to speak first.

"I fear you are greatly disappointed," he said, at a loss. "I am sorry for your loss, and sorry that you must return to Scotland both empty-handed and bereft."

Sally Partlow stood up and extended her hand to him, while her brother retrieved her cloak and shawl from the end of the sofa. "We trust we did not take up too much of your time at this busy season," she said. "Come, Thomas." She curtseyed again, and he bowed and opened the door for her. She hesitated a moment. "Sir, we are quite unfamiliar with Portsmouth. Do you know . . . ?"

". . . of a good hotel? I can recommend the Spithead on the High."

The Partlows looked at each other and smiled. "Oh, no!" she said. "Nothing that fine. I had in mind an employment agency."

He shook his head. "I couldn't tell you. Never needed one." *Did they want to hire a maid?* he wondered. "Thanks to Boney, I've always had plenty of employment." He bade them good day and the best of the season and retreated behind his paper again as Miss Partlow quietly shut the door.

Two hours later, when Mrs. Brattle and the maid were serving his supper, he understood the enormity of his error. Mrs. Brattle had laid the table and set a generous slice of sirloin before him when she paused. "Do you know, Captain, I am uneasy about the Partlows. She asked me if I needed any help around the place."

Mystified, he shook his napkin into his lap. "That is odd. She asked me if I knew of an employment agency."

He sat a moment more in silence, staring down at the beef in front of him, brown and oozing pink juices. Shame turned him hot, and he put his napkin back on the table. "Mrs. Brattle, I think it entirely possible that the Partlows haven't a sixpence to scratch with."

She nodded, her eyes troubled. "She'll never find work here so close to Christmas. Captain Lynch, Portsmouth may be my home, but it's not a place that I would advise a young woman to look for work."

He could only agree. With a speed that surprised him, considering how slowly he had dragged himself to the rooming house only yesterday, he soon found himself on the street, looking for the Partlows and hoping deep in his heart that their dead uncle would forgive his captain's stupidity. He stopped at the Spithead long enough to tell his brother officers that they would have to find another fourth to make up the whist table tonight and then began his excursion through town. It brought him no pleasure, and he berated himself for not being more aware—or even aware at all of the

Partlows' difficulties. *Am I so dense?* he asked himself, and he knew the answer.

Christmas shoppers passed him, bearing packages wrapped in brown paper and twine. Sailors drunk and singing stumbled past. He thought he saw a press-gang on the prowl as well, and his blood chilled at the thought of Lieutenant Partlow's little nephew nabbed and hauled aboard a frigate to serve at the king's good pleasure. Granted he was young, but not too young to be a powder monkey. *Not that*, he thought as he turned up his collar and hurried on, stopping to peer into restaurant kitchens over the protestations of proprietors and cooks.

He didn't even want to think about the brothels down on the waterfront where the women worked day and night on their backs when the fleet was in. *She would never*, he thought. Of course, who knew when they had even eaten last? He thought of the beef roast all for him and cursed himself again, his heart bleak.

When it was full dark and his cup of discouragement had long since run over, he spotted them on the fisherman's wharf, seated close together on a crate. Their arms were around each other, and even as he realized how awful their situation was, he felt a tug of envy. *There is not another soul in the world who would care if I dropped dead tomorrow*, he thought, *except possibly my landlady, and she's been half expecting such an event all these years of war.*

He heard a sound to his left and saw, to his dismay, a press-gang approaching, the ensign ready with his whistle and the bosun with a cudgel should Tom Partlow choose to resist impressment in the Royal Navy. As an ensign, Lynch had done his own press-gang duty, hating every minute of it and only getting through it by pretending that every hapless dockyard loiterer that he impressed was his brother.

"Hold on there," he called to the ensign, who was putting his whistle to his lips. "The boy's not for the fleet."

At his words, the Partlows turned around. Sally leaped down from the packing crate and stood between her brother and the press-gang. Even in the gloom, he could see how white her face was, how fierce her eyes. There was something about the set of her jaw that told him she would never surrender Tom without a fight.

"Not this one," Lynch said, biting off each word. He recognized the bosun from the *Formidable*, whose captain was even now playing whist at the Spithead.

To his irritation—he who was used to being obeyed—the young officer seemed not to regard him. "Stand aside," the man shouted to Sally Partlow.

"No," Sally said, and backed up.

Lynch put a firm hand on the ensign's arm. "No." The ensign stared at him and then looked at his bosun, who stood with cudgel lowered. "Topkins, as you were!" Lynch shouted.

The bosun shook his head. "Sorry, Captain Lynch!" he said. He turned to his ensign. "We made a mistake, sir."

The ensign was almost apoplectic with rage. He tried to grab Lynch by the front of his cloak, but in a moment's work, he was lying on the wharf, staring up.

"Touch me again, you pup, and I'll break you right down to able seaman. This boy is not your prey. Help him up, Topkins, and wipe that smile off your ugly face."

The bosun helped up his ensign, who flung off his assisting arm when he was on his feet. He took a good look at Lynch, blanched, and stammered his apologies.

"There's those in the *Formidable*'s fo'castle who'd have paid to see that, Captain Lynch," the bosun whispered. "Happy Christmas!"

Lynch stood where he was between the Partlows and

the press-gang until the wharf was deserted again. "There now," he said, more to himself than them. He turned around to see Sally still standing in front of her brother, shielding him. "They won't return, Miss Partlow, but there may be others. You need to get yourselves off the streets."

She shook her head, and he could see for the first time how young she really was. Her composure had deserted her, and he was embarrassed to have to witness a proud woman pawn her pride in front of practically a stranger. He was at her side in a moment.

"Will you forgive me for my misunderstanding of your situation?" he asked in a low voice, even though there was no one else around except Tom, who had tears on his face. Without a word, Lynch gave him his handkerchief. "You're safe now, lad," he said and looked at the boy's sister again. "I do apologize, Miss Partlow."

"You didn't know because I didn't say anything," she told him, the words dragged out of her by pincers. "No need to apologize."

"Perhaps not," he agreed, "but I should have been beforehand enough not to have needed your situation spelled out for me."

Tom handed back the handkerchief, and Lynch gave it to the boy's sister. "But why were you sitting here on the dock?"

She dabbed at her eyes and then pointed to a faded sign reading FISH FOR SALE. "We thought perhaps in the morning we could find occupation," she told him.

"So you were prepared to wait here all night?" he asked, failing to keep the shock from his voice, which only increased the young woman's own embarrassment. "Have you no funds at all? When did you last eat?"

She looked away, biting her upper lip to keep the tears back, he was sure, and his insides writhed. "Never mind that," he said briskly. "Come back with me now, and we can at least remedy one problem with a meal." When she still hesitated, he picked up her valise and motioned to Tom. "Smartly now," he ordered, not looking over his shoulder, but praying from somewhere inside him that never prayed that the Partlows would follow.

The walk from the end of the dock to the street seemed the longest of his life, especially when he heard no footsteps behind him. He could have sunk to the earth in gratitude when he finally heard them—the boy's quicker steps first and then his sister's accompanied by the womanly rustle of skirt and cloak.

His lodgings were blessedly warm. Mrs. Brattle was watching for him from the front window, which filled him with some relief. He knew he needed an ally in such a respectable female as his landlady. Upstairs in his lodgings she had cleared away his uneaten dinner, but it was replaced in short order by the entire roast of sirloin this time, potatoes, popovers that she knew he liked, and pounds of gravy.

Without even a glance at his sister, Tom Partlow sat down and was soon deeply involved in dinner. Mrs. Brattle watched. "When did the little boy eat last?" she asked in round tones.

Sally blushed. "I . . . I think it was the day before yesterday," she admitted, not looking at either of them.

Mrs. Brattle let out a sigh of exasperation and prodded Sally Partlow closer to the table. "Then it has probably been another day beyond that for you, missy, if you are like most women. Fed him the last meal, didn't you?"

Sally nodded. "Everything we owned was sold for debt. I thought we would have enough for coach fare and food, and we almost did." Her voice was so low that Lynch could hardly hear her.

Bless Mrs. Brattle again, he decided. His landlady gave Sally a quick squeeze around the waist. "You almost did, dearie!" she declared, turning the young woman's nearly palpable anguish into a victory of sorts. "Why don't you sit yourself down—Captain, remember your manners and pull out her chair!—and have a go before your brother eats it all."

She sat without protest and spread a napkin in her lap, tears escaping down her cheeks. Mrs. Brattle distracted herself by admonishing the maid to go for more potatoes, and hurry up about it, giving Sally a chance to draw herself together. The landlady frowned at Lynch until he tore his gaze from the lovely woman struggling with pride and took his own seat next to Tom. He astounded himself by keeping up what seemed to him like a veritable avalanche of inconsequential chatter with the boy and removed all attention from his sister until out of the corner of his eye, he saw her eating.

Having eaten, Tom Partlow struggled valiantly to stay awake while his sister finished. He left the table for the sofa and in a minute was breathing quietly and evenly. Sally set down her fork, and Lynch wanted to put it back in her hand, but he did nothing, only watched her as she watched her brother. "'Tis hard to sleep on a mail coach," she said in a low voice.

He didn't know why it should matter so much to him, but he felt only unspeakable relief when she picked up her fork again. She ate all that was before her like a dutiful child but shook her head at a second helping of anything. Weariness had stamped itself upon all the lines of her body. She seemed to droop before his eyes, and he didn't know what to do for her.

Mrs. Brattle came to his aid again. After the maid had taken the dishes down the stairs in a tub, his landlady sat next to Sally Partlow and took her by the hand. "Dearie, I have an extra room downstairs and you're welcome to it tonight," she said. "Tom will be fine right here on the captain's sofa. Come along now."

Sally Partlow looked at him, distress on her face now, along with exhaustion. "We didn't mean to be so much trouble," she said. "Truly we didn't."

She was pleading with him, and it pained him that he could offer her so little comfort. "I know you didn't, Miss Partlow," he assured her as Mrs. Brattle helped her to her feet. "Things happen, don't they?"

It sounded so lame, but she nodded, apparently grateful for his ha'penny wisdom. "Surely I will think of something in the morning," she told him and managed a smile. "I'm not usually at my wit's end."

"I don't imagine you are," he commented, intrigued by the way she seemed to dig deep within herself, even through her own weariness. It was a trait he had often admired in her uncle. "This will pass too. If you have no objections, I'll think on the matter myself. And don't look so wary! Call it the Christmas present I cannot give your uncle."

After she left, he removed Thomas's shoes and covered the sleeping boy with a blanket, wondering all the while how someone could sleep so soundly. He sat by the boy, asking himself what David Partlow would have done with a niece and nephew thrust upon him. Tom could be bought a midshipman's berth if there was money enough, but Sally? A husband was the obvious solution, but it would be difficult to procure one without a dowry.

He spent a long time staring into his shaving mirror the next morning. His Mediterranean tan had faded to a sallow color, and nothing that he knew, short of the guillotine, would have any effect on his premature wrinkles, caused by years of squinting at sun and sails and facing into the wind. *And why should I ever worry*, he considered as he scraped away at his face.

He had waked early as usual, always wondering if he had slept at all, and moved quietly about his room. When he came into his sitting room, Tom Partlow was still asleep. Lynch eased into a chair and gave himself over to the Partlows' dilemma. He knew she could not afford to purchase a berth for Tom, and oddly, that was a relief to him. *Life at sea is no life, laddie*, he thought as he watched the boy. *After all, you might end up like me, a man of a certain age with no more possessions than would fit in two smallish trunks and not a soul who cares whether I live or die.*

But I did have a mother once, he reminded himself, *so I did*. The idea hit him, stuck, and grew. By the time Tom woke and Sally Partlow knocked on the door and opened it for Mrs. Brattle and breakfast, he had a plan. Like some he had fallen back upon during years of toil at sea, it had holes a-plenty and would never stand up to much scrutiny, but it was a beginning.

"Miss Partlow," he announced over bacon and eggs, "I am taking you and Tom home to my mother's house for Christmas."

On his words, Mrs. Brattle performed an interesting juggling act with a teapot, recovering herself just before she dumped the contents all over the carpet. She stared at him, her eyes big in her face.

"We couldn't possibly intrude on your holiday like that," Sally Partlow said quietly, objecting as he had no doubt that she would.

Here I go, he thought. *Why does this feel more dangerous than sailing close to a lee shore?* "Miss Partlow, it is not in the nature of a suggestion. I have decided to visit my mother in Lincolnshire and would no more think of leaving you to the mercies of Portsmouth than, than . . . writing a letter of admiration to Napoleon, thanking him for keeping me employed for all these years!"

She opened her mouth to protest, but he trod on inexorably and felt himself on the firmer deck of command. "If you feel a burning desire to argue, I would not recommend it. I suspect that your uncle has funds on 'Change. Once the probate is done—and I will see that it is going forward—you should have funds to repay me, even with interest. Until that moment, I won't hear of anything else."

He returned to his eggs with what he hoped was the semblance of serenity. Miss Partlow blinked, favored him with a steady gaze, and then directed her attention to the egg before her. "Captain Lynch, I suppose we will be happy to accompany you to . . . where was it? Lincolnshire?" she murmured.

"Lincolnshire," he said firmly. "Yes, indeed. Pass the bacon, would you please?"

They finished breakfast in silence. He knew that Mrs. Brattle was almost leaping about in her eagerness to have a word in private with him, so he directed Tom and Sally to make themselves useful by taking the dishes below stairs to the scullery. To his amusement, the Partlows seemed subdued by his plain speaking, a natural product of years of nautical command.

The door had scarcely closed behind them when Mrs. Brattle began. "I never knew you had a mother, Captain Lynch," she declared.

He looked at her in mock horror. "Mrs. B, everyone has a mother. How, pray, do you think I got on the planet?"

His landlady was not about to be vanquished by his

idle wit. "Captain, I am certain there are those of your crew who think you were born fully grown and stalking a quarterdeck! I am not numbered among them. I am not to be bamboozled. Captain, is this a good idea?"

"I don't know," he was honest enough to admit. "They have nowhere to go, and I have not visited my mother in twenty-two years."

She gasped again and sat down. "You would take two perfect strangers to visit a lady you have not seen in twenty-two years? Captain . . ." She shook her head. "Only last week I was saying to my daughter that you are a most sensible, steady, and level-headed boarder, and wasn't I the lucky woman!"

"Yes?" he asked, intrigued again that he would come to anyone's notice. "Perhaps it is time for a change."

"It's been so long, sir," Mrs. Brattle reminded him. "Twenty-two years! Is your mother still alive?"

"She was five years ago," he told her. "I have kept in touch with the vicar, at least until he died five years past and my annual letter was returned."

She looked at him with real sympathy. "A family falling out, then?"

"Yes, Mrs. Brattle, a falling out."

And that is putting too kind a face upon it, he decided as he sat down after noon in the post chaise with the Partlows, and they started off, with a call to the horses and a crack of the coachman's whip. Even after all these years—and there had been so many—he could not recall the occasion without a wince. It was more a declaration of war than a falling out.

"Captain?"

He looked up from the contemplation of his hands to see Sally Partlow watching him, a frown between her fine eyes. "What is it?" he asked, clipping off his words the way he always did aboard ship. As he regarded the dismay on her face, Michael regretted the sharpness of his inquiry.

"I . . . I didn't mean any disrespect," she stammered. "I just noticed that you looked . . . distressed," she concluded, her voice trailing off. She made herself small in her corner of the chaise and drew her cloak more tightly about her.

"I am quite in command, Miss Partlow," he replied, the brisk tone creeping in, even though he did not wish it this time.

She directed her attention to the scenery outside the window, which amounted to nothing more than dingy warehouses. "I didn't mean to intrude."

And she did not intrude again, through the whole long afternoon. He heard her sniff once or twice and observed from the corner of his eye that she pressed her fingers against her nose several times; there were no tears that he could see. She put her arm about her brother with that same firm clasp he had noticed yesterday. When Thomas drifted to sleep, secure in his sister's embrace, she closed her eyes as well, with a sigh that went directly to his heart.

I have crushed her with my grudging generosity, he realized, and the revelation caused him such a pang that he longed to stride back and forth on his quarterdeck until he wore off his own irritation. But he was trapped in a post chaise, where he could only chafe and wonder how men on land ever survived such confinement. *I suppose they slam doors, kick small objects, and snap at well-meaning people as I have done*, he decided, his cup of contrition full.

He couldn't think of a remedy except apology or explanation, and neither suited him. *Thank goodness my father forced me to sea years ago*, was the thought that consoled him. He found himself counting the days when he could be done with this obligation to the Partlows, which had forced him into a visit home that he knew he did not want.

The time passed somehow, and Sally Partlow was obliging enough to keep her eyes closed. Whether she slept, he had no idea. Darkness came even earlier than usual, thanks to the snow that began to fall as they drove north toward Lincolnshire. Inwardly he cursed the snow, because he knew he could not force the coachman to drive on through the night and end this uncomfortable journey. When after an hour of the slowest movement he saw lights ahead, he knew the driver would stop and insist that they spend the night.

The village was Firch, the shire Cambridge, one south of his own, but there was no budging the coachman, who looked so cold and bleak that Michael felt a sprinkling of sympathy settle on the crust of his irritation. It was an unfamiliar emotion; he almost didn't recognize it.

"We have to stop here," the coachman said, as Michael opened the carriage door. "No remedy for it, Captain."

"Very well." He joined the man outside the carriage, grateful for his boat cloak and boots. He noticed the other carriages in the yard and made the wry observation that Christmas continued to be a challenge for innkeepers. "Can you find a place for yourself?" he asked the coachman.

"Aye, sir. I'll bed in the stables with t'others." The man scratched his chin. "You're the one who might not be so lucky, beggin' yer pardon."

He feared the man was right. With no allowance for argument, Lynch told the Partlows to move along smartly and follow him inside. He started across the yard, leaning against the snow and wind and wondering as he had before on the Portsmouth docks if they would follow him. He slowed his steps, hoping they would catch up with him, but they did not, hanging back, not wishing—he was sure—to trouble him beyond what they were already doing.

Hoping for the best, even as he suspected the worst, he asked the innkeep for two rooms and a parlor. "Sorry, Captain," the man said, properly cowed by what Lynch suspected was the height of his fore and aft hat and gold braid, if not the look on his face. The keep glanced beyond him, and he felt some relief that the Partlows must have followed him inside.

His relief was momentary. The keep asked him, all hesitation and apology, "Can ye share a room just this once with your son and daughter?"

"She's not my daughter," he said before he thought.

"Sorry, sir," the keep apologized. "Then you and your lady'll have to have"—he hesitated, as if trying to determine the relationship—"the boy on a pallet in your room, I'm thinking. There's no parlor to be had. Once you take that room, there won't be another for anyone else, it's that full we are."

"Very well," Lynch said, disconcerted right down to his stockings but determined not to make it worse by saying more. "It seems we have no choice."

"None, sir," the keep replied.

Lynch was too embarrassed to look at Sally Partlow, so he ignored her and followed the keep's wife up the narrow stairs to a room at the back of the inn. Again he listened for the Partlows behind him, because he knew that only the weather outside was keeping them tethered to his side.

The keep's wife apologized for the size of the room, but he could find no fault with the warmth from the fireplace and the general air of comfort in small places that he was used to, from life aboard a frigate. When the woman left the three of them, Sally removed the plaid about her head, shook the flakes into the fireplace, and put the shawl on the narrow cot.

"I was thinking I should take that berth," he told her. "You and Tom can have the bed."

"Nonsense. I am fully a foot shorter than you, sir," she said, and nothing more; he had the wisdom not to argue.

He knew he would dread dinner in the common parlor, but he did not, even though the setting was not one he was accustomed to. No matter how rough his life at sea, his infrequent sojourns on land, in whatever port of the world, had always meant private parlors and deference. He sat at the long table next to Sally and followed her lead, passing the common dishes around to the next diner and engaging, eventually, in small talk with the farmer to his left, an act that would have astounded his late first mate. He decided to enjoy conversation about crop prices and even yielded far enough to tell a sea story.

He never embellished tales, and he did not now, so he was amazed that anyone would care to listen to his paltry account of life at sea. Maybe he was trying to explain himself to the Partlows; he didn't understand either, beyond a sudden need to offer some accounting of himself.

When dinner concluded, he could bear no retreat to a private parlor; before he could say something about sitting for a while in the public room, Sally told him that she was going to settle Tom upstairs in bed. "It was a long day, sir," she murmured, and he realized with a start that it was only the second thing she had said to him since his unkindness at noon.

I suppose it was a long day, he thought as he watched her escort her brother upstairs, her hand upon his back, her motion on the stairs so graceful that he felt like a voyeur. He went into the public room, content to prop his booted feet by the fender and enjoy the warmth of the fire. He even leaned back against the settee and called it a luxury.

He had thought that his hearing was going after years of cannonading, but he knew her steps on the stairs when she came down later. Before he could say anything—had anything occurred to him—she was out the door and into the snow. He debated a moment whether to follow—surely she would never leave her brother behind—and then rose, pulled his cloak around him, and head down, went into the snow after her.

He could barely see her in the dark, but he watched her pause at the fence beyond the high road. The wind swirled the snow, but she raised her face to it, as though she hated super-heated rooms as much as he did. He walked across the road to stand beside her.

"I was not running away, Captain," she said without looking at him.

"I know that. You would never leave Tom."

"It is just that I do not like being an object of charity, sir," she said.

The candor of her words startled him, until he recalled her uncle, who never feared to tell him anything. "Who does, Miss Partlow?" he asked. "May I remind you that you can repay me when your uncle's funds on 'Change are probated."

"There won't be any funds, sir."

She spoke so firmly that he did not doubt her.

"How is this?" he asked. "He has always had his share of the salvage."

"Uncle Partlow sent his money home for my father to invest." She hesitated, took a deep breath, and forged on. "My father had no more notion of wise investments than a shoat in a piggery." He could hear the tears in her voice. "He wrote such glowing letters to Uncle Partlow, and truly

I think Da believed that he could recoup his losses. Year after year he thought so." She sighed and faced him for the first time. "We are objects of charity, Captain. What will you do with us?"

"I could leave you here and continue by myself in the morning," he said. "Every town of any size has a workhouse."

The look on her face told him that was exactly what she expected him to say, and her assessment of him bit deep. She did not flinch or try him with tears, but merely nodded and turned back to the fence to lean upon it again, accepting this news as though he told her that snow was cold and winter endless.

"But I won't leave you here," he assured her. He surprised himself and touched her arm. "I have a confession of my own, Miss Partlow."

"You have not been home in years and years," she said. "Mrs. Brattle told me."

He leaned on the fence, same as she, and stared into the snowy field. "I have not," he agreed, perfectly in charity with her as though they were of one mind. What happened just then between them he never could have explained, not even at a court of inquiry convened by the Lords Admiral themselves.

"I suppose I should hear the gory details," she said at last, and he could not fail to note the amusement in her voice.

"Not out here in the snow. Your feet would freeze before I finished my tale of family discord, love unrequited, and blood in the orchard," he replied, turning toward the inn. He shuddered in mock terror and was rewarded with a small laugh.

Funny, he thought as they ambled back together, *but I have never made light of this before. Could I have made too much of it through the years? Surely not.* He stopped her with one hand and held out the other one to her, which she took. "Let us be friends, Miss Partlow," he said and shook her hand. "If you will help me keep my temper among my relatives, all of whom may wish me to the devil, I will figure out something for you and Thomas to do that won't involve the slave trade." It sounded so lame, but he had nothing else to offer that was remotely palatable. "Come, come, Miss Partlow, it is Christmas, and we just shook on it. Have a little charity."

She laughed, and he knew he was backing off a lee shore. "This could be a Christmas of desperate proportions, sir," she joked in turn, and his relief increased. "Oh, very well, then!"

Once inside, he told her that he would remain in the parlor and give her time to prepare for bed. She thanked him with that dignity he was becoming accustomed to and went upstairs. When he retired a half hour later, the room he shared with the Partlows was dark and quiet. By the light of glowing coals in the hearth, he undressed and lay down with a sigh, content to stare at the ceiling. His years at sea had conditioned him to brace himself against the ship's pitch and yaw, but the only movement was Tom sliding closer, seeking his warmth. He smiled and stretched out his arm, and the boy curled up beside him. He slept.

A nightmare woke him an hour later or so, but that was not unusual. He lay in bed, his heart pounding, his mind's eye filled with explosions and water rising and the ship—his first ship, well before the *Admirable*—slowly settling in the water: the usual dream, the usual time. After the moment of terror that never failed him, he closed his eyes again to let the dream fade, even though he knew he would not sleep again that night.

He opened his eyes in surprise. Miss Partlow had risen from her cot and was now perched on the side of his bed. Without a word, she wiped his face with her handkerchief and then pinched his nostrils gently with it until he blew his nose. His embarrassment was complete; not only had she seen his tears and wiped them away, she had made him blow his nose like a dutiful child.

"I would have been all right, Miss Partlow," be said in a whisper, unwilling to add Thomas to the audience. "Surely I did not cry out. I . . . I don't usually."

"You weren't loud, Captain," she whispered back. "I am a light sleeper, perhaps because I took care of Da for months before he died. Go back to sleep."

So he had cried out. *The devil take her*, he thought. He wanted to snap something rude at her, as he had done innumerable times to his steward, until the man never came into his quarters, no matter how intense the nightmare. But his steward was dead now, and he held his tongue in time.

"I thought your father was your ruin," he said without thinking.

She stared at him as if he had suddenly sprouted a dorsal fin. "And so why was I nice to him?" she whispered, after a moment in which she was obviously wondering what he was saying. "Captain, you mustn't throw out the baby with the bathwater! He had his failings but he was my Da." She rested her hand for too short a moment on his chest. "Have you never heard of forgiveness this far south?"

"See here, Miss Partlow," he began, but she put her hand over his eyes, and he had no choice but to close them.

"Good night, Captain."

He must have dreamed the whole matter, because in the morning, Miss Partlow made no mention by blush or averted eyes that he had roused her from her bed. When he and Tom trooped downstairs to the common wash-room, leaving her to complete her morning toilet in the privacy of the chamber, she was seated by the window, Bible in her lap. When they returned, she was still seated there, but her marvelous hair was now captured in a bun and she wore a fresh dress. And she looked at him—he couldn't describe the look, except that it warmed his heart.

He waited until they were some hours into their journey and Tom was dozing before he explained himself. "You wanted the gory details, Miss Partlow," he began. "Let me lay the bare facts before you."

She looked down at her brother, whose head rested in her lap. "Say on, Captain Lynch."

He told his story for the first time in twenty-two years of avoiding any mention of it, astounded at how easy it was to talk to this sweet-faced woman. "I was young and stupid and hotheaded, Miss Partlow, and quite in love with my brother Oliver's fiancée," he told her.

"How old?"

He almost smiled, because in the actual telling, it seemed almost ridiculous. "Fourteen, and—"

"Heavens, Captain Lynch," Sally interrupted.

"Yes, fourteen!" he retorted. "Miss Partlow, have you never been in love?"

She stared back at him and then smiled. "Not at fourteen, sir!"

"Is it warm in here?"

"No, sir."

"Miss Partlow, you are a trial. Amelia was eighteen, and I was a slave to her every glance. Did a boy ever fall so hard?"

"You were young," she said in agreement. "And did she . . . did she encourage you?"

"I thought she did, but I may have been wrong."

He sighed, thinking of all the years he had hung on to that anguish and wondering why now it felt so remote. "At any rate, Oliver found out and challenged me to a duel."

She looked up from her contemplation of her sleeping brother and frowned. "That does seem somewhat extreme, sir."

He nodded. "I can't say that Oliver and I ever loved each other overmuch before and certainly not since. Twenty paces in the orchard with our father's dueling pistols. I shot him and ran away."

"Worse and worse," she murmured. When he said nothing more, she cleared her throat. "Possibly you could discard economy now, Captain, and fill in the narrative a little more?"

He could, but he didn't want to tell her about foggy days shivering on the Humberside docks at Hull, wondering if his brother was dead, wondering how soon his father would sic the Runners on him, and all the while eating potato peels and sour oats gleaned from ash cans in a city famous for its competitive beggars. He told her, and not even all his years, prizes, and honors could keep the distress from his voice.

As he spoke, Sally Partlow slipped out from beside her sleeping brother and came to sit next to him. She did not touch him, but her closeness eased the telling. "It's hard, not knowing what to do," she commented. "And to be alone." She looked at Tom and smiled. "I've been spared that."

And why do you seem unafraid? he wanted to ask her. *Your future is even bleaker than mine was.* "The magistrate nabbed me after a week of dockside living," he said instead.

"And returned you home?"

He shook his head. "Father would not have me. He

wrote that Oliver was near death, and what did I think of that?"

"Was he?"

"No." He looked down at his hands where they dangled between his knees. "I learned that much later from the vicar, who also told me that Oliver from his bed of pain had assured my father that the duel was all my idea, and that I was a demon, impossible of correction." He clapped his hands together. "That ended my career as son and brother, and I was invited—nay, urged—at age fourteen to seek a wider stage beyond Lincolnshire."

He could feel Sally's sigh. "The world can be a frightening place, eh, Miss Partlow?" he said. He hesitated, and she looked at him in that inquiring way. "Actually, I sometimes wonder if I even shot him."

"I don't understand."

"Well, when the smoke cleared, Oliver was on the ground. I just ran, and do you know, I heard a shot when I was on the edge of the orchard." He shifted in the seat, uncomfortable as though the event had just happened. "I sometimes wonder if he shot himself after I left. You know, just the veriest flesh wound to paint me blacker than I already was."

She stared at him with troubled eyes and then leaned against him for the smallest moment. Or perhaps the chaise lurched in the slushy snow; he couldn't tell.

"My father—bless his nipfarthing heart—did buy me a midshipman's berth with Nelson's fleet, even though I was a little beyond the usual age." He couldn't help a laugh, but it must not have sounded too cheerful, since it made Sally put her hand on his arm. "In the first and only letter I ever received from him, he said he was in high hopes that I could not long survive an adventure with the Royal Navy." Another laugh, and the pressure of her hand increased. "Deuce of it was, I did. I hope that knowledge blighted his life, Miss Partlow."

"Oh, dear, no," she whispered.

"He was a dreadful man!"

"He was your father."

On this we will never see eye to eye, he thought. He turned to face her, sitting sideways. "I wrote to my mother every time we made landfall, but never a word in reply did she send. It is likely that there will be no welcome for me, even at Christmas, even after all these years. I have wanted Oliver to suffer every single day of those twenty-two years." He wished he had not moved, because she had taken her hand from his arm. "If that is the case, then Miss Partlow, I've put you in an uncomfortable position."

"We can go to a workhouse and you can go back to sea, Captain," she said as calmly as though they discussed whether to take tea in Barton or Fielding. She leaned toward him slightly. "But to harbor up such bitterness, Captain! Has your life been so horrible since that duel?"

What a strange question, he thought. *Of course it has.* Under her steady gaze, he considered his life again, his thoughts directed down an avenue he had never explored before and even less considered. "Well, no," he told her finally after he had thought through twenty-two years of war at sea, shipwreck, salvage prizes, foreign ports, exotic women, rum from tin cups, and the odd cat curled and warm at the end of his berth. He smiled. "I've actually rather enjoyed the Navy. Certainly I have done well." He lowered his voice when Tom stirred. "I doubt that Oliver's led such an exciting life."

"I daresay he has not," Sally agreed. "Uncle Partlow's letters were always interesting enough to share with the neighbors." She touched his arm again. "Think what a nice time of year this would be to let it all go, sir, and forgive Oliver."

"You must be all about in your head," he blurted without thinking. "Never, Miss Partlow. Never." He made no effort to disguise the finality in his voice, which he knew sounded much like dismissal. She sat up straight again and directed her attention to something fascinating outside in the snow.

"It was just a thought," she said quietly, after some miles had come and gone, and then she said nothing else.

"Rather a totty-headed one," he growled back and then quickly gave himself a mental slap. *See here*, he thought, irritated with himself, *can you not remember for half a minute that she is not a member of your crew and doesn't deserve the edge of your tongue?*

He looked at her and noticed that her shoulders were shaking. *And now I have made her cry*, he thought, his mortification complete. His remorse grew, until he noticed her reflection in the glass. She was grinning, and for some odd reason—perhaps he could blame the season—that made all the difference. *I see before me a managing woman*, he thought, observing her reflection. *We scarcely know each other, and I know I have not exactly been making myself charming. Indeed, I do not know how. She is a powerless woman of no consequence, and yet she is still going to make things as good as she can. I doubt there is another woman like her.*

"Miss Partlow, what on earth are we to make of each other? And what is so deuced funny?" he asked when he nerved himself for speech. She laughed out loud as though her mirth couldn't be kept inside another moment, her hand over her mouth to keep from waking her brother. She looked at him, her eyes merry, and he knew he had never seen a prettier woman. "I tell you a sad story—something that has been an ulcer all of my adult life—and all you can do is ask me if I really minded the Navy all that much! Drat your hide! I'm almost thinking now that going to sea was probably the best thing that happened! It's your fault! And you want me to give up my grudges too? Whatever happened to the ... the shy commentary of scarce acquaintance? Have you no manners?"

"None whatsoever, I suppose," she told him when she could speak without laughing. "Do I remind you of my uncle?"

That was it, of course. "You do indeed," he replied. "David would twit me all the day long." He paused to remember, and the remembering hurt less than it had a week ago. "I don't know ... what to think at the moment, Miss Partlow."

She was silent a long time. "We are both of us in an impossible situation, and I say at least one of us should make the best of it. I am determined that you at least will have a happy Christmas."

My stars, but you have a way about you, he marveled to himself. "If I must, I must," he said. "Can you think of any subterfuge that will explain your presence and that of your brother?"

"Not any," she said cheerfully. "Paint us how you will. There's no denying that while Tom and I are genteel, we are definitely at ebb tide in our fortunes at present. Just tell them the truth, because they will believe what they want anyway. We are objects of charity, sir."

Who of us is not? he thought suddenly and then dismissed the notion as stupid in the extreme. *I am not an object of charity! I have position and wealth and every right to be offended by my brother. She is lovely, but she is wrong.*

Thomas was awake then, and Sally moved over to sit by him again. Captain Lynch envied the way the boy so matter-of-factly tucked himself under her arm. *He belongs there*, Lynch thought and could not stop the envy that rose in him.

"Do you know, Sally, I rather think I will give up the idea of the sea," Tom announced.

"That is probably best," she replied, "considering that I cannot buy you a midshipman's berth. What will you do then, sir?"

She spoke as though to someone her own age and not to a little brother with wild ideas, and he knew she was serious. Lynch knew that this woman would never trample on a boy's heart and cause him pain. He watched them and remembered a Benedictine convent—more of a hospital—in Tenerife where he was brought during a terrible bout of fever. From his pallet he could see a carving in Latin over the door. He read it over and over, stupidly at first, while the fever still tore at him, and then gradually with understanding: "Care must be taken of the sick as though they were Christ in person." *That is how she treats people*, he told himself and was warmed in spite of himself.

"I think I will go into business in Fort William," Tom announced to Sally. "Wool. We can buy a large house and take in boarders and be as merry as grigs."

"I think we should do that too," Sally replied and kissed the top of his head. "We'll serve them oatmeal twice a day at least and cut up stiff if anyone asks for hot water."

They both laughed, and Lynch wondered if that was their current lot. He wanted to ask them why they were not burdened down by their circumscribed life or the bleakness of their future, but his manners weren't entirely gone. And besides, they didn't seem to be as unhappy as he was.

As they drew closer to Lynch Hall, he knew that

Sally Partlow was not a chatterbox. She was content to be silent and asked only one question as dusk arrived. "What is your mother like?"

He was irritated for a moment as she intruded on his own growing misgivings, and then he had the charity to consider her question. "I suppose you would call her a frippery lady," he said at last, "always flitting here and there, running up dressmaking bills, and spending more on shoes than you would ever dream of." He smiled. "I doubt my mother ever had two consecutive thoughts to rub against each other."

"But you loved her?"

"I did."

They arrived at Lynch Hall after dark. He wished the Partlows could have seen it in daylight. "I hope Oliver has not changed too much about the place," he murmured into the gloom. "Do you think anything will be as I remember?"

Sally leaned forward and touched his hand, and he had the good sense not to pull back even though she startled him. "People change, Captain."

"I don't," he said quickly.

"Perhaps you should."

Cold comfort, he thought and turned himself so he could pointedly ignore her.

"You never told me. Did your brother marry that young lady you loved?"

He sighed. *How much does this woman need to know?* "He did. I have this from the vicar. Apparently there have been no children who have survived even to birth."

"Seems a pity," Sally said as the manor came into view. "What a large house, and no children."

He knew she was quick, and in another moment, she looked at him again. "Heavens, does this mean you will inherit someday?" she asked.

He nodded. "I suppose it does." He thought of the long nights standing watch and watch about on the *Admirable*, staring at the French coast and thinking about riding back to Lynch Hall in triumph. He never thought much beyond that and the sour knowledge that Oliver would be dead then, and what was the point in triumph? "I suppose it does."

He was certain his voice had not changed, and he knew in the dark that Sally Partlow could not distinguish his features, but she leaned across the space separating them and touched his face, resting the palm of her hand against his cheek for a brief moment.

And then she was sitting up straight again, as though the gesture, the tenderest he could ever remember, had never happened. Her hand was grasping Thomas's shoulder as before, and she had returned her gaze to the window.

There were few lights burning inside Lynch Hall when the post chaise drew up at the door and stopped. He remembered nights with lights blazing in all the windows, and he wondered if there was some great shortage of beeswax this year, some wartime economy he had not heard of before.

"Does . . . does anyone live here?" Sally was asking.

"I believe so," he replied, no more sure than she.

The coachman said he would wait there until he was "sartin, sor, that you'll not be needing me." Lynch helped Sally from the post chaise. He was prepared to let go of her hand, but she wouldn't turn loose of him. Or maybe he did not try hard enough. However it fell out, they walked hand in hand up the shallow front steps, Tom behind them. She did release his hand so he could knock.

After what seemed like an age, a butler he did not recognize opened the door, looked them over, informed them that the master and mistress were out for the evening, and prepared to shut the door. Lynch put his foot in the space. "I am his brother, and we will wait," he said. "Inside," he concluded, when the butler continued to apply the pressure of the door to his foot.

"I do not believe Sir Oliver has ever mentioned a brother," he said.

"I doubt he ever has," Lynch replied. "I am Captain Michael Lynch of the White Fleet, home for Christmas from the blockade."

The butler peered closer, as if to determine some family resemblance and then looked beyond him to Sally and Thomas, who were standing close together on a lower step. "Pray who, then, are these young persons?"

"They are my friends," Lynch said quietly, stung to his soul by the butler's condescension.

"Then may you rejoice in them, sir, at some other location." The butler pressed harder against the door.

"Where is my mother?" Lynch asked, his distress increasing as the Partlows left the steps and retreated to stand beside the coachman.

"If you are who you say you are, then she is in the dower house," the man replied. "And now, sir, if you would remove your foot, perhaps I can close this door before every particle of heat is gone."

Lynch did as the butler asked but stood staring at the closed door, embarrassed to face the Partlows. He hurried down the steps and took Sally by the arm. "Miss Partlow, I do not believe there is a more toplofty creature in all England than a butler! You must have formed such an opinion of this nation."

She leaned close to whisper, "I cannot think that Tom and I will further your cause with your mother if the butler is so . . . so . . ."

She couldn't seem to think of anything to call the man, even though Lynch had half a hundred epithets springing to mind as he stood there in the snow. *These two are babes*, he thought. *She is too kind even to think of a bad name, and Thomas, if I know that expression, is getting concerned. Look how closely he crowds his sister.* He looked at the coachman. "Suffer us a little longer, sir, and drive around on the road I will show you."

No one spoke as the coachman followed his directions. They traveled through a smallish copse that he knew would be fragrant with lilacs in April. Somewhere there was a stream, the one where he sailed his first frigates years ago.

The dower house was even smaller than he remembered, and lit even less well than Lynch Hall. He took a deep breath, and another, until he felt light-headed. *Be there, Mother*, he thought. *I need you.*

The post chaise stopped again. He could see a pinpoint of light somewhere within, and he remembered the breakfast room at the back of the house. Silent, he helped down an equally subdued Sally Partlow. "I think I am home now," he told the coachman, walking around to stand by the box.

The man, his cloak flecked with snow, leaned down. "Sor," he whispered, "I know this trip has been on sufferance for you, wha' wi' your standin' an' all. No skin off me to take Sally and Tom wi' me. My missus'll find a situation for the girl wot won't be amiss, and Tom can 'elp me at stable."

Stables and Christmas, Lynch thought, *and curse my eyes for acting so put upon because I have had to do a kindness. The man means well.* "Thank you for the offer, but I will keep them with me," Lynch whispered back.

The coachman did not appear reassured, but after a moment of quieting his horses, he touched whip to hat and nodded. "Verra well, sor." With a good-bye to Tom and another touch of his hat to Sally, he was gone.

"Well, then, shall I knock on this door and hope for better?" he asked no one in particular.

"I think we are a great trouble," Sally said. "What will you do if no one answers, or if . . ." She stopped, and he could almost feel her embarrassment.

"Or if she will have nothing to do with me?" he continued. "Why then, Miss Partlow, I will marry you promptly, because I've compromised you past bearing already!"

He meant it to sound funny, to lighten what he knew was a painful situation for them both, but when the words left his mouth, he knew he meant them, as much, if not more, than he had ever meant anything. *Say yes and then I will kiss you right here in front of Tom and all these trees*, he thought, filled with wonder at himself.

To his disappointment, she smiled. *Come, come, Michael. You know that was what you wanted her to do*, he told himself. "You're being absurd, Captain," she said.

"So are you, my . . . Miss Partlow," he answered.

"I think we are both deserving of good fortune at this very moment."

"I know I am," she said in such a droll way that his heart lightened and then sank again when she added, "But please remember that you are under no real obligation to us, no matter how you felt about my uncle."

It was just as well that the door opened then, because he could think of no satisfactory reply. She was right, of course. He turned his attention to the door and the old man who opened it.

Simpson stood there, older certainly, but Simpson.

"You have aged a little, my friend," Lynch said simply. "Do you remember me?"

After a long moment of observation, the butler

smiled and bowed. "I did not expect this day," he said simply. "Your mother will be overjoyed. Do, do come in." He looked at the Partlows, and Lynch could see none of the suspicion of the other butler in the darkened house. "Come, come, all of you! Coal's dear. Let's close the door."

They stood silent and close together in the small entranceway while Simpson—dignified, and yet with a little spring to his step—hurried down the hall. He listened intently, shamelessly almost, for some sound of his mother, amazed at his own discomposure. For the first time in his life, he understood why so many of his men died with the word "Mother" on their lips.

He felt a great longing that brought tears to his eyes. He could only be grateful that the hall was ill lit. And then his mother was hurrying toward them from the back of the house, and then running with her arms outstretched. She threw herself at him and sobbed into his shoulder, murmuring something incomprehensible that eased his soul in an amazing way.

"Mother, I am so sorry for all those years," he managed to say when her own tears had subsided and she was standing back to look at him.

Her eyes roamed him from hat to boot, assessing him, evaluating him. He smiled, familiar with that gaze from a time much earlier in his life. "I still have all my parts, Mum," he said finally as he looked her over as well.

She was still pretty, in an older way now, a calmer way than he remembered, but her clothes were drab, shabby even, which caused his eyes to narrow in concern. She was no longer the first stare of fashion that he remembered, not the lady he never tired of watching when she would perch him on her bed while she prepared herself for a dinner party or evening out.

She must have known what he was thinking, because

she touched her collar, which even to his inexpert eyes looked frayed. "La, son, things change. And so have you, my dear." She rose on her toes and he bent down obligingly so she could kiss his cheek. "Now introduce me to these charming people. Are you brother and sister?" she asked, turning to the Partlows.

"These are Tom and Miss Partlow," he said. "Next of kin to David Partlow."

"Your first mate?" she asked as she smiled at the Partlows.

He stared at her. "How did you know that, Mama?" he asked. "We . . . you and I . . . have not communicated."

She tucked her arm in his and indicated the Partlows with a nod of her head. "Come along, my dears, to the breakfast room, where we will see if Simpson can find a little more coal and possibly another lamp. In fact, I will insist upon it."

This is odd, he thought as they walked arm in arm.

He remembered being a little taller than his mother when he left at age fourteen, but he fairly loomed over her now. The gray of her hair did not startle him, and then he remembered that the last time he saw her she wore powder in her hair. *It was another century*, he thought in wonderment. How much had happened in that time!

As his mother sat them down in the breakfast room, he looked around in appreciation. Simpson was well ahead of the game. Even now he was bringing tea, and there was Cook, her sparse hair more sparse but her smile the same, following him with Christmas cakes. "One could almost think you have been expecting us, Mama," he said, taking a cup from the butler.

To his alarm, tears welled in her eyes. He held out his hand to her, and she grasped it. "I have done this for twenty-two Christmases, son," she said when she could manage. "Oliver and your father used to scoff, but I knew that someday . . ." She could not continue.

He sat back in amazement. "You astound me, my dear," he told her. "When I never heard anything, not one word from you, I knew that you must be of the same mind as Oliver and Father." He took a sip of the tea and then glanced at Sally, who was watching him with real interest. "After fifteen years, I quit writing to you."

His mother increased her grip on his arm until it became almost painful. "You . . . you wrote to me?" she asked, her voice so low he could hardly hear it.

"Every time I reached a port where the natives didn't have bones through their noses or cook Englishmen in pots," he replied with a smile. "Must've been two times a year at least."

He knew he wouldn't have started to cry if his mother hadn't leaned forward, kissed his hand, and rested her cheek on it. "Oh, son," was all she said, but it wore him down quicker than any lengthy dissertation ever could. After a moment he was glad to accept the handkerchief Sally handed him and had no objection when she rested her own hand on his shoulder.

"You never got them, I take it," he said, after he blew his nose. "And you wrote?"

"Every week." She said nothing more but stared ahead with a stony look. "I left those letters in the bookroom, Simpson, along with my husband's correspondence. Did you never see them?"

"Madam, I never did," the butler said.

Lynch felt more than heard Sally's sharp intake of breath. She dropped her hand from his shoulder and sat down heavily in her chair. "Simpson, none of my letters ever arrived here?" he asked.

"Never, Captain."

No one said anything. It was so quiet in the breakfast room that Lynch could hear the clock tick in the sitting room. Then his mother sighed and kissed his hand again. "Son, if the scriptures are true and we are held to a grand accounting some day, your father may find himself with more debt than even Christ chooses to cover."

She spoke quietly, but Lynch felt a ripple go down his back and then another, as in that long and awful moment before a battle began. He couldn't think of a thing to say, except to turn to Sally and say more sharply than he intended, "And weren't you just telling me about forgiveness, Miss Partlow?"

She stared right back. "Nothing has changed."

"All those years," his mother murmured. She touched his face. "You want to know how I am acquainted with your first mate?"

He nodded, relieved almost not to think of the hot tears he had shed—a man-child of fourteen—wanting her arms about him when he lay swinging in his hammock over the guns. He thought of all the tears he had swallowed to protect himself from the laughter of the other midshipmen, some of them younger than he, and hardened already by war. "Mama, was it the vicar? I can think of no other."

"My dear son, Mr. Eccles was on his deathbed when he asked me to attend him. Oh, my, hadn't I known him above thirty years! He was too tired to talk, really, but he said he would not be easy if I did not know that for five years he had been hearing from you."

"It was never much, Mama, but I did want to know how you got on, even if you never wanted to speak to me . . . or at least, that was what I thought," he corrected himself.

She stood up, as if the telling required activity, and

in her restless pacing, he did recognize the woman of years ago. *I do much the same thing on a quarterdeck, Mama,* he thought. To his gratification, she stopped behind his chair finally and rested her arms upon his shoulders. He closed his eyes with the pleasure of it. "He woke and dozed all afternoon, but before he died that evening, he told me that you were well and in command of a frigate." She kissed his head. "He told me a story or two that included David Partlow and ports from Botany Bay to Serendip." She sat beside him, taking his hands again. "He never would tell me if you wanted to hear from me or not; indeed, he feared that he was betraying your confidence."

"I didn't know what to think, Mama, when I never heard from you. All I had ever asked of him in letters was to let me know how you were." He squeezed her hands. "And that he did." He hesitated a moment. "He told me that Father died ten years ago."

"He did," she said, and he could detect no more remorse in her voice than he felt. "Since then, Oliver has had the managing of me."

"And a poor job he has done, Mama," Lynch said, unable to keep his voice from rising.

To his surprise, Lady Lynch only smiled. "I thought that at first, too, son." She looked at the Partlows. "Thomas—does your sister call you Tom? I shall then too. Tom, you're drooping! I hope you will not object to sharing a chamber with my son. Miss Partlow—"

"Do call me Sally," she said. "It's what everyone calls me, even if the captain thinks I should be Miss Partlow."

"And here I thought he would know nothing of the niceties, after all those years at sea!" Mama exclaimed with a smile in his direction. "Sally it is, then. My dear, there is the tiniest alcove of a bedroom next to my room, with scarcely a space for a cat to turn around. How fortunate that you are economical in size." She looked around the table, and Lynch could see nothing but delight in her face. "We will be as close as whelks in a basket, but I dare anyone in Lincolnshire to have a merrier Christmas."

She had directed her attention to the Partlows, but he followed them upstairs, leaning against the doorframe of the little chamber he was to share with Tom while Sally tucked him in. "I want my own bed," he heard the boy say to his sister as she bent over him for a good-night kiss. "I want to be home." *Don't we all?* Lynch thought, remembering years and years of writing unanswered letters, letters where he pleaded with his parents to forgive him for being a younger son, for being stupid, for being a child who thought he was a man, until the day came when he could think of nothing that warranted an apology and stopped writing, replacing remorse with bitterness. *I was intemperate and wild*, he thought as he watched the Partlows, *but these are forgivable offenses. Too bad my father never thought to forgive me and Mama was never allowed the opportunity.*

He thought his cup of bitterness, already full, should run over, but he was filled with great sadness instead. *My parents have missed out on my life*, he thought with regret but no anger this time. He remained where he was in the doorway while Sally conferred with his mother in low whispers. He heard "nightmare" and "mustn't trouble you" and looked away while they discussed him. *I am in the hands of managing women*, he thought, and again he was not irritated. It was as though someone had stretched out a wide net for him at last, one he could drop into without a qualm.

He said good night to Sally there in the hall, standing close because it was a small corridor, and then followed his mother downstairs, where she gave a few low-voiced orders to Cook and bade Simpson good night. She took his hand and just looked into his face until he wanted to cry again. "Have I changed, Mama?" he asked at last. She nodded, her eyes merry. "You're so tall now, and—"

"That's not what I mean," he interrupted. "You've changed in ways I never thought you would. Have I?"

"You have," she said quietly. "How much, I cannot say, because you have only returned."

"For better or worse?"

"We shall see, Michael," she replied. "Oh, why that look? Does no one ever call you Michael?"

No one ever did, he realized with a jolt as he heard his Christian name on her lips. "No, Mama. I am Captain to everyone I know."

She stood on tiptoe to kiss his cheek. "Then we will have to enlarge your circle of acquaintances." She pulled him down to sit beside her. "And you must not look at me as an object of charity, son! I am nothing of the kind."

He knew he must only be pointing out the obvious, but he did it anyway. "Mama, there is little coal in this house, few candles, and I have never seen you in a dress so shabby!"

But she only smiled at him in a patient, serene way he had never seen before in his parent and tucked her arm in the crook of his. "I don't know that any of it matters to me, son, now that you are home for Christmas."

"That is enough?"

"Why, yes," she replied, even sounding startled at his question. After a moment, she released his arm and stood up. "My dear, morning comes early, and we can be sure that Oliver will be over soon."

He stood up with her, more bemused than agitated. "I don't understand, Mama."

She kissed his cheek again and stood up. "I don't know that things are ever quite as bad as we imagine they are, son. Good night."

Oliver was the last person he thought of when he finally slept and the first person he saw when he woke hours later. He was dimly aware that at some point in the night someone came into his room and sat beside him, but he could not be sure who it was. He sank himself deep into the mattress and did not open his eyes again until much later when he heard someone clearing his throat at the foot of the bed.

My, how you've changed, was his first thought as he stared—at first stupidly, and then with recognition—at the man gripping the footboards and glaring at him through narrowed eyes. "Oh, hullo, Oliver," he said with a yawn. "How are you?"

Comfortable in the way that only a warm bed and a venerable nightshirt allow, he gazed up at his older brother and decided that if he had passed the man on the street, he would not have known him. He folded his hands across his stomach and observed his brother. *So this was the object of my bitterness all these years*, he thought as he took in a man thin to the point of emaciation but dressed in a style much too youthful for him. *If I am thirty-six, then he is rising forty-four*, Lynch thought, *and there he is, dressed like a popinjay.* Sir Oliver looked like a man denying age, with the result being that he looked older than he was.

"Why did you think to come here now?"

To Lynch, it sounded more like a challenge than a question. "Well, Oliver, I have it on the best of authority that people who are related occasionally choose to spend certain calendar days together. I realize there's no accounting for it, but there you are," he replied. "And do you know, even though I am sure no one in the White Fleet believes me, I have a mother." He sat up then. "Is there some problem with the estate that she must dress like an old maid aunt no one cares about?"

Oliver smiled for the first time. "Economy, brother, economy! On his deathbed, our father made me swear to keep a tight rein on his widow, and so I did."

My word, two rogues in as many generations, Lynch thought. *Vengeful even to death, was the old man? I imagine the next world was a jolt to his system.*

"We have order and economy and—"

"—tallow candles cut in half and coal doled out by the teaspoon!" He couldn't help himself. Lynch knew his voice was rising. "You won't object if I order more coal and beeswax candles for Mother, will you?"

"Not if you pay for them," his brother replied. "Through the years Amelia and I have been frugal with everything."

"You have indeed," Lynch agreed, remembering with some slight amusement that his brother had no progeny. "Last night we were even wondering if the manor was inhabited. Scarcely a light on in the place."

His brother shrugged and sat down. "Why waste good candles when one is not home?" He leaned closer. "And when you speak of 'we,' brother, surely you are not married to that . . . that rather common person downstairs?"

A number of intemperate words bubbled to the surface, but Lynch stifled them all, determined for his mother's sake not to continue the fight where it had begun twenty-two years ago over a woman. "No, I am not married to her. She and her brother were wards of my late first mate, with nowhere to go for Christmas."

To his further irritation, Oliver waggled a bony finger

at him. "That's the sort of ill-natured charity that makes dupes of us all! I'll wager you don't even know them!"

Better than I ever knew you, he thought, *or wish to know you.* He got out of bed and pulled down his nightshirt at the same time that Sally Partlow entered the room with a tray and two cups of tea. He wasn't embarrassed because she seemed unconcerned. "Your mother thought you two would like some tea," she said, her glance flicking over him then coming to rest on the wall beyond his shoulder. Her face was only slightly pink and dashed pretty, he considered. He took a cup from her and sat down again, remembering that this particular nightshirt—long a favorite—had been from Bombay to the Baltic and was thin of material. "And you, sir?" she said, indicating his brother. "Would you like some tea?"

Oliver shook his head. "Tea at midmorning smacks of waste and profligacy," he said, so smug that Lynch itched to smack him. "I ate my mush at daybreak and will make it last until luncheon."

Over the rim of the cup, Lynch glanced at Sally and knew without question precisely what she was thinking. He turned his head so Oliver would not see his smile. *I do believe, my dear Sal, that it would not be beyond you to tell my prig of a brother just where to put his mush,* he thought.

He feared that Oliver must be wondering at the expression on his face, but his brother was staring at the tray Sally carried. The color rose up from his scrawny neck in blotches. "I cannot imagine that Lady Lynch would ever permit someone she cannot know to be handling our silver!"

"It's just that old teapot even I remember," Lynch said, stung into retort. "I hardly think Sally will . . . will stick it up her skirt and trot to the pawnshop!"

"That is precisely what I mean!" Oliver replied. "We

have had years and years of order and serenity, and now you are back one morning with ... with heaven knows who this woman is—and things are going to ruin! I am going downstairs directly to tell Mama to count her—my silverware carefully!"

Sally gasped. Without a word she picked up the teacup on the tray and dumped it over his brother's head. Oliver leaped to his feet, his hand raised, but Lynch was on his feet as well, and he grabbed his brother's arm. "I wouldn't," he said.

"But she poured tea on me!"

"I don't blame her," Lynch replied. "You're dashed lucky this isn't the Middle Ages and it wasn't hot tar! How dare you accuse her of having designs on the family silver?"

Oliver looked at them both, his eyebrows pulled close together, his face in a scowl. "I'm going to talk to Mother about the wisdom of house guests at Christmas," he said primly as he left the room.

Sally stared after him and then looked down at the empty cup in her hand. Lynch smiled at her and sat down. "You should have a little charity, Miss Partlow," he said. "Didn't you tell me only yesterday that it was high time I forgave my brother?"

He decided that she must not have realized what she was doing, because she sank down beside him on the bed. "Perhaps I was hasty," she amended. "I hadn't met him yet." Lynch shouted with laughter. After a long moment, she smiled, if only briefly. She stood up then, as if suddenly aware of him in his nightshirt. "He may be right, Captain," she said as she replaced both cups on the tray and went to the door. "I really don't have much countenance, do I?"

"Probably not," he agreed, in perfect charity with her, although he was not certain that she appreciated the fact.

"It doesn't follow that the matter is disagreeable." To his utter delight, she made a face at him as she left the room.

He lay back down, hands behind his head, content to think of Sally, when she stuck her head in the room again. "Your mother said most particularly that you are not to do what you are doing now! She wants your escort to the vicarage this afternoon."

"Shrew," he said mildly. "When am I to have the nap I so richly deserve after nine months of watch and watch about on the blockade?"

Sally Partlow sighed and put her hand on her hip, which only made him want to grab her, toss her down beside him, and abandon naps forevermore. "Captain, I believe that one must rise before one can consider the next rest as a nap."

To his relief, Oliver was gone when Lynch made his appearance in the breakfast room. The table was covered with material and dolls—dolls large and small, with baby-fine hair of silk thread and abundant yarn hair. Sally was diligently embroidering a smile onto a blank face, and even Tom was occupied, pulling nankeen breeches onto a boy mannequin. Lips pursed, eyes narrowed in concentration, his mother—who to his knowledge had never plied a needle in her life—pushed the last bit of cotton wadding into a disembodied leg.

He kissed her cheek and cleared a little spot for himself at the table, which only brought a protest from Sally and the quiet admonition of his mother to please eat his breakfast standing up at the sideboard. He didn't wish to spill eggs or tea on the dolls, did he?

Mystified at the doll factory on the table, he did as he was told. "Is this one of Oliver's cottage industries?" he asked finally when he had finished and sat himself at the table.

"La, no," his mother said as she attached a leg to a comely doll with yarn ringlets. "Ever year he complains when I ask for a few shillings to make dolls for the orphanage. He can be wearing at times."

He leaned closer to her, wishing with all his heart that he had come home sooner. "I can change things for you now, Mother," he said.

If he expected to see relief in her eyes, he was doomed to disappointment. With a few expert stitches, she concluded the limb attachment and picked up another leg. "I suppose Oliver is onerous at times, son, but do you know that his nipfarthing ways at my expense have quite brought out a side of me I never knew?" She looked around the table, and Lynch could see nothing in her face but contentment. "When I think how little I used to do with much and now how much I do with little, it fair amazes me!" She patted his arm, handed him an empty leg, and pushed the stuffing closer. "And I owe Oliver this revelation of character."

"I . . . I suppose I never thought of it that way, Mother," he said, picking up the stuffing. He saw with a frown that his fingers were too large to make any headway on the leg. To his relief, Sally came to the rescue, moving her chair closer until her glorious hair touched his cheek as she expertly worked the stuffing in place with her own slim fingers. *I'm in love*, he thought simply as he breathed deep of her fragrance—probably nothing more than soap and water—and tried to think when any woman had stirred him as completely as this one. The deuce of it was that he didn't think she had the slightest idea of her effect on him.

The thought niggled at the back of his brain all morning as he sat at the table and brought his mother up to date on twenty-two years of his life. He had no need to enlarge upon his experiences because they were vivid enough with war, shipwreck, illness—which set Sally to sniffling, even though she heatedly denied it when he teased her—salvages, and exotic ports as his topics. Before he brought his recitation to a close, even Simpson and Cook had joined them around the table.

"The blockade is the least pleasant duty of all, I believe," he commented.

"We will have it, too, son, since you have told us everything else," his mother said.

"No!" he exclaimed, louder than he had intended. Sally looked at him in surprise. "It's . . . it's not worth the telling."

He watched his mother gather the dolls together and motion to Tom to put them in the pasteboard box Simpson provided. "And now the *Admirable* is in dry dock, and I find myself in a strange position for a seafaring man."

"On land and hating it?" Sally asked, her voice soft.

She hadn't stirred far from his side but had continued to work on the doll in her lap.

Twenty-four hours ago he would have agreed with her, but now he could not say. "Let us say, on land and not certain where to go from here," he told her, "or even what to do." He was deeply conscious of the fact that he was aware of every breath she took, so close there to him.

"Then that makes two of us," Sally murmured. She put down the doll. "Captain Lynch, do you ever wish, just once, that you could be sure of things?"

He shrugged. "Life's uncertain," he told her. "I suppose that is what I have learned."

"Not that it is good?" she asked. "Or at least satisfactory on occasion?"

"That has not been my experience, Miss Partlow," he said, his voice sharp. "If it has been yours—and I cannot see how considering your own less-then-sanguine circumstances—then rejoice in it."

To his shame, Sally leaped up from the table as though seeking to put real distance between them as fast as she could. If he could have snatched his spiteful words from the air, crammed them back into his mouth, and swallowed them, he would have, but as it was, Sally only stood by the window, her head down, as far away as the moon.

"That was poorly done, son," his mother murmured.

"I told you I had changed, Mother." *Where were these words coming from?* he asked himself in anguish.

"Not for the better, apparently."

The room was so hot that he wondered if he had been wise to order more coal.

"Excuse me, please," he said as he left the table.

He kicked himself mentally until he passed through the copse and could no longer see the dower house. In his mind he could still see the calm on Sally's face and the trouble in her eyes. *It takes a thoroughly unpleasant customer to tread on a woman's dignity, Lynch,* he told himself, *and you've just trampled Sally's into the dust. Too bad the Celerity's carronade didn't belch all over you instead of her uncle. She'd certainly have a better Christmas.*

He wanted to cry, but he wasn't sure he could stop if he started, so he swallowed the lump in his throat and walked until he looked around in surprise, the hair rising on his neck.

He stood in the orchard, barren now of leaves and any promise of fruit, the branches just twisted sticks. *How does it turn so beautiful with pink blossoms in the spring?* he wondered. *I have been so long away from land and the passage of seasons.* He closed his eyes, thinking of summer in the orchard and then fall, especially the fall twenty-two years ago when two brothers had squared off and shot at each other.

Why did I let him goad me like that? he thought. *Why did I ever think that his fiancée preferred me, a second son, greener than grass, unstable as water in that way of fourteen-year-olds?*

He stood a moment more in thought and then was aware that he was not the orchard's only visitor. He knew it would be Oliver and turned around only to confirm his suspicion. "Does it seem a long time ago, brother?" he asked, hoping that his voice was neutral.

Oliver shook his head. "Like yesterday." He came closer. "Did you mean to kill me?"

I was cruel only minutes ago, so what's the harm in honesty? Lynch thought. "Yes. I'm a better aim now, though."

Oliver smiled. "My pistol didn't fire."

"I thought as much. And then you shot yourself later, didn't you?"

His brother nodded. "I wanted to make sure you never returned."

"It worked."

They both smiled this time. Lynch noticed that Oliver was shivering. "Your cloak's too thin for this weather," he said, fingering the heavy wool of his own uniform cloak. "Oliver, why do you live so cheap? Is the estate to let?"

He didn't think Oliver would answer. "No! It pleases me to keep a tight rein on things," he said finally. "The way Father did."

"Well, yes, but Father lit the house at night and even heated it," Lynch reminded him.

"I control this estate."

To Lynch, it seemed an odd statement. He waited for his brother to say more, but the man was silent.

They walked together out of the orchard, and Lynch wondered what he was feeling, strolling beside the person he had hated the most in the world for twenty-two years. "You ruined my life, Oliver," he said as a preamble to the woes he intended to pour out on the skinny, shabby man who walked beside him.

Oliver startled him by stopping to stare. "Michael, you're worth more than I am! Don't deny it, I've checked the Funds. You've done prodigious well at sea. You aren't ruined."

"Yes, but—"

"And you don't have a wife who is so boring that you must take deep breaths before you walk into any room she is inhabiting. And someone unfeeling enough to . . . to drop her whelps before they're big enough to fend for themselves!"

"I doubt that Amelia ever intended to miscarry," Lynch said, startled, and he wondered if now he had finally heard everything.

"And the deuce of it is, brother, I cannot unburden myself of her and take another wife who might get me an heir!"

Dumbfounded, Lynch could think of no response to such a harsh declaration, beyond the thought that if Amelia Lynch had been a horse with a broken leg and not a wife with an uncooperative womb, Oliver could have shot her. He had the good sense not to mention it. "No heir," was all he could say, and it sounded stupid.

Oliver turned on him. "Oh, I have an heir," he declared, "a by-blow got from the ostler's daughter at the public house, for all the good that does anyone. Naturally he cannot inherit. There you are, free to roam the world, tied to nothing and no one. As things stand now, you will inherit this estate."

As they walked on, Lynch felt a great realization dawning on him. It was so huge that he couldn't put it into words at first. He glanced at his brother, feeling no anger at him now but only the most enormous pity and then the deepest regret at his own wasted time.

"Brother, can it be that we have been envying each other all these years?"

"I doubt it," Oliver snapped, but his face became more thoughtful.

"You were the oldest son and successor to the title, and you won Amelia's affection, but I wanted her then—and Father's love," Lynch said. "Didn't you get what you wanted?"

Oliver sighed. "I discovered after six months that Amelia only loves lap dogs. Father never loved anyone. And Mama, who used to be such a scatterbrain, has turned into the most . . . the most . . ."

". . . respected and wise woman in the district," Lynch concluded, smiling at the irony of it all. "You and Father broke her of bad habits out of your own meanness, didn't you? And she became someone worth more than all of us. That must've been a low blow."

"It was," Oliver said with some feeling. "And look at you—a handsome big fellow. I've been ill used."

The whole conversation was so unbelievable that Lynch could only walk in silence for some minutes. "So for all these years, you've either been wishing me dead or wishing to change places. And I've been doing the same thing," Lynch said, not even attempting to keep the astonishment from his voice. "What a pair we are."

If it weren't so sad, he would have laughed. *Father sentenced me to the sea, and I was the lucky one,* Lynch thought. *I've not been tied to a silly, barren woman, forced to endure years with that martinet who fathered us or tethered to an estate when just maybe I might have wished to do something else. And Oliver thinks I am handsome. I wonder if Sally does?*

He took his brother by the arm, which startled the man into raising both his hands, as though in self-defense. "Settle down, Oliver. I have an idea. Tell me how you like it." He hesitated only a moment before throwing his arm around the smaller man, enveloping him in the warmth of his cloak. "I've given some serious thought to emigrating to the United States. I mean, since I refuse to die and oblige you that much, at least if I became a citizen of that nation, I certainly couldn't inherit a title, could I? Who would the estate devolve upon?"

"Our cousin Edward Hoople."

"Hoople." Lynch thought a moment and then remembered a man somewhat near his own age.

"Yes! He has fifteen or twenty children at least, or it seems that way when he troubles us with a visit and as many dogs," Oliver grumbled. "But I'd much rather he had this estate than you."

"Done then, brother. I'll emigrate," Lynch said. "At least, I'll do it if I survive another year on the blockade, which probably isn't too likely. My luck has long run out there. That satisfy you?"

"I suppose it must," Oliver said. He looked toward Lynch Hall. "Do you want to put it in writing?"

Lynch shook his head. "Trust me, Oliver. I'll either die or emigrate. I promise."

His brother hesitated, nodded, and then hesitated again. "I suppose you can come to luncheon," he said, his reluctance almost palpable. "I usually only have a little bread and milk."

"I'll pass, Oliver. I think I've promised to take some dolls to the vicarage for Mama."

Oliver sighed. "That woman still manages to waste money!"

Lynch surprised himself by kissing Oliver on the forehead. "Yes, indeed. She must have spent upward of ten shillings on all those dolls for orphans. What can she have been thinking? Tell you what I will put in writing. I'll take care of Mother from now on and relieve you of that onerous burden and expense." He looked at Oliver closely, trying to interpret his expression. "Unless you think you'll miss all that umbrage."

"No, no," Oliver said hastily and then paused. "Well, let me think about it."

They had circled back to the orchard again. Lynch released his brother and put out his hand. "What a pair we are, Oliver."

Oliver shook his hand. "You promise to die or emigrate."

"I promise. Happy Christmas."

Oliver turned to walk away and then looked back.

"You're not going to marry that chit with the red hair, are you? It would serve you right to marry an object of charity."

The only objects of charity are you and I, brother, Lynch thought. "That would please you if I married her, wouldn't it?" he asked. "You'd really think I got what I deserved."

Oliver laughed. "It would serve you right."

"I'll see what I can do," he offered, "but my credit with Sally is on the ground right now. I think she wants me dead too."

Oliver was still laughing when Lynch turned away.

He didn't hurry back to the dower house, because he knew they would have gone on without him. He sat at the table in the breakfast room for a long moment, wondering if it would be better if he just left now. He could make arrangements with his solicitor in Portsmouth for his mother and add a rider to it for Sally and Tom, even though he knew that scrupulous young woman would never touch it. In only a day or two he could be back on the blockade conning another ship.

The thought of the blockade turned him cold and then nauseous. He rested his forehead against the table until the moment passed. He knew that he needed Sally Partlow far more than she would ever need him.

The vicarage was much as he remembered it, but this new man—vicar since his old confidant had died five years ago—had taken it upon himself to organize a foundling home in a small house just down the road.

"My good wife and I have no children of our own, Captain," the man explained after Lynch arrived and introduced himself. "This gives us ample time to help others."

Lynch nodded, thinking of his own childless brother, who spent his time pinching pennies, denying his mother, and squeezing his tenants. "It seems so . . . charitable of you," he said, realizing how lame that sounded.

"Who among us is not a beggar, sir?" the man asked.

Who, indeed? Lynch thought, turning to watch Sally Partlow bend over a crib and appropriate its inmate, a child scarcely past birth. He watched as the baby melted into her, the dark head blending into her own beautiful auburn hair. He thought of years of war and children without food and beds, left to shiver in odd corners on wharves and warehouses and die. "I am tired of war," he said, his voice quiet. *I need that woman.*

"How good that you can leave war behind now," the vicar said.

"Perhaps," he told the man as he watched Sally. *She has an instinct for the right thing. I wish I did.* He sighed. *If she turns me down flat, then my sentence is the blockade and I will die.*

He shuddered at the thought; he couldn't help himself. The vicar looked at him in surprise and then touched his sleeve. "*Can* you leave it behind?" he asked.

That, apparently, is the question, he asked himself as he went to Sally. "Please forgive me," he murmured, and without another word, he took the sleeping child from her. To his deep need and intense gratification, the baby made those small sounds of the very young but did not even open her eyes as she folded into his chest. He felt himself relax all over. Her warmth was so small, but as he held her close, he felt the heat of her body against his hand and then his chest as it penetrated even the heavy wool of his uniform. He paced up and down slowly, glad of the motion, because it reminded him of his quarterdeck. The baby sighed, and he could have wept when her little puff of breath warmed his neck.

He wasn't aware of the passage of time as he walked up and down, thinking of nothing beyond the pleasure of what he was doing, the softness of small things, and the impermanence of life, its little span. *What would it have cost me to forgive my brother years ago? Nothing.*

Stung by his own hypocrisy, he walked on, remembering the Gospel of Matthew, which he read from the quarterdeck to his assembled crew on many a Sunday after the required reading of the Articles of War. With painful clarity, he recalled the parable of the unmerciful servant, who was forgiven of a great debt, and then inflicted his own wrath on another who owed him a tiny portion of that which had been forgiven. " 'Shouldest not thou also have had compassion on thy fellowservant, even as I had pity on thee?' " he whispered to the baby.

He never prayed, but he prayed now, walking up and

down in the peaceful room with a baby hugged to his chest. "*Forgive us our debts,*" he thought, "*as we forgive our debtors.*" *How many times as captain have I led my crew in the Our Father and never listened? Forgive me now, Father,* he thought. *Forgive me, Sally. Forgive me, and please don't make me go back on the blockade. For too many years I have nourished my animosities like some people take food. Let us now marry and breed little ones like this sweet child and walk the floor of our own home and lie down at night with each other. Please, not the blockade again.*

He stood still finally. The baby stirred and stretched in his embrace, arching her back and then shooting out her arms like a flower sprouting. He smiled, thinking that in a moment she would probably work up to an enormous wail. *It must be dinnertime,* he thought. She yawned so hugely that she startled herself and retreated into a ball again. He kissed her hair and walked on until she was crying in earnest and feeling soggy against his arm. In another moment, the vicar's wife came to him, crooning to the baby in that wonderful way with children that women possessed: old women, young women, barren, fertile, of high station, and lower than the drabs on the docks. "The wet nurse is waiting for you, little one," she whispered. "And did you soak Captain Lynch's uniform?"

"It's nothing," he said, almost unwilling to turn loose of the baby.

She took the baby and smiled at him, raising her voice so he could hear over the crying, "You're a man who likes children."

I know nothing of children, he thought, *except those powder monkeys and middies who bleed and die on my deck.* "I think I do," he replied. "Yes, I do."

He stood another moment watching the woman with the baby, and then he took his cloak from the servant, put it on, replaced his hat, and stood on the steps of the vicarage. Sally Partlow waited by the bottom step, and he felt a wave of relief wash over him that he would not have to walk back to the dower house alone, he who went everywhere alone.

"I sincerely hope you have not been waiting out here all this time," he said.

She smiled that sunny smile of hers that had passed beyond merely pleasing to absolutely indispensable to him. "Don't flatter yourself! I walked home with your mama and Thomas, and then she told me to return and fetch you." She tugged the shawl tighter around her glorious hair. "I told her that you had navigated the world and didn't need my feeble directions. Besides, this is your home ground."

"But you came anyway."

"Of course," she said promptly, holding out her arm for him. "You're not the only biped who likes to walk. The path is icy, so I shall hang on to you."

He tucked her arm in his gladly, in no hurry to be anyplace else than with Sally Partlow. "I am thirty-six years old," he said and thought to himself, *that ought to scare her away. Why am I even mentioning my years to this woman?* was his next thought, followed by, *I have not the slightest idea what to say beyond this point.*

"Only thirty-six?" Sally said and gathered herself closer. "I'd have thought you were older." She smiled at him.

"Wretched chit."

"I am twenty-five." She gripped his arm tighter. "There, that's in case my advanced years make you want to flee."

"They don't." To his gratification, she didn't let loose of him.

They walked on slowly, Lynch gradually shortening

his stride to make it easier for the woman beside him to keep up. *I'll have to remind myself to do that*, he thought, *at least until it becomes second nature.*

In far too short a time, he could see the dower house at the bottom of the slight hill. Beyond was the copse and then the manor house, all dark but for a few lights. It was too close, and he hadn't the courage to propose.

He sighed, and Sally took a tighter grip on his arm.

"I hoped this would be a happy Christmas for you," she said.

He shook his head. "Perhaps we can remember this as the necessary Christmas, rather than the happy one," he replied and wondered at his effrontery in using the word "we."

She seemed not to heed his use of the word, as though something were already decided between them. "Well, I will have food for thought, at least, when I return to the blockade," he continued, less sure of himself than at any time in the last decade.

"Don't return to the blockade," she pleaded and stopped.

He had no choice but to stop too, and then made no objection when she took the fork in the path that led to the village and not the dower house. "You're going the wrong way," he pointed out.

"No, I'm not," she said in that unarguable tone that he had recognized in her uncle. "We're going to walk and walk until you have told me all about the blockade." She released his arm so she could face him. "You have told us stories of the sea, and personally I thank you, for now Tom has no urge to follow his uncle's career! You have said nothing of the blockade, beyond watch and watch about, and you look so tired."

"Say my name," he said suddenly.

"Michael," she replied without hesitation. "Michael. Michael."

"No one says my name."

"I noticed how you started the other day when your mama did." She took his arm again, this time twining her fingers through his. "I can walk you into the ground, Michael. No more excuses."

You probably can, he told himself. He yearned suddenly to tap into her energy. "I'm tired. Watch and watch about is four hours on and four hours off, around the clock, day after week after month after year. We are a wooden English wall against a French battering ram."

She rested her cheek against his arm, and he felt her low murmur rather than heard it. "At first it is possible to sleep in snatches like that, but after a few months, I only lie in my berth waiting for the last man off to summon me for the next watch."

"You never sleep?" she asked, and he could have cringed at the horror in her voice.

"I must, I suppose, but I am not aware of it," he said after a moment of thinking through the matter. "Mostly I stand on my quarterdeck and watch the French coastline, looking for any sign of ship movement." He stopped this time. "We have to anticipate them almost to sense that moment when the wind is about to shift quarters, and be ready to stop them when they come out to play in our channel."

"How can you do that?" Her voice was small now. "It is not possible."

"Sally, I have stood on the deck of the *Admirable* with my hat off and my cloak open in the worst weather, just so I won't miss the tiniest shift in the wind."

"No wonder you tell us of fevers."

"I suppose." He took her arm again and moved on.

"Not only do we watch the coast, but we watch each other, careful not to collide in fog, or swing about with a sudden wind, or relax our vigilance against those over our shoulders who would sneak in under cover of the dark and make for shore."

"One man cannot do all that," she whispered, and she sounded fierce.

"We of the blockade do it." He patted her hand, and they walked on into the village, strolling through empty streets with shops boarded for the long winter night. Through all the exhaustion and terror he felt a surge of pride and a quiet wonder at his own abilities, despite his many weaknesses. "We do it, my dear."

He knew she was in tears, but he had no handkerchief for her. *I don't even know the right words to court this beautiful woman and flatter her and tell her that she is essential to my next breath*, he told himself. *I've never learned the niceties because they're not taught aboard ship. In the middle of all my hurt and revenge, I hadn't planned on falling in love.* He knew he had to say something. They were coming to the end of the village. Surely Sally did not intend just to keep walking.

To his amazement, she did, not even pausing as they left the last house behind. She kept walking on the high road as though it were summer. She walked, eyes ahead, and he talked at last, pouring out his stories of ship fevers and death and cannonading until his ears bled from the concussion, and splinters from masts sailing like javelins through the air, and the peculiar odor of sawdust mingled with blood on the deck, and the odd patter of the powder monkeys in their felt slippers, bringing canister up from the magazine to the men serving the guns, and the crunch of weevils in ship's biscuit, and the way water six months in a keg goes down the throat in a lump.

She shuddered at that one, and he laughed and took both her hands in his. "Sally Partlow, you amaze me!" He looked at the sky and thought he saw the pink of dawn. "I have told you horrible stories all night, and you gag when I mention the water! If there is a man alive who does not understand women, I am he."

Holding her hands like that, he allowed himself to pull her close to him. If she had offered any objection, he would have released her, but she seemed to like what he was doing and clasped her hands across his back with a certain proprietary air.

"I'm keeping England safe so my brother can squeeze another shilling until it yelps, and . . ." He took a deep breath and his heart turned over. ". . . and you can lie safe at night, and mothers can walk with babies, and Thomas can go to school. Marry me, Sally."

She continued to hold him close. When she said nothing, he wondered if she had heard him. He knew he didn't have the courage to ask again. The words had popped out of his mouth even before he had told her he loved her. "Did you hear me?" he asked at last, feeling as stupid as a schoolboy.

She nodded, her head against his chest, and he kissed her hair. "I love you," he said.

She was silent a long moment. "Enough to leave the blockade?"

His heart turned over again, and he looked up to see dawn. He had told her all night of the horrors of the blockade and in the telling had come to understand his own love of the sea and ships and war and the brave men he commanded. It terrified him to return, but he knew that he could now. With an even greater power than dawn coming, he knew that because he could, he did not need to.

"Yes, enough to leave the blockade," he said into her

hair. "I will resign my commission with the new year. Mind now, the Lords Admiral will object, because we remain at war, but I will wear them down eventually." He waited for such a pronouncement to rip his heart wide open, but all he felt was the greatest relief he had ever known. *This must be what peace feels like*, he told himself in wonder. *I have never known it until now.*

She raised her head to look at him, and he wanted to drop to his knees in gratitude that for every morning of the rest of his life, hers would be the first face he saw. She put her hands on his face. "You are not doing this because I am an object of charity?" she asked.

"Oh, no!" He kissed her until she started to squirm for breath. "My dearest love, you are the one marrying the object of charity." He smiled when she did. "Of course, you haven't said yes yet, have you? You're just clarifying things in your Scottish way, aren't you?"

"Of course," she replied calmly. "I want to know precisely where I stand. Your brother will be horrified, your mother will be ecstatic, and Thomas will follow you about with adoration in his eyes. You've lived solitary for so long. Can you manage all that?"

"Actually, Oliver will be ecstatic when I marry you. I'll explain later. I wish you would answer my question, Sally, before you start in with yours! My feet are cold, and do you know, I am actually tired right down to my toenails." *That was not lover like*, he thought, but it didn't matter, because Sally was pressing against him in a way that sharpened his nerves a little more than he expected there on a cold road somewhere in the middle of Lincolnshire. "Where the deuce are we?" he asked.

"Somewhere in Lincolnshire, and yes, Michael, I will marry you," she said and took her time kissing him. When they stopped, she looked at him in that intense way that warmed him from within. "I love you. I suppose I have for a long time, ever since Uncle Partlow started writing about you in his letters home."

"Preposterous," he said, even as he kissed her once more.

"I suppose," she agreed after a long moment. "There's no use accounting for it, because I cannot. I just love you." She held up her hands, exasperated at her inability to explain. "It's like breathing, I think."

"Oh, Sally," he said and kissed her again, until even the air around them felt as soft as April.

They learned from a passing carter (who must have been watching them, because he could hardly contain himself), that they were only a mile from Epping. It was an easy matter to speak for breakfast at a public house, admire his blooming Sal over tea and shortbread, and then take the mail coach back to Lynch. Pillowed against Sally, he fell asleep as soon as the coachman gathered his reins. He probably even snored. Hand in hand they walked back to the dower house. He answered his mother's inquiries with a nod in Sally's direction and then went upstairs to bed, leaving his pretty lady to make things right.

She must have done that to everyone's satisfaction.

When he woke hours later, the sun was going down, and she was sitting in a chair pulled close to the window in his room, her attention on yet another doll in her lap. He lay there admiring her handsome profile and beautiful hair, and hoped that at least some of their children would inherit that same dark red hue. He chuckled at the thought. She turned in his direction to give him an inquiring look.

"I thought I would prophesy, my dearest," he said, rising up on one elbow.

"I almost shudder to ask."

"I was merely thinking that a year from now it will probably still be watch and watch about."

She put down her needlework, and he recognized that Partlow glint in her eyes. "You promised me you were going to give up the blockade."

"I am! Cross my heart! I was thinking that babies tend to require four on and four off, don't they? Especially little ones?"

To his pleasure, she pinked up nicely. She took up her sewing again and turned back to the window, even as her shoulders started to shake. "I can see that you will be a great deal of trouble on land," she said when she could speak again.

"I'll do my best."

She finished a seam on the little dress in her lap and turned it right side out. "I think it would be prudent if we don't settle anywhere close to Lynch, my love," she told him. "I'm sure Oliver thinks I am a great mistake."

"I'm open to suggestion," he said agreeably and then shifted slightly and patted the bed. "Let's discuss it."

She shook her head. "Not from there! My uncle Partlow always told me to beware of sailors."

"Excellent advice. See that you remember it." They were still debating the merits of a return to the Highlands over a bolt across the Atlantic to Charlotte because he liked the Carolinas, when Mama called up the stairs that dinner was ready.

He took Sally by the arm as she tried to brush past the bed. She made not a single objection as he sat her down next to him. Sally leaned closer to kiss him. "I thought your uncle told you to beware of sailors," he reminded her and then pulled her closer when she tried to sit up. "Too late, Sal."

She seemed to feel no melancholy at his admonition.

"I am tired, love! I do not plan to walk all over Lincolnshire tonight. "

"Let me make a proposal, dearest Sal."

"You already did, and I accepted," she reminded him, her voice drowsy.

"Another one, then. What do you say if after dinner we hurry to the vicarage where I can ask about the intricacies of obtaining a special license? We can get married right after Christmas, and I will see that you get to bed early every night."

She blushed, even as she nodded. He folded her in his arms, and to his gratification, she melted into him like the baby he had held yesterday. He thought briefly of the *Admirable* in dry dock and then put it from his mind forever. He smiled to think of the Gospel of Luke, another favorite quarterdeck recitation—"and on earth peace, good will toward men."

"Happy Christmas, Sally," he whispered in her ear as goodwill settled around him like a benediction and peace became his second dearest companion.

THE *Three Kings*

Pay attention, Sarah, you silly, she told herself as she stood before General Clauzel—was it Bertrand? Did enemies have first names?—and tried to follow his French.

He was speaking slowly and distinctly for her benefit, eyeing her thoughtfully when he finished. He sighed and motioned for his orderly to come forward with quill and ink. He spread out the piece of paper before him, regarded her again—not unkindly—and began to write.

He scratched along on the paper as if he had all the time in the world and then looked up. "Your name, mademoiselle. All of it, please."

Wake up, Sarah, she scolded herself. *This will never do. Only a half-wit would doze off on her feet in the presence of so august an enemy.* "You can sleep when you're dead," her brother James used to joke when she complained of exhaustion among the mounds of red tape in the library.

The library! At the thought of it and of James, tears sprang to her eyes. They were large brown eyes, and quite her best feature besides her marvelous English skin and tidy figure. She had not slept in two nights because of what happened at the library. Every time she closed her eyes, she relived the experience.

Sarah bit her lip and glanced at the general, who was watching her with a certain male trepidation that knew no language barriers. Had he been a German or a Russian, she would have stifled her tears at all expense to herself, but since he was French and this was Spain, she allowed her tears to well up in her eyes, magnifying them, and then spill onto her cheeks. She sniffed, stifled a sob, and was not at all surprised when General Clauzel leapt to his feet, took her in his arms, and patted her back in the foolish fashion men have attempted ever since Adam first consoled Eve over her sudden change of address.

Sarah let him console her and went so far as to rest her blonde head against his chest. He smelled divinely of too much cologne, good French perfume that she had not smelled in years. Clauzel's careful embrace was a decided improvement over that of the old priest into whose care she had surrendered the still-warm James, and who had thought to comfort her too.

Because General Clauzel was French, he knew what to do with his hands, despite his own discomfort. Sarah allowed him to pat her back because she was tired and in desperate need of someone to lean on, and because he was so comfortable and she needed that safe-conduct in the worst way.

At last Sarah made a movement and he released her.

She scrubbed at her eyes with hands that shook, in spite of herself, and accepted the general's handkerchief.

"*Merci, mon général,*" she said in precise French. "Excuse my womanly weakness. These, sir, are trying times."

He nodded. "They are, mademoiselle. Please be seated."

She sat, and he returned to his side of the desk. He glanced behind him at his adjutant. "Is it December twenty-second already? Where has 1812 gone?" He looked at Sarah expectantly as he dipped the quill in the ink pot one more time.

"Sarah Brill Comstock," she said. "Lady Sarah," she amended.

She spelled Brill for him, overlooking the fact that he left the "h" off Sarah.

The general finished writing, leaned back, and allowed his orderly to sprinkle the page with sand. When the sand was back in the bottle, he took the safe-conduct and waved it slowly.

"There it is, my dear, safe-conduct from Salamanca to the Spanish border, preferably Ciudad Rodrigo."

Now that the deed was done, Clauzel allowed himself a touch of humor and began to tease her. "That means no side trips to Madrid to admire the paintings—the ones we have left there—or no jaunts to Seville to sketch those smelly gypsies. You are to take the most direct route southwest to Ciudad Rodrigo. The border and Portugal are not far, *ma chère*."

Sarah nodded, her eyes on the safe-conduct. "As you wish, *mon général*."

"You will, of course, leave immediately."

Sarah nodded again, resisting the urge to grab the paper and sprint for the nearest exit, scattering soldiers before her. Instead, she took the pass and blew on it for a moment to make sure the ink had dried, hoping that she exhibited true British phlegm and that he could not see the beads of perspiration forming on her upper lip in that cold room.

"There is not a healthy horse to be had in all of Salamanca," the general said. "Your countrymen have seen to that in their—shall we say?—precipitate retreat. I can offer you a plug only, and there is no guarantee that someone else will not take it from you. But I do recommend that you hurry."

She nodded, suddenly worn out with translating Clauzel's impeccable French. With a slight smile in his direction, she followed the orderly into the hallway.

After James's shocking murder, the French had moved her to the university itself. Her protests at being separated from her clothes and other possessions had met only with a roll of the eyes, Gallic expressions better left untranslated, and laughter. She thought never to see her bandboxes again or the sturdy trunk that had traveled just that summer from Kent to Lisbon and then east over hot, shimmering roads to Salamanca in the wake of Wellington's army.

But there they were now, taking up the better part of the windowless little room. Sarah dropped on her knees in front of the trunk and pulled it open, pawing through her petticoats and chemises to the bottom. She pounded on the trunk in frustration. The money was gone. All she had remaining were the few coins in her reticule that the guards had somehow overlooked.

She sat back and waited for fear to wash over her.

It did not. She felt nothing. She had felt nothing since James had staggered back from the archive doorway, his chest covered with blood, his eyes unbelieving, even as he shook his head in amazement and said, "Bless me, Sarah, what a plaguey turn of events," and then died in her arms.

The cold floor roused Sarah from her reverie. She touched the massive ring on her thumb, encircling it with her whole hand. While the breath was still sighing out of James's body and the soldiers still stood, transfixed, in the archive doorway, she had whisked the signet ring with the family crest off James's finger and crammed it on her thumb. There had to be something to take home to Papa.

"I will get it home, Papa," she said out loud. "I promise."

She looked over the clothes that had seemed so important to her only two days ago. She shook out her riding habit and, after a careful look around, closed the door behind her and hurried into the outfit. She pulled on two layers of stockings and glanced about her again.

The soldiers had piled James's possessions against the far wall. She hunted through his clothes, holding her breath against the familiar smell of the Caribbean lime cologne that he had favored, until she found his wool hunting shirt and pulled it on over her habit.

There was one thing more. She put her ear to the door and heard the soldiers coming up the stairs again. She darted to her pallet and raised the corner.

No one had disturbed the bloody papers that she had so carefully transcribed and that James had tossed in the air when the gun went off at such close range. The papers had fluttered about him as he lay dying. She had watched them settle on his body and had scrambled them together even as the soldiers were shouting at her and trying to drag her to her feet.

The papers lay hidden where she had left them, the blood brown now, old already, but not as old as the words from the fifteenth century she had been copying.

"*Cristóbal Colón*," Sarah whispered. "Christopher Columbus. Let us go on a journey." She stuffed the sheaf of papers into a leather pouch and pulled it over her head, easing it down the front of her riding habit.

For the first time since her interview with Clauzel, tears stung her eyes. Had it been only two days ago, before the soldiers had bashed on the archive door with their rifle butts, that James had remarked to her how much he was looking forward to turning those pages over to the Bodleian Library?

"Sarah, only think," he had said, his eyes sparkling,

even though she knew how tired he was with the effort of translation. "Perhaps the last chapter hasn't been writ on Columbus's first voyage, now that we know the precise landfall. How I shall relish presenting these papers!"

She sank back on her heels. "Ah, why did we do it?" she whispered.

When word had come to James through one of his Continental sources about the possibilities in the Salamanca library, why had she allowed herself to be swept along by his enthusiasm?

She had been as eager as James to hurry to Papa with the news and then to plead and argue and urge Sir William Comstock to exert his considerable influence to permit them, in the name of scholarship, to follow in the wake of the triumphant army. A word here, some coins there, a promise given, and the deed was done.

She thought of Papa and his great excitement. He had kissed her on both cheeks, a thing of rare excess in itself, and declared that the Comstock papers from Salamanca would soon be as well known as Lord Elgin and his marbles.

The pleasure of presentation would be hers now, but Sarah Comstock took no joy in it. She jammed her hat upon her head, took one last look around the room, and consigned herself to the French guards outside her door.

The miserable horse that awaited her in the great courtyard of the University of Salamanca looked as resigned as she felt. Snow was beginning to fall. Sarah turned her face up to the sky, absorbing in one last breathtaking moment the venerable spires of ocher and pink that she had clapped her hands over when they rode in better style into Salamanca that summer. Never mind that French soldiers in green uniforms ringed the court-yard now. She did not notice them as she put her fingers to her lips and blew a kiss to the university and to James, resting in a vault of San Miguel in the Wall.

And there was Clauzel again, his kind face wrinkled with worry. "You know the road to Lisbon?" he asked.

"*Oui, mon général,*" she replied, her voice scarcely a whisper.

He gave the horse a prod. "It is never hard to find an army, Mademoiselle Comstock. And they are not far."

She should have smiled at him at least. Throughout the misery of the last few days, he had been nothing but concerned—and aghast, at least in her presence over the shocking death of her brother. "My dear," he had said over and over, "we do not fire upon scholars. I cannot understand how this happened."

No more could she. She nodded in his direction, dug her heels into the horse's side, and took her leave of the University of Salamanca.

Lady Sarah Comstock rode in silence for the better part of the day. Her early fears that someone would steal her horse or molest her soon disappeared. While nobody made a move to help her—and how could they, with the French back again?—the Spanish eyes that watched her from hovels and meticulously picked-over grain fields showed only respect and some sorrow at her situation.

When she dismounted at noon for a nuncheon of water from a stream that tumbled ice-cold beside the road, she discovered a slice of bread and five dried-out olives in one of the innumerable shrines found on every Spanish byway. She sniffed the bread. It was not fresh, but it was bread.

"You see, sir," she said out loud to the saint, who looked at her out of mildly surprised eyes from his niche, "I am hungrier than thou art."

Sarah spoke in polite Spanish, such as she would

use to address her betters or a recent older acquaintance. While not a superstitious person, she had no desire to offend the sensibilities of one who might consider, in this Christmas season, some heavenly intervention.

Snow was falling faster as she walked her horse into the afternoon, following the trail of Wellington's retreating army that had passed through Salamanca less than two weeks ago. There were broken bottles, bloody bandages, and wooden biscuit crates that didn't even hold a whiff of victuals anymore.

She rode off and on as the shadows lengthened and the sun struggled out from its weight of clouds. Over one more rise, and the army was before her.

Her relief fled as quickly as it had come as she rose up in the stirrups and shaded her eyes with her hand. It was only the smallest group of soldiers and camp followers, the last straggling detachment from this part of Spain.

What did you expect, Sarah? she asked herself and swallowed her disappointment. Wellington was probably sitting before a fire in Lisbon even now, writing up his report of the failed siege of Burgos and the retreat to Portugal. He probably didn't even know about this group.

She clucked to the horse and it moved faster, heading for the company of animals and the potential of food. As they bumped and jogged over the stony road, Sarah could make out the scarlet regimentals of British troops and the drabber brown of Spanish allies.

"Thank goodness," she said out loud.

Some of the horses were already milling around behind the picket line. Sarah sniffed the fragrance of campfires and the sharper smell of food cooking. Her mouth watered and she felt hungry again for the first time in several days.

She rode into the encampment and was met by a

familiar face, hiding behind a layer of dirt and several days of whisker. Sarah held out her hand.

"Well, Dink, I didn't expect to see you here!" Lord Wetherhampton—Dink to his Oxford cellmates—looked at her in some confusion. "Gracious, Sarah, have a little pity and call me Lieutenant Markwell at least!"

The officer on horseback next to him, dressed in Spanish brown, caught her attention out of the corner of her eye. He turned away quickly to hide a smile, even as his horse did a little dance in the snow.

"I'm sorry, Lieutenant," she amended as the Spaniard turned his back to her, his shoulders shaking.

And then it was Dink's turn to stare, as if he had only just then realized that he was looking at Sarah Comstock.

"Goodness, Sarah, what are you doing here? And where is James? Don't tell me that brother of yours is still in Salamanca." He screwed up his eyes in that familiar gesture she remembered. "Oh, I would like to thrash him."

Sarah sighed. In another moment Dink would be dithering. She laid her hand on his arm, even as he muttered, "Hookey will kill me for leaving you behind."

"You couldn't have known we were there. James . . ." Her voice changed and she looked down at her hand that grasped the reins. The Spaniard had steadied his horse and was facing her again, as if compelled to turn around by the despair in her voice. She looked at him instead of Dink. "James is dead. Killed by French troops. Dink, I hope you can get me out of Spain."

After the amazement on his face was followed by chagrin, she waited for him to utter the expected phrases of condolence and reassurance. Dink Markwell did none of those things. He sat on his horse, slapping his gloves from hand to hand, until Sarah wanted to grab him and shake him.

"Well, I'll do what I can," he said at last, but there was little resolution in his voice and none whatsoever in his eyes.

He was on the verge of saying something else when a Spanish woman of indeterminate years stormed up to him and latched on to his reins. The animal snorted in surprise but no more surprise than Dink Markwell showed as he lurched forward and clutched the saddle's pommel.

"We are hungry," the woman pleaded, her voice low and intense.

When her pleadings produced no look of interest on Markwell's rather spotty face, she tugged at the reins. "What are we to do, sir, we who stayed behind to nurse your wounded?" she asked pointedly, following his eyes with hers, forcing him to look at her.

She was joined by other women and then by the children, who set up such a clamor that Sarah looked away in embarrassment. Trust Dink not to have a single clue what to do. She and Dink had grown up on neighboring estates in Kent, and she knew him too well.

After another moment of silence, followed by one last, desperate look around to see if there were someone else to take the burden, Markwell retrieved his reins and glanced over at the Spanish officer, who, like Sarah, had found something else to occupy his vision.

"Colonel, these are your people," he snapped in exasperation. "You tell them what to do!"

"Lieutenant, this is your command," the Spaniard replied. "I joined you only this noon, do you not recall? You have your orders. I have mine."

Dink wheeled his horse about in exasperation and faced his sergeant, who, with some difficulty, managed to compose his face.

"Sergeant, find these people something to eat," he ordered.

The sergeant saluted, grinned when the lieutenant turned away, and herded the little group toward the one remaining pack mule. The lieutenant watched him go and then dismounted and gestured to the Spaniard, who dismounted too.

"Colonel, since you remind me that my attention is fully occupied by this ragtag, pestilential gathering of camp followers and stragglers, I would ask you to be Sarah Comstock's escort. Lady Sarah Comstock, that is, until such time as we reach the battlements of Lisbon."

The Spaniard bowed but shook his head. "Lieutenant, I am going no farther than Ciudad Rodrigo." He looked back at Sarah. "And then I ride south along the border to Barcos to spend Christmas with my children. I am sorry, Lady Sarah, but there you have it."

Take it or leave it, she thought.

"Then you will be her escort until Ciudad Rodrigo," Dink said smoothly as he accepted a cup of tea from his servant. "Sarah, is it agreed?"

"I . . . I suppose," she replied, "if it is agreeable to the colonel."

She spoke in Spanish and was rewarded with a flicker of a smile from the colonel.

She held out her arms to him, and he lifted her from the sidesaddle.

"Do you have many children, Colonel?" she asked as Dink handed her a cup of tea.

"Two," he said. "Two daughters. The young one is two and will not remember me. The older is four, I think."

"But you do not know?" she asked and then colored. The question sounded so impertinent, especially in Spanish, which is a peremptory language.

"It has been a long war, *doña*," was all he said.

He took off his gloves and walked, stiff-legged, toward the nearest fire. Sarah noticed that he limped.

Lieutenant Markwell put his hands on his hips and watched him go. "He never said that much to me at one time," he said, his tone disagreeable, childish. He laughed then. "You must be an inspiration. Oh, these are dour people. One would think they were Scots."

Sarah could summon no reply. She felt less than inspiring. Her backside flamed from an entire day in the saddle, and she was so hungry that tears sprung to her eyes when Dink's servant handed her a lump of nearly cooked horse meat. She scraped a little salt on it from the gray lump that the older Spanish woman offered her and ate it with surprising relish.

The Spanish colonel—she did not even know his name—made no move to speak to her while she ate, and she wondered if she had offended him. And then she did not care. She gobbled up a handful of burned onions and washed it all down with beer.

"That was the worst meal I ever ate, Dink," she said as she passed the bottle to the private who sprawled next to her, half-asleep.

"Not exactly plum pudding and eggnog?" Dink rubbed his eyes and yawned. "Sarah, when we are next in London, I will take you to dinner at Claridge's."

"Very well, sir," she replied, and then spent the remainder of the brief meal in sleepy contemplation of the fire, her chin in her hand.

The Spaniard sat across from her through the fire, and she watched him, interested in him mainly because he was not interested in her and there was no one else in her line of vision.

He was not a big man, and he was lean, but it was the

leanness that comes from starvation. Probably if peace ever returned to Spain and he were given the opportunity, the colonel would put on pounds and flesh until he looked like the little priests who strutted about the University of Salamanca like so many pouter pigeons.

But now he was lean. Even his fingers were lean and elongated, like the hands of an El Greco saint she had seen in one smoky church or other. His hair was black and in need of trimming, and he wore a moustache shorter on one end than the other, as though he chewed on it. His eyes were far and away the thing about the nameless colonel that drew her attention. They were a most startling blue, the blue of a subzero morning, the blue of ice rimming a deep pond.

She had seen enough blue-eyed Spaniards before, but none with eyes so pale, the pupils circled about with deeper blue. The effect was memorable. Sarah found herself looking at him through the flames, wondering about those eyes, until the sun went down and he turned into a silhouette.

He spoke to no one. When the sun was down, he had one of the Spanish soldiers tug off his boots. He sat cross-legged before the fire, gently massaging the instep of the foot that he favored. When he finished, he pulled on the boots again, wrapped his cloak about him, leaned his head forward against his chest, and was still.

Dink Markwell sat down beside Sarah. He followed the direction of her gaze. "That is an art I have not yet perfected, m'dear," he said, more to himself than to her. "I will be infinitely more rested when I can sleep sitting up." He laughed softly. "Think what an advantage it will be when I finally take my seat in the House of Lords." He winked at her. "Wouldn't James have a laugh at the thought of me in the House?"

He paused then and remembered, his eyes instantly sorry. "I am a beast, Sarah. Forgive me," he said. "It just doesn't seem possible that James . . ." His voice trailed off.

Sarah touched his arm and then rested her hand on the front of her riding habit. "I have saved his work, Dink. Oh, such wonderful things we learned about Columbus's first voyage." Her voice was animated despite her exhaustion.

The figure across from her through the fire raised his head and watched her. She was not a person of much prescience, but Sarah Comstock was acutely aware of his gaze.

"You'll take it to Oxford?" the lieutenant asked.

"I will," she answered, surprised by the fervency in her voice. "No power can stop me. I will, Dink, I will."

And then she was filled with an enormous sadness that left her gasping for breath. With great effort she controlled it and sat once again in silence.

Dink was fidgeting beside her. "Well, old thing," he said at last, "you'll be in Lisbon soon enough. Colonel Sotomayor and I will see to it."

She swallowed her tears and leaned closer to the lieutenant. "Dink, what is his name? You never introduced us."

"I am sorry, m'dear." Dink passed a hand in front of his eyes. "Can't believe how easy it is to forget the social graces in this scummy country. Luís Sotomayor, and there's more, of course," he whispered back. "How these garlic-eaters tack on name after name and then use the middle one baffles me."

"Alargosa de Meném," said the voice through the fire, not even raising his chin from his chest. "And it is not a scummy country, my lord. Devil take you Englishmen."

Dink leapt to his feet in confusion, looking about him for help and finding none. "Beg your pardon, Colonel.

I am sure I did not mean any of that." There was no reply. Sotomayor was silent. They might have dreamed his pithy comment.

Sarah sat alone for another hour, her eyes on the flames and then on the embers when the flames were gone and the others had begun to wrap themselves in cloaks against the snow that was falling again.

Sarah rose at last and shook the snow off her cloak. She tugged James's wool shirt up tighter under her chin and arranged her cloak around her again. There was no grass to cushion her sleep. She smoothed off a spot close to the fire but away from the soldiers.

On the trip from Lisbon to Salamanca that summer, James had showed her how to burrow out a little hollow for her hips. Remembering him, she did as he had shown her so many months ago, and then sobbed out loud at the memory of James riding in the wake of the triumphant army; James in the archives, crowing over his discovery among the red tape; James lying still, his eyes wide open but not seeing her as the papers fluttered about.

Sarah took a deep breath and forced herself into silence. She lay down and drew her knees up toward her chest, her head pillowed on her arm. She closed her eyes.

It was hours later when she opened them. The Spaniard sat beside her now. He had covered her with his cloak too. She sniffed and smiled to herself as she thought of Dink Markwell and his stupid prejudices. It smelled of horse and garlic.

Sarah made no sound, but the colonel seemed to know she was awake. He looked at her, and he was deadly serious.

"Lady, do you know," he said in Spanish, "you would feel much better if you cried now."

She said nothing.

"No one will hear you." He looked about him elaborately, and his voice was dry and filled with something close to contempt. "Everyone sleeps. Even the guards your friend almost forgot to place until I reminded him. It would be a good time to cry."

Deep sobs shook her. Sotomayor sat close by in silence for only a moment before he wrapped both arms about her and pushed her head down onto his shoulder. In a pleasant baritone, he hummed a little tune that resonated in his chest and brought her surprising comfort.

Sarah let him console her. He hummed and rubbed her back until the tears were gone, replaced by a quiet calm that she wished would never end.

And then, suddenly, she was shy. She shifted her position and he released her immediately.

"You're awfully adept with weepy women," Sarah murmured, embarrassed.

He laughed. "I told you I have two little girls. Tempestuous creatures!" He sighed then and tugged on his moustache. "And Liria."

He said nothing more, and Sarah did not press him.

After another moment he handed her a handkerchief. She wiped her eyes, blew her nose, and lay down to sleep, more reassured than at any time since she and James left Lisbon last summer.

The attack came at dawn, when she was most comfortable. All she was aware of at first was that someone— the colonel most likely—had whisked a cloak off her. She mumbled something and burrowed deeper in her own cloak.

"Get up."

The words were low and she might have been mistaken, but there was no mistaking the sharp slap to her backside.

Sarah sat up, angry now, even as she was still groggy, and ready to tell him what she thought, but the colonel was already running toward the horses, which had begun to mill around and whinny to one another.

No one else was up. The sky was dark still; it threatened snow. Sarah rose to her knees, mystified by the low rumble in the distance and the trembling of the earth under her. She looked in the direction of the horse herd, wondering that so few animals could cause such a sound.

And then she saw the French cavalry on the rim of the hill she had crossed only yesterday and leapt to her feet, her heart in her mouth. She picked up her skirts and ran for the horses, the sound of the charge in her ears and another sound of men wailing in high, banshee voices that raised the hair on her neck. In one wild moment, she remembered the stories the officers had told her of that terrible noise and how grateful she had felt never to have heard that eerie, warbling cry.

Her pitiful excuse of a horse that yesterday could scarcely put one hoof in front of the other was snorting and rearing now, its eyes rolling in terror. The colonel had managed to bridle the animal—how, she couldn't imagine—but it would not stand still for her sidesaddle.

Other soldiers were up now, some running for the horses, others just huddling together in the fog of sleep. Sarah couldn't see Dink anywhere.

Her attention was yanked back forcibly to her horse.

With a scathing oath, the colonel threw down the sidesaddle and leapt into his saddle. He held his hand out for her, but she backed away.

"I left my duffel bag by the fire," she said breathlessly. "Everything I value is in there. My clothes, some food. I can't leave it behind."

The French were firing now, some dismounted and taking deliberate aim at the British soldiers only beginning to wake to the chaos of early morning. Others had drawn their swords and were slashing among the wounded.

"Lady, please," said the colonel. He leaned out of the saddle and tried to grab her, but she danced out of his reach, confused by the noise and the smell of gunpowder.

Driven by the demon of panic, she turned to run, heedless of the danger, crazy to gather up her few pitiful belongings and the odds and ends of James's scholarship in the Salamanca archives. She picked up her skirts and ran, mindful suddenly of the thunder of hooves behind her, and the horrible whooping and warbling that would not go away.

The colonel leaned down and grabbed the waistband of her dress, hauling her unceremoniously into the saddle in front of him.

Children were running about like rabbits now, women screaming, the wounded raising their arms for someone to help them into a saddle. Bending low over Sarah and without a backward glance at the others, the colonel sailed his horse over the picket line and down a small embankment, where he dismounted and pulled Sarah after him.

"We would only be followed," he said as he tugged her after him into the hollowed-out overhang of the dry riverbed. "Let us pray they have short memories and other matters to occupy them." He whistled twice to his horse, which sank suddenly to the ground and lay still.

As Sarah watched, her eyes wide, all protest died in her throat. She offered no objection when the colonel clasped his hands over her ears as the main body of French cavalry struck the helpless troopers with an audible smack. She closed her eyes and made herself as small as she could against the dirt embankment, her fingers digging into the colonel's hands.

And then it was quiet. Colonel Sotomayor gradually removed his hands from Sarah's ears and then whispered to her, his voice a mere tickle. "Now it becomes dangerous. Don't even breathe."

She remained absolutely silent as the Spaniard grabbed the hem of her long riding habit and pulled it tight into their hiding place. The skirt was full and seemed to fill the space. As she watched, he dropped handfuls of dirt on her skirt until someone looking down from above would see no telltale fabric.

The eerie silence hummed in her ears. After several minutes of intent listening that seemed like hours, she tried to rise to her knees.

The colonel clamped his arms tighter around her waist. "Don't move," he whispered, and she had the wisdom to obey.

They lay close together, sheltered by the overhang of the embankment, and then in another moment, they were not alone. A group of soldiers stood above them on the bank. One of them even sat down, dangling his legs over the embankment and practically in Sarah's face. Her eyes wide with fear, she drew back as far as she could in the limited space and glanced at Sotomayor.

The Spaniard's face was devoid of all expression. He released his grip on Sarah's waist and fingered the cross about his neck, his lips tight together and thin. With his other hand he pulled the dagger from his belt and laid it across Sarah's lap.

After silence that stretched out like warm taffy, the soldiers finally stirred. Sarah flinched at the sound of a sword slamming home in its scabbard.

"Gone," exclaimed one of the Frenchmen. "And now what will we tell the general?"

"Nothing," said another. "We will follow, as we have been following. The border is far away in winter."

The others laughed.

"I wonder if Hook Nose can find the border by himself," said the first soldier.

After another long moment, the men left the embankment. Sarah let out the breath she had been holding. She was being followed, she assumed. That much was certain. What possible use could General Clauzel have with the Columbus papers? Why had he allowed her to leave Salamanca with them in the first place? And he had seemed so kind. It made no sense to her.

Still not moving and scarcely breathing, Sarah and the colonel remained where they were, listening as the cavalry, augmented by the remaining animals of the British retreat, moved off to the west at a walk, and then a trot.

Colonel Sotomayor shook his head as Sarah stirred. "We will wait a little longer," he said. He grinned. "'Patience—and shuffle the cards.' You have heard this saying?"

She nodded. Not until another hour had passed did the colonel move. He climbed quickly up the embankment and whistled twice again to his horse, which rose immediately and scrambled up the embankment after him.

Sarah crept from the hiding space and then looked back in amazement. What a tiny space it was. She shook the dirt from her skirt and held up her hand to the colonel, who stood, hands on his hips, staring at the sight before him.

"Help me, sir," she asked at last.

He shook his head. "No, lady. Stay where you are."

Sarah sat down, suddenly cold at the thought of what lay above her. *Dink! Where are you?* Her eyes filled with tears, but she blinked them back.

Before her imagination forced her down blind alleys better left unexplored, the colonel returned. He dangled his legs over the embankment and then leapt down. He had a campaign hat in his hand, Dink's hat. Sarah took it from him and brushed at the dirt.

"They stole everything else." The colonel turned away and spat. "Even his smallclothes. I hate the French."

Sarah clutched the battered hat. The colonel nodded at the look in her eyes, and she did not have to ask anything. "The wounded, the soldiers. . . . it is as you imagine. The women and children have fled."

He sighed and looked to the southwest. "The cavalry has moved down the road to Ciudad Rodrigo." He sighed. "I suppose we must go another way." He stood still, hands on hips again, as if working through his next strategy. He shook his head. "Happy Christmas," he muttered in English, and held out his hand to her.

Sarah hung back, suddenly shy and ill-at-ease with this competent man. "I am sorry . . ." She gulped and began again. "Sorry I gave you such trouble over the duffel bag."

"It is nothing," he replied, his hand still outstretched.

She held her own out. "You could have been long away from here, Colonel, if I had not slowed you down."

The colonel pulled her up the embankment. "I made a promise to get you to Ciudad Rodrigo, and I will keep it." He looked at her the way she used to stare at the menagerie in Philip Astley's Amphitheater. "Don't you English keep promises?"

"Of course we do," she said immediately, and then had the good grace to blush. "And I am impertinent to think you would not do likewise."

"You are," he agreed, his tone affable, friendly almost. "But we will overlook it." The colonel mounted and pulled her up behind him.

They rode quickly from the massacre, the colonel talking to his horse in the softest Spanish as the animal picked its way among the dead. Sarah buried her face in the colonel's back and tightened her arms around his waist.

There was nothing to say. The skies threatened snow again as Colonel Sotomayor followed the Ciudad Rodrigo road a mile and then turned south to another road, a shepherd's track through the scrub trees that shivered without their leaves and swayed in the biting wind.

Sarah relaxed as much as she dared, but she did not loosen her grip on the colonel. The silence stretched on, and she remembered Dink's joke that the colonel was not given to many words. She would have to supply the conversation.

"Sir," she began at last, "did you say that you had two daughters?"

He nodded, the subject covered.

She tried again in another mile, where the trees surrendered to a windswept valley.

"Sir, what are their names?"

He was silent for another mile or more, and then he sighed. "Mariana and Elena."

"Beautiful names," she returned.

"Yes," he agreed. They were now on the other side of the wide valley. "My wife named them."

"Your wife?" Sarah asked, determined to pursue this line of inquisition to take her mind off the cold that bore down from higher mountains about them.

"Liria." He paused again. "She is dead."

"Oh, poor man," Sarah exclaimed involuntarily. The

colonel said nothing for many miles then, and Sarah did not force her conversation on him. The cold seeped up her legs, and she wished she had taken the time to pull on a pair of James's socks before she left Salamanca. Her own hose were too thin for the Spanish wind.

"She died a week after Elena was born, trying to stop the French from burning our home."

Luís Sotomayor's words, coming as they did out of the air, startled her, and she let go of him. The colonel reached around behind him and grasped her hand, and she regained her grip.

"I was away with Wellington's army. My sister in Barcos took my daughters into her household. I visit when I can. You see, we are all miles from home."

"How difficult for you," Sarah murmured.

The colonel nodded and directed his attention to the stony path before them.

"Was she pretty?"

Sarah could hardly fathom where such a rude question had come from.

Sotomayor shifted in the saddle, as if surprised, but he did not hesitate to answer this time.

"She was"—he hesitated—"about your size. She was . . ." Again he paused and then shrugged. "She was beautiful to me."

He said nothing more until long past noon, when Sarah's stomach set up an insistent growl that would not be silenced. She pressed her free hand against her middle and then laughed at the thought of her famished stomach suddenly reaching out through her skin to munch down her fingers, or turning about to gnaw on her backbone.

"Lady Sarah?"

She laughed and leaned her forehead against the

colonel's back for a brief moment. "I laugh because I do not know how to deal with such a bit of social inelegance."

"You English," was all he said, but Sarah detected a smile in his voice, the first she had heard.

They rode until they were well into the trees again; then the colonel dismounted beside a trickle of a stream. He untied a tin cup from the front of his saddle, where he had lashed it tight so it would not rattle, dipped it in the stream, and handed it to her.

The cold water cramped her stomach and she made a face. The colonel drank the rest with evident relish and dipped it in the stream for more.

"You will forget for a while that you are hungry, if you drink some more," he said.

"I will not," she declared. "My stomach is not so easily fooled." Sarah pressed her hands to her middle. "Especially in December," she said, her eyes merry with remembrance, "when it knows there should be pastries, and fruited pies, and plum pudding, and a roast so thick, and goose with crackling skin . . . Oh, don't let me go on like this."

The colonel did not appear to be listening to her. His hands were on his hips again, the pose Sarah had already begun to associate with deep thought. A decision arrived at, he clapped his hands together and reached into the small canvas pouch next to the tin cup. He pulled out a small object wrapped in tissue paper and handed it to Sarah.

She pulled back the paper. It was a pear. No, it was not a pear. It was beautifully decorated marzipan, delicate green with just a blush of red.

"I have two of these, one for each daughter," he said as he took the candy from her, sliced it in half, and handed one portion back to her.

"Oh, I couldn't take their present," Sarah protested, even as her mouth watered and she longed to grab both pieces.

"I can," he said and ate his share. "Even the one that is left, divided between them, will be such a treat."

Sarah ate the candy, holding the almond paste in her mouth until it melted, and remembering a time—was it only last year?—that she would have turned her nose up at Christmas marzipan and called it childish.

The colonel wiped his hands on his uniform. "Well, it is only fitting, I suppose that we should lose a gift. That is the way of the Three Kings."

"Three Kings?"

"Yes. They travel to Belén bearing many gifts for the Child and leave things on the way for others who need them more."

To Sarah's surprise and utter delight, he struck a pose, threw back his head, and sang:

Ya viene la vieja, con el aguinaldo,
Le parece mucho, le viene quitando:
Parnpanitos verdes, ojas de limón,
La Virgen María, madre del Señor.

Sarah clapped her hands. "I heard that one night in Salamanca! Little children were singing it and teasing me for coins."

He bowed and grinned at her. "Ah, then you know about the little old lady and her presents of limes and lemons and her basket too full."

Sarah nodded. "And isn't the second verse about the Three Kings that you spoke of?"

"Yes, yes. I will not tease you for coins." He winked at her. "Maybe other things, but not money."

Sarah blushed suddenly for no reason she could possibly think of. "It is a funny song."

"Yes, lady, and we have need of laughter." He touched her cheek with the back of his hand. "Let us go."

They walked the horse then, the colonel careful to keep well back in the trees. Silently, he scanned the horizon, his eyes alert and a frown on his face as he squinted into the distance.

Not pacified by marzipan, Sarah's stomach growled again.

"This is a hungry part of Spain, not like my part," the colonel said. "All armies prey here, and they are pardonably suspicious." He chuckled. "And I have no money to buy food, anyway, even if there were any." His tone became rueful. "I left Burgos in a hurry."

"Burgos? But isn't that in French hands now?" Sarah asked and then wished she had remained silent, for the colonel said nothing more.

Sarah fingered her earrings, gold posts with diamond drops. Her reticule with its few pitiful coins seemed like a joke as she considered the journey ahead. *At least I have my ear bobs,* she thought. She looked about her at the enormous emptiness of the high Spanish plain. *We might as well be on the moon,* she thought and tightened her grip on the colonel's belt even as she inched closer to him.

Sotomayor patted her hand. "Don't worry. It takes more than a day or two to die of hunger."

They reached the monastery of San Pedro entre los Montes after dark, long after Sarah had given up hope of ever seeing another building again. She had already memorized the weave in the back of the colonel's uniform cape and the way his hair curled over his ears.

Her entire horizon had been reduced to Colonel Sotomayor's back. She was weary with the cold, grumpy with hunger, and too frightened to look around, for fear of what she might see.

The colonel reined in his horse far short of the monastery's barred entrance. He handed Sarah down and dismounted.

"Surely you could go closer," Sarah exclaimed, dismayed at the pain in her legs.

The colonel shook his head. "Lady, I trust no one. Not even priests."

She fell in beside him as he started toward the monastery, and the dogs began to bark. "You can trust me," she said on impulse.

"I know that," was all he said.

He jangled the bell, and Sarah jumped in spite of herself. The tinny little sound seemed to trumpet their arrival. She pulled her cloak tighter about her shoulders and waited for the French to leap out of their hiding places, screeching and yelling as before.

"Good evening, my son."

It was an old priest, his face a map of lines and crevasses. He peered closer at Sarah. "And to you, my daughter."

"Are there French about?" the colonel asked, moving closer to the half-open gate and pulling Sarah with him.

The priest looked about him elaborately and winked.

"They have come . . . and gone." He put his finger to his lips. "But not far. Come inside."

Silent, a black crow among the pale walls, the priest led them into the refectory. Other priests—none looked younger than Methuselah—huddled close to the fireplace. Other than a glance in their general direction, no one marked their arrival.

"Is there something to eat?" Sotomayor asked, his voice hushed.

"Be patient, my son. Sit down," said the priest, who motioned to a bench far from the fitful warmth of the fireplace and left them.

Time passed. Sarah shivered and pulled her cloak closer. Sotomayor went to the door through which the old cleric had vanished. He stood there, looking for a long moment, and then stepped aside for the priest, who carried two bowls of gruel.

The fragrance of the cooked wheat tore at Sarah's insides. She smiled up at the priest and took the spoon he offered her. She was acutely conscious of eyes watching her. The other priests stared at the two bowls on the table.

Sarah glanced up at the colonel, who still stood in the doorway. "For heaven's sake, sit down and eat before the old man changes his mind," she declared, her voice louder and more strident than she wished.

Instead, the colonel came to the table and held out his hand for her. "I am sure you would be pleased to wash your hands."

Not really, she thought, her mind crowded with wheat that smelled more divine than a brace of roast pheasant. She sighed, took his hand, and let him pull her toward the kitchen.

Sarah stood still on the threshold. Four children stared up at her, children small and dwarfed by clothes rendered too large by hunger. No one moved. No one cried.

Sotomayor was careful not to look at her. "This is why the priests are not eating," he said. "Here is the washbasin, lady."

She made no move to wash her hands. Her stomach growled, and suddenly she was ashamed.

"Christ declared that the poor are with us always,"

said the priest behind her, "even in this time of His birth, my lady."

Sarah nodded, her eyes on a small girl, scarcely more than a baby, who stared at her out of grown-up eyes and leaned against an older girl.

"Have they anything to eat?" she asked when she could find her voice.

The priest shrugged. "The Lord provides."

Sarah put her hands on her hips in unconscious imitation of the colonel and then went back into the refectory. She gathered up the bowls and returned them to the kitchen, sitting on the floor and drawing the child onto her lap. She patted the floor beside her and the older girl sat.

Sarah handed the spoon to the older girl. "If you feed her a bite and take two yourself, that will be fair," she said.

Without a word, the child took the spoon in fingers that trembled and fed her sister, who opened her mouth like a fledgling bird. Sarah cuddled the little one close and then looked up at Sotomayor.

"Well, Colonel, there are two other children. And didn't you say a while back that hunger was the best sauce?"

The ghost of a smile flickered across his lean face.

"I did."

She nodded. "And I suppose you have that other piece of marzipan in your pocket."

"I do. It will divide nicely into four parts, and we will sniff the wrapper."

Sarah laughed and the little girl turned around, startled. Sarah's smile died on her lips as tears filled her eyes. "Oh, little one, have you never heard anyone laugh?" she whispered into the child's curls. "How long has this war been going on?"

And why was I never aware of it back in England? she

thought as she watched the colonel portion out the gruel among the other children and then divide the marzipan. She thought of the food she used to push around on her plate, the courses she ordered back to the kitchen because the garnish was not just so, or the meal slightly overdone.

Soon the gruel was just a memory. The child on her lap licked the spoon clean and then leaned back against Sarah with a sigh. It was a sound that went straight to Sarah's heart, and she sobbed out loud. Quickly Colonel Sotomayor took the little girl off her lap and tucked the child in the crook of his arm, singing to her, walking her close to the kitchen fire, which burned lower and lower.

Sarah wiped her eyes and got to her feet. She shook her reticule and was less than satisfied. She sighed and reached into it anyway, avoiding the colonel's eyes. She handed a coin to the priest, and it disappeared up his sleeve.

"You cannot always trust the Lord to provide, Father, especially in time of war, when so many others require His assistance," she explained, her voice low.

He nodded, bowed, and handed her a cup of hot water with a single potato peel in it. "Excellent for the digestion, my lady."

Sarah sipped the hot water without a murmur. With a smile, the colonel began to hum again and rock the child in his arms. Soon the girl slept, the spoon still tight in her hand.

Sarah came closer to the colonel. "She is asleep now, Colonel Sotomayor," she said. "You can put her down."

He nodded. He fingered the little one's curls, but his eyes were far away. He made no move to put down the child, but cradled her closer to his chest.

Is it Mariana or Elena that you are thinking of, Colonel? Sarah thought as she watched him with his small burden.

She sat where she was on the floor and drank the rest of the hot water.

Suddenly she was in a pelting hurry to be off, to drag the colonel out the door and walk and walk until she could see the battlements of Lisbon. *I will whine and cry and chivvy Wellington until he picks me up and tosses me on board the next frigate, man-of-war, or garbage scow bound for Portsmouth. And I will never, ever leave England again.*

The older girl tugged on the colonel's sleeve finally, recalling him to the moment, and he stopped pacing the floor with the sleeping child. She held out her arms, and Sotomayor surrendered the baby. The priest shepherded the children out of the kitchen.

The colonel watched them go and then sank down against the wall on the floor beside Sarah. He closed his eyes and was asleep before she could complain. All her hasty words stopped in her throat as she looked at his face, as tense in sleep as it was when he was awake, the frown line between his eyes deeply etched. She went to the table to retrieve his cloak and bumped into a stool. At the slight noise, Sotomayor's eyes popped open, and his hand went to his sword.

Sarah gathered up his cloak and put her finger to her lips. "Shh, Colonel," was all she said. She covered him with his cloak, and he closed his eyes again. Without thinking, she touched his hair, smoothing it down, and then ran her finger lightly over the line between his eyes.

When she was satisfied that he would sleep, Sarah sat down next to him again. The little light from the fireplace gave off no heat, and as she watched, the embers winked out until the room was dark.

Sarah touched the leather pouch with the Columbus papers, the parchment crackling in her fingers. Sotomayor twitched in his sleep but did not waken. The leather ties tugged at the skin on her neck, but she did not pull the pouch from its hiding place.

There was no comfortable place on the rough flagstones of the kitchen floor. After a moment of serious thought, Sarah scooted closer to the colonel and rested her head on his legs. He tensed, sat up from the wall, patted her hair, and then leaned back against the wall again. Soon he was breathing evenly.

The room was still dark when Sarah woke. A priest knelt by the fireplace like a Muslim facing Mecca, trying to breathe some life into the coals. He blew and coughed and wiped his ash-filled eyes, then blew again patiently until the coal glowed again. In another moment Sarah heard the crackle of the fire and felt the colonel tense and then waken.

Sotomayor stared at her, as if willing his mind to register who she was and where they were. He looked no more rested than when he had closed his eyes the night before.

The priest rose from his obeisance to the fire. *"Dios los bendiga,* my son," he said. "We have been watching the cut to the southwest where the French were camped. They have left. It would be good if you would do the same, you and your lady."

"Have we outstayed our welcome already?" Sarah burst out, stung by the priest's unctuous tone. "Can't you see that the colonel is tired?"

The priest bowed and smiled. If anything, his tone was more intractable. "My good lady, we have had enough of soldiers in this valley."

Sarah opened her mouth to protest, but the colonel took her by the arm in a grip surprisingly strong and pushed her in front of him to the doorway. "But aren't we on his side?" she whispered to Sotomayor as the colonel hurried her along.

"Lady, I don't press my luck," he hissed back.

"But . . ."

The colonel set his lips in a tight line and did not relinquish his grip, even though he slowed down. "Oh, how can I explain it? They have all been at war too long. I am not sure we are on anyone's side, as you put it. We are only more trouble."

"I refuse to accept that for an answer," Sarah stormed. She stamped her foot, furious with this stubborn man and all those countrymen of his who had raised intrigue to such a fine art. "I'll have you know I am an English-woman, and we expect answers that make more sense."

He stopped in his tracks and threw up his arms. "I don't care if you are the antipope of Canterbury. It's the only answer I have. Now quit nagging me."

Sarah stared at him. To her horror, tears pooled in her brown eyes and trickled down her cheeks. She dabbed at her cheeks and sobbed, "I don't understand you Span-iards. You're not at all like the English."

Colonel Sotomayor shook his head, but there was a smile in his eyes. He held out his arms, and she walked into them. He hugged her close, rocking her back and forth, until she felt like the little child in the kitchen last night. She sobbed into his shoulder in good earnest.

"Maybe if you spent less time in dusty archives, you would get to know us," he said at last. "No, we're not like the English. Is that so bad?"

She dried her eyes and blew her nose on Sotomayor's handkerchief she had appropriated yesterday. "I didn't mean it to sound so rude," she said.

He held her away from him by the shoulders. "I know this is difficult." He put his arm around her shoulder and

walked her across the courtyard to the stable. "I wasn't
going to tell you. Those children. They saw their parents
cut down because they hid a British soldier. Some fool
that wandered away from Wellington's army."

"Oh, no!"

"Yes. You see, we are only more trouble."

She nodded and sat down on the empty manger as the
colonel saddled his horse. The animal nosed the manger
and bumped her hip, searching for oats. There was nothing. Sarah sighed and went back into the monastery.

The children were sleeping in the refectory, jumbled
together like spoons in a drawer. The air was so cold that
Sarah could see her breath. She knelt by the older girl,
who clutched her little sister to her, her grip tense even
in sleep. Sarah watched them a moment, her resolution
wavering.

"And now you must rely on the kindness of strangers,
even as I? Ah, me," she said.

She looked around her. She heard the priests down
the hall in the chapel singing some out-of-tune morning
hymn. Quickly she took the last coin from her reticule
and placed it in the girl's free hand, curling her fingers
around it.

Sarah patted the little one's head and smiled as the
child nestled closer to her sister. Sarah touched the older
girl, careful not to wake her. "You look resourceful, my
dear," the Englishwoman whispered. "Make it last as long
as you can." Sarah drew her cloak tight around her again
and tiptoed from the dining hall.

The horse was saddled. Colonel Sotomayor gave
the cinch another tug and turned to her. "We can get
very close to the border this day," he said. "Excuse me a
moment." He went back into the building.

Sarah shivered as the wind teased her skirts. Was it

two days to Christmas? Was it one day? Had Christmas come and gone and left her still cold, still hungry, still in want? She rubbed her arms against a deeper chill. In all the days of trial since James's death, she had never felt quite so powerless.

It was an unwelcome emotion. She thought back to the only time in her life she had been hungry before, and it was the occasion of a horse ride through the Kentish countryside that went on much longer than she had anticipated. Even as her stomach had growled, she knew that at the end of the ride there would be food and people to make a commotion over her. On the Spanish high plains, there was nothing like that. No one cared that she was hungry or cold or frightened.

She managed a crooked smile. *Maybe that is why these people are such realists*, she thought. *They don't fool themselves.* In another moment she was embarrassed at her harsh words to the colonel, at her childish behavior. *Goodness, I haven't stamped my feet since I was in the nursery.* Her cheeks flamed, and she felt the most acute sort of misery, followed by a savage resolve to never be so foolish in front of Colonel Sotomayor.

She touched the front of her dress, feeling the outline of the leather bag. *James, I will get this to Oxford. I will.* The tears came back. *It is my only Christmas gift of any value this year.*

And there was the colonel in the arched doorway, pulling on his gloves. Sarah sighed, feeling immensely calmed to see him there. She smiled her biggest smile at him, the one that set the lights dancing in her eyes, the smile she usually saved for Almack's.

Surprised, the colonel smiled back. "You English are peculiar," was all he said as they hurried into the courtyard.

She stopped him with a hand on his arm. "Maybe if you would spend less time in dusty marches, you would get to know us." She lowered her head then, unable to look at him. "And I do apologize for my silliness."

He grinned at her and touched his forehead in salute. "*Muy bien.* I have already forgotten it."

He looked closer at her, his eyes troubled. "What is the problem, my heart?" he asked, the endearment out of his mouth unaware.

"I am afraid," she replied quietly, wondering if she had heard him right, then certain she had not. "Just . . . afraid."

The colonel took her by the hand and kissed her fingers. "I understand," he said, his voice as soft as hers. "I would infinitely prefer to be riding among my orange trees, with a little one in front of me in the saddle, helping me with the reins and ordering me about." He paused, and the memory filled his face. He squeezed her hand tight. "But Spain has need of me now."

"Are you never afraid?" she asked.

"All the time. It is this way, Lady Sarah. When there is no choice, it's better to be brave."

He kissed her cheek quickly. "Let us leave this place. Now what are you staring at?"

"Colonel, you left your cloak in the refectory. I know you had it a moment ago."

He could not ignore her pointed scrutiny. A flush rose to his cheeks. "I thought I would help the Lord provide a little too, as you put it, and the boys looked so cold. Now, are we going to leave this place or not?"

Sarah already knew better than to remark upon the colonel's philanthropy. Instead, she unfastened her cloak and handed it to him. "If you insist upon being Father Christmas—goodness, do Spanish children have Father Christmas?—then you had better take my cape and let me ride in front. That way, you can wrap it around both of us. I still have James's shirt, and it is quite warm."

He took the cloak, fastened it on, and lifted her into the saddle, swinging up behind her. He took the reins from the pommel and tucked his elbows in close to her sides. "Very well, Lady Sarah. I will not argue. And if you remember, Father Christmas does not come to Spain. There are the Three Kings on the sixth of January that children here look for." He leaned closer, his lips brushing her ear. "I tucked that coin under the edge of her skirt. She will still find it, and better yet, the priest will not. Was that the last of your money?"

Sarah shrugged. "It doesn't matter. You said we are close to the Portuguese border. The British army will feed me across Portugal to the sea. When I get to Lisbon, it's a simple matter to make an arrangement with a solicitor there on Papa's bank." She touched her earrings. "If worse comes to worst, I have these. We'll get by."

They rode into the early-morning fog, picking their way slowly along the stony path that led from the barren valley behind them to another barren valley before them. The colonel reined in his horse and rose up slightly in the saddle, looking over Sarah's head.

"See here," he said at last, pointing into the far distance. "I think it is the French. Well, they have not found us yet, and I have another path to try, once we leave this place."

He settled back down and put one arm around her waist as they began the steep descent. In another moment, his fingers rested against the leather bag that was outlined more distinctly under her habit. He moved his thumb across the pouch.

"Lady Sarah, what is that?" he asked finally. "I am rude to ask, but I am also curious."

"You needn't prod," she said briskly, and his hand left her waist.

Sarah tugged on the strings and pulled out the pouch.

She spread out the closely written pages in front of the colonel's eyes and told him about their remarkable find in the Salamanca archives.

"You see, sir, everyone has assumed for years and years that any papers of Columbus would be in the Cadiz archives, or at Simancas." Her voice warmed to her subject. "James had an inkling about the Salamanca archives, and he arranged for a friend to check his hunch. Here it is." Her voice grew doubtful then. "We stayed behind to copy it all."

"You stayed too long."

The colonel was silent then for a long time, and Sarah wondered if he had reverted once more to the monosyllables of yesterday. She folded the papers and replaced them in the pouch, dropping it down the front of her habit again.

"Was it worth it?" he asked simply, when they were in the safety of the trees again.

"I'm not sure," she replied. "I feel so angry at James for doing what he did and insisting that I stay with him and at Papa for urging us both on. And then I am angry at myself for not demanding that we leave with the army." She touched her chest. "And still, there are these papers. It is the only gift I have left to give, isn't it?"

She thought of the French then and turned around slightly to look at the colonel. "I need to tell you. It's only fair that I should tell you . . . Colonel, I think the French found out I have these papers, and they are after them. I cannot imagine any other reason they seem to be looking for us, can you?"

He made no reply.

"I truly am sorry," she said. "I don't understand why they want these papers, but there it is."

"Perhaps they want to wish us Happy Christmas," Sotomayor said at last. "Lady, I did not know you were a dangerous lady when I agreed to escort you to Ciudad Rodrigo."

"I am sorry, sir. Please do not leave me now."

"Not a chance," and his voice was stiffly formal again. "I believe we already discussed Spanish honor on this issue."

"Oh, don't remind me," she murmured. "I always seem to be apologizing to you, Colonel." She turned around again. "I wish you would call me Sarah, Colonel, instead of lady." She smiled at him and then turned back to her previous view of the horse's ears. "I harbor a vast suspicion that you have many more titles than I, anyway."

"It's possible . . . Sarah. And you must call me Luís. I have titles and land, but the estates are all burned and the sheep and cattle run off."

"You can get more someday."

"I can get more someday," he agreed. "Right now, I would give it all up for a bowl of wheat mush."

Sarah laughed. "And a sausage."

"A piece of cheese."

"An orange."

He laughed then too. "I have oranges, only they are on trees so far away." His voice was wistful as he tightened his grip on her. "You can't imagine the perfume when the blossoms come out in the spring. Liria used to . . . She would leave the windows open, and the petals would fall all over the floor. It was beautiful."

His tone was so wistful that Sarah felt the familiar prickle of tears behind her eyelids.

"Do you miss her?" she asked suddenly. Sotomayor

showed no surprise at the bald question, even though Sarah blushed as soon as the words left her lips.

"*Virgen santa*, how I miss her," he said, unconsciously slowing his horse to a walk. "I was so far away and so busy when she died. I would have given the earth to see her one last time . . ." He sighed and prodded his tired horse into motion again.

It was many words for the colonel, but he did not stop. It was as though Sarah's impudent question had opened a door closed too long.

"I miss her at night, Sarah, when I turn over and she is not there." He smoothed his hair. "I used to tease her about taking the middle of the bed and leaving me the sides, but I would gladly tolerate that again."

"Poor colonel," Sarah whispered. "Was it love at first sight?"

He laughed, and the free sound of his laughter relieved her. "No. Our papas arranged the whole thing. I didn't see Liria until the day we were married." His voice became reflective again, subdued. "We were just luckier than most."

He shifted in the saddle, and Sarah knew how badly he wanted to move about and walk off the agitation that her questions were causing.

"Do you know what I miss the most, all other things set aside?"

"No, Luís."

"When I used to do something she did not like, she would get such a look in those brown eyes and scold me and call me a thickheaded orange-grower."

Sarah laughed then, thinking of the times her father had peered over her shoulder and jabbed his finger at those places where her translations were weak. Or how James, his lips thin in that familiar gesture of agitation, would shake his head over her penmanship as she scribbled to keep up with his enthusiastic dictation.

"You can't seriously miss that, Colonel."

He slewed himself around to look her in the face. "Sarah, when someone scolds you, that means they care. Don't you see? If people don't care about you, they don't say anything."

"I suppose I never thought of it like that," she replied.

"And then, when I was properly contrite, Liria would give me such a hug. Yes, I miss her."

"Now?" Sarah asked, her voice low.

"Well, not so much. The feelings are there, but they have changed. Time smooths the emotions, like water on rock, and thank goodness for that. I am grateful for the time we had, and for our daughters, but life does go on . . ."

He was silent then, and she did not press him. The wind picked up and she shivered. The colonel drew her cape in closer. "But right now we are cold. Too bad there are no dead Frenchmen about."

She made a face. "What are you talking about?"

"On more than one occasion, I have dumped French bodies from caskets and burned the coffins to keep warm."

Sarah gasped and clutched the pommel. *No, these people are not like we are. They are immensely practical, enormously resourceful.*

"But didn't the smoke smell . . . well, funny?" The colonel threw back his head and laughed. He hugged her tighter about the waist until she gasped again.

"You are a bit of a *pícara* yourself, no, Sarah?"

"No," she said firmly and pulled his arms from her waist. "I would never dream of burning a coffin."

"Warm's warm, Sarah. Don't forget it. And also don't forget, trust no one."

They traveled in silence and hunger across high,

wild-country, windswept land that seemed to stretch beyond her puny vision, out of the edge of her sight. What must it be like in the spring, when the oceans of grass were lime green again and lambs dotted the hillsides like so much cotton wadding?

But now it was stark and cold and frozen in the deepest winter such as she had never known. There was no snow. The ground was bare right down to the center of the earth. She shivered, grateful for the colonel's arms around her.

As the day wore on, they began to see houses, one here, one there, widely separate on the vast plain, and then closer together, as if seeking mutual comfort from the wind that never stopped. Luís circled the houses at a distance, coming no closer than was necessary.

Finally Sarah could hold back her complaint no longer. "Oh, Luís, could we stop for food? Surely someone—"

He cut her off. "Not as long as the French army is in front of us," he said. "They will be ordering every *campesino* to look for"—he paused, as if unsure what to say—"a woman in a blue cloak, and maybe a soldier too." He shrugged and tightened his grip on her waist. "And if they are behind us, well, that would be worse. Then the French would know precisely where we are. We dare not trust anyone."

The cold was making Sarah drowsy. She nodded to sleep, only to be elbowed awake by the colonel.

"No, Sarah," he said, his voice filled with an urgency that startled her, and yanked back the blanket of sleep. "You must stay awake."

He stopped his horse, plucked her off the front of the saddle, and set her on the ground. "Walk alongside for a while. It will wake you up."

She made no protest, where yesterday she would have sighed and scolded. Without a word, she took hold of the stirrup and plodded beside the animal, her eyes straight ahead. Soon she was colder than before without the protection of her cape and the colonel's warmth, but she was wide awake. Hunger had gnawed a hole through her middle and lighted a flame in her forehead that kept her moving. Over and over she thought, *I will get these papers to Oxford. I will, I will.*

Sarah didn't realize she was speaking out loud until the colonel leaned down and touched her head. "Of course you will," he said. "Come up now. I think you will stay awake."

He took her by the elbow as she put her foot over his and climbed back into the saddle. She settled herself in front of the colonel with a sigh, pleased to the point of caricature to be warmer again. *I can be content with so little now*, she thought as the cloak came around her.

"Are you warm enough?" he asked.

She nodded and rested her head against him, enjoying the comfort of his nearness.

They traveled a shepherd's path then, high into the mountains, rocky and difficult, and when they came out of the pass, the army was gone.

"I did a foolish thing!" the colonel exploded.

Sarah looked around. The plain was bare, with no sign of the French army before them raising a cloud of dust. The colonel swore again and turned around in the saddle. "Where are they now, Sarah?" he asked, more to himself than to her.

"Perhaps they have gone back," she offered helpfully.

"Then I am the king of Spain, bless that royal cuckold," was the colonel's reply. "Well, let us be more watchful."

The afternoon shadows lengthened across the land,

which gradually yielded to a forested area dotted with ice-flecked ponds and frozen grass. The colonel stopped frequently to allow his horse to graze, while Sarah dipped the tin cup over and over into the ponds and drank until her stomach gurgled. The colonel joined her, squatting on his heels, and accepted the cup from her.

"We're close to the border. I wonder that we have seen no Spanish troops yet, or British. They command a presence here." He drank and then tossed the rest over his shoulder. "Or, at least, they used to."

"Do you mean—"

"I don't know. I don't know anything right now," said the colonel, his voice filled with frustration. "I don't even know where the enemy is, and that is the worst blunder of all."

Sarah put her hand on his arm. "You have done magnificently, Luís. I would never have gotten this far with Dink."

He smiled at her. "You are more than kind, Sarah."

He rose and pulled her up after him, looking at her. "I wonder that you have never married. Excuse the impertinence, but is there something wrong with the English?"

Sarah laughed and then pressed her hands to her middle. "Oh, that hurts! There is nothing wrong with Englishmen," she said, "only I suppose no one was ever interested in someone so bookish. I am what you would call a bluestocking. It was always more fun to tag along after James into archives than to bow and dance, and knot a fringe, or paint a dreary watercolor." She looked about her. "But I would like to come back here in the spring and try something else in oils. Spain is not watercolor country."

The colonel shook his head and then bowed playfully. "You have my permission when—*ojalá*—there is peace again, to paint my orange groves in the south. In fact, it may be that I will insist upon it."

"Insist?" she teased playfully, delighted at the way his blue eyes widened when he smiled.

"Yes. I have been known to order people about. For their own good, of course, dear lady," he said.

She clapped her hands and curtsied back. "We shall see about your orange groves. Are there archives nearby?"

"Silly woman," he scolded, but there was a twinkle in his eyes. "Did no one ever tell you that brains are a frivolous ornament on a woman?"

"Many times," Sarah replied quietly, "but I chose not to believe them."

"Brava, bravissima," the colonel said as he helped her to her feet. "My Liria was a woman of great intelligence. It is good she was smarter than I."

He limped back to the horse and just stood there watching the animal. He shifted his weight from one foot to the other.

"Do you know, Luís, you should have your foot looked at by the British doctors when we get to Ciudad Rodrigo."

He turned around in surprise. "What? What are you talking about?"

"Well, your limp," she said in confusion.

He shook his head. "It will be better soon enough. Nothing to worry about."

They rode into the afternoon. Dark was coming fast as the valley narrowed. Sarah could see lights in the near distance. She pointed to them.

"Ciudad Rodrigo?"

The colonel shook his head. "No. Probably La Calera, or maybe Cailloma."

He started to say something else but jerked forward, a grunt of surprise forced from him. Nearly thrown from the saddle, Sarah grabbed the pommel and then the reins as they fell from his hands. In another second, the colonel's head drooped onto her shoulder, and she felt a wet warmth spreading over her back.

"Colonel Sotomayor!" she screamed as she pulled back on the reins and the horse stopped. The animal tossed its head, nervous at the smell of blood, sidestepping even as she tugged on the reins. The colonel was a deadweight against her. She reached behind and felt him.

"Don't stop, Sarah," he said, his voice heavy, sleepy, and faint in her ear. "I think we found the . . . the . . ."

"French army," she concluded, her thoughts jumbled together. Not this, not now. They fired at someone in a blue cloak. It was meant for me.

Without another word, Sarah grabbed for the colonel's hands and pulled them around her waist. She held them there until he managed to dig his thumbs into the waistband of her riding habit.

With a savage tug of the reins, she wrestled the colonel's horse under control and then dug her heels into the animal. They shot across the plain, the exhausted animal grunting in its exertions.

The colonel managed a look over his shoulder.

"Nothing," he muttered. "Where are they?"

Sarah looked back once as twilight settled in, and the sight drove all hunger and cold from her mind. It was a column of troopers, not riding fast in pursuit, but loping along like wolves to the rear of a wounded deer, animals of prey with all the time in the world.

She headed toward the village, and the colonel tried to take the reins from her.

"Not there," he gasped. "Sarah, not these border villages. They have even less loyalty than the *campesinos*. Find a small farmhouse, anything else."

She ignored him and forced the horse into a gallop, her heart and mind trained on the village. "At some point, Colonel, you have to trust someone," she murmured and then rubbed her cheek against his in a gesture of comfort.

His breathing grew more labored as he leaned so heavy against her back. "Sarah, I wanted to tell you something," he gasped.

"Can it wait?" she said. "Oh, please don't exert yourself. Luís, just hang on!"

They galloped into the village as dark took hold, still in front of the soldiers. She rose in the stirrups and then covered her mouth with her hand to stifle a cry. French soldiers were camped across the bridge just beyond the village. As she watched, another detachment rode in from the north.

What have I done? she thought wildly.

And there was the village. The comforting smell of wood smoke greeted her and made her mouth water, even as her stomach grew into a tighter ball from fear. As she sat on the lathered horse, wondering what to do next, a procession of villagers wound their way through the street, singing. At their head was a woman wrapped in blue, seated sidesaddle on a donkey. A bearded man led the animal, and children skipped alongside.

The colonel opened his eyes at the singing. "Bless us, a *posada*," he said. "Oh, Sarah, help me off this horse."

She sat where she was, remembering. Was it only nine days ago that she and James had watched a similar procession wind its way through the narrow streets of Salamanca, as Joseph sought a bed for Mary? This was the ninth night. Soon he would knock and knock and then the innkeeper would finally let them in.

Sarah threw herself from the horse and steadied Luís as he dismounted and then dropped to his knees. She ran to the head of the procession, which had stopped in confusion.

Her hands clasped in front of her, she ran to the Joseph. "Oh, please, please help us," she cried. "The French."

Startled, the man stepped back and stared at her. He shook his head.

Tears sprang into Sarah's eyes and then she realized that in her agitation she had spoken in English. She took a deep breath and tried again in Spanish, her words tumbling out. "The French! They are after me. Oh, please, the colonel said not to trust anyone, but I must."

There was silence and then sudden activity as the villagers swarmed around her. Almost quicker than sight, someone grabbed the colonel, ripping off a waistband and cinching it tight around his middle, stopping the bleeding, while another took his horse by the reins and ran with it into the darkness.

As she watched in openmouthed surprise, the children stomped in the dirt and covered the blood on the ground, while a woman gently removed the bloody cloak and motioned to Mary, who leapt from the donkey, pulling off her cloak as she ran to Sotomayor. She whirled the cape around his sagging body as Joseph lifted the colonel in his arms and placed him on the donkey. He pulled the veil far over the colonel's face and took his place at the head of the procession again, even as another man, singing loud again, jerked Sarah to his side and covered her with his cloak.

The procession moved on again as the French troopers rode into town and shouted at them to stop. The villagers continued to move until the officer spoke to them in terrible Spanish.

"Have you seen any strangers in this village, one of them bleeding?"

Joseph shrugged. He looked up at Colonel Soto-mayor. "María, you would have noticed, wouldn't you?"

The colonel shook his head. Sarah clenched her fists and turned her face toward the villager who held her tight.

Joseph looked back at the soldier, who scowled and struck him.

"I know he is here, and that woman!" the man shouted.

Joseph only wiped the blood from the corner of his mouth and rested an arm on the colonel's leg. "We are only poor pilgrims on our way to Belén, if it please your worship. Honorable sir, it is the ninth evening of our *posada*. Soon the Child will be born." He gestured toward the colonel. "I must find a place for María this night. Let us pass, noble one. It is a small thing we do, something we have done for centuries."

As the Frenchmen stood beside the colonel and Joseph, the other soldiers ran down the procession, peering at the villagers. Scarcely breathing, Sarah burrowed in closer to the man who held her. The soldier scrutinized her and passed on down the line.

The French stood together in conference at the head of the procession. The colonel swayed slightly in the saddle, and Sarah bit down on her knuckles and closed her eyes. She clutched at the leather pouch under her habit, cursing herself for being such fearful trouble to the colonel and wondering why she had not thrown the papers away hours ago, to let them flutter about the landscape. What terrible secret did they hold? Were they worth a man's life?

She let her breath out slowly as the soldiers moved off. The leader returned and shook his fist at Joseph. "Continue your procession, you superstitious savages," he shouted and struck the man again for good measure.

Joseph reeled under the blow and then bowed again.

"Happy Christmas to you, my lord," he said.

As the soldiers watched, the procession moved down the street to another door. Joseph let go of the colonel and knocked on the door.

A man with an apron drooped about his paunch opened the door. "What is wanted?" he bellowed and then sang in old, pure Spanish as quaint as the writing on the Columbus papers. "We have a party within, and our house is full of travelers."

Joseph bowed his face to the ground. "We seek a room for the night," he sang, gesturing to the colonel. "Here is María, great with child, and it is her time. Oh, sir, is there room in this inn?"

"Please sir, I am weary," sang the woman who stood beside the colonel and steadied him. "Please, sir, it is the Christ Child."

The French soldiers drew closer again, intrigued by the ragged pageantry before them. Sarah gritted her teeth. *Would they never go away?*

Joseph looked about him as if he had no greater concern than María, who clutched at the donkey's mane with bloodstained hands. Gently he covered the colonel's fingers with the edge of the robe and sang to the innkeeper again, adding something at the end of the song that made the man's eyes widen.

The innkeeper nodded then and gestured to Joseph.

"All may enter and find rest," he sang, his voice loud and with a certain defiance that gave Sarah hope and put heart back in her again.

Joseph bowed low once more and lifted María from the donkey. The colonel groaned, and his head flopped against the man's shoulder.

The French troopers applauded. "Such acting," shouted one and tossed a coin to the colonel. "Three cheers for María!"

The soldiers shouted their approval, laughed, and then moved off down the street toward the campfires across the bridge. The villagers poured into the house, throwing off their cloaks and gathering around Sotomayor, who lay in front of the *nacimiento*. He opened his eyes as Sarah knelt beside him and gripped his hand. Slowly, slowly, he drew her hand closer, kissed her fingers, and fainted.

One of the women led Sarah to a stool close to the fire as Joseph cut away the colonel's uniform and the men gathered around to offer advice. They chatted companionably among themselves as Joseph and another man poked and prodded the colonel and then uttered "Ahh," and plinked a ball into a basin.

A call from one of the men brought a wife close with a sewing basket and more advice, followed by grunting and shallow breathing from the colonel and then a long silence that was even harder on Sarah's nerves. She leapt to her feet, but the woman pulled her back and handed her a bowl of wheat mush.

Famished, Sarah ate the mush as a call went out for cloth. The usurped María offered her petticoat, which was accepted and ripped into strips and wrapped tight around the colonel, who had long ago drifted into unconsciousness.

Her eyes on the men, Sarah ate another bowl, wondering how she could sit there in that room and stuff herself as the drama of life and pain unfolded in front of her. *I shall have such a story to tell the neighbors back in Kent*, she thought and then dismissed the idea. They would never believe her.

In another minute the colonel, swaddled in María's petticoat and clad only in his smallclothes, was carried into the next room and put between rock-warmed sheets.

Sarah followed and watched from the doorway as the priest blessed him and the innkeeper's wife drew the blankets up to his chin. She glanced at Sarah and put her finger to her lips.

"He will feel much better in the morning, my lady, and so will you."

Feeling strangely empty, Sarah went into the other room again. A pallet was prepared for her close to the fire, and she sat down upon it. Joseph came and stood before her.

"Accept the hospitality of our village, my lady," he said simply and held out his hand to her.

Sarah got to her feet again and took his hand. "I cannot express my gratitude, *señor*," she said.

He patted her cheek. "There is only one payment, my lady. You must do likewise for another."

She nodded. "Thank you," she said again and sat down, more tired than she had ever been before in her life.

As she sat staring into the fire, one of the women brought the colonel's bloody clothes to her and held out the boots. In her hand was a wad of paper, tightly folded.

"My lady, you should see this. It fell out of the colonel's boot."

Mystified, Sarah accepted the paper and unfolded it.

She frowned over the tiny writing, pages of numbers and letters. They made no sense to her at first, but as she studied them, a growing chill covered her body. She moved closer to the fire. They were regimental numbers, French regiments, and a census of artillery. She put them aside and picked up the other papers, also in French. She saw the names Soult, and Ney, and the signature of . . . She looked closer: Bonaparte.

The letters dropped from nerveless fingers. Sarah took a deep breath. "And you thought the French were after you, you silly widgeon," she whispered. "Colonel Sotomayor, you dear, wonderful, aggravating man! What game have you been playing?"

And then suddenly Sarah was furious with him. She tried to resist the anger that shot through her like a ball from a French carbine, irrational anger that left her weak and shaking as it passed quickly.

She folded the papers again, her mind going a thousand miles an hour, even as her body cried out for sleep. The colonel had mentioned Burgos once and then brushed past the word as though he had not said it. "Were you spying on the French, Colonel Sotomayor?" she asked out loud.

The papers formed a sizable wad in her hand. "No wonder you had such a limp, Colonel," she said in English and then laughed.

The woman beside her looked at Sarah in concern.

Sarah touched her arm. "I am not hysterical, *señora*," she assured her. "But I am so tired."

The woman nodded and spread back the blanket. Sarah shook her head. "If you do not mind, could we carry this into the colonel's room? I would feel better if I were there when he woke up."

"Very well, my lady."

They carried the pallet into the room where Joseph kept watch over his unconscious María. He beamed at Sarah and helped make a space for the pallet at the foot of the bed.

Sarah lay down then, clutching the papers tight in her hand, and was asleep before Joseph pinched out the candle.

When she woke, startled out of sleep by a dream of soldiers in pursuit of Joseph and Mary, the colonel was sitting up in bed, letting himself be fed by the lady of the house. Two bright spots of fever burned in his cheeks, but he was single-minded in his devotion to wheat mush. Someone had wrapped a shawl around his bare shoulders, and his curly hair was tousled.

He winked at Sarah, and she smiled back, noting the very small seep of blood through the bandage.

He followed her glance. "Our host is a barber, Sarah, or so his good wife tells me. We fell into excellent hands."

Sarah nodded. She straightened herself around and then sat on the end of the bed until the woman spooned in the last of the mush and wiped the colonel's mouth. She withdrew from the room, a smile on her face.

Without a word, Sarah held out the wad of paper. He took it from her, wincing as he leaned forward. He spread the papers out as she had done the night before, looking at them as if for the first time.

"Bless my soul," he said at last. "Where could these have come from?"

Sarah glared at him. "You know perfectly well," she said indignantly. "Why didn't you tell me I was riding with the most dangerous man in Spain?"

He tried to shrug, winced, and then gave it up as a poor attempt. "I thought you would be afraid."

She could only sigh and look away.

"Happy Christmas, Sarah," he said, and her cup ran over again.

"How could you do that?" she scolded and shook her finger at him. "When I found those papers last night and realized what a game you have been playing—"

"No game," he interrupted, a twinkle in his eyes that mystified her as much as it enraged her.

"You made me so angry! I wanted to march in here and clobber you with your own boot." She paused for breath and narrowed her eyes. "But I never throttle people who are down, no matter how much they deserve it. Consider yourself lucky, you . . . you . . ."

"Thickheaded orange-grower?" he offered helpfully.

She stared at him and nodded slowly, realizing exactly what he meant and why he was looking at her with such love.

"Yes, you marvelous person. I don't wonder that Liria used to scold you."

"As you just did, *querida.*"

"Well, someone has to," she finished lamely, too shy to look at the man in the bed.

The colonel moved carefully, made a face, and lay back against the pillow. "I wish I were equal to this occasion, Sarah. Maybe in a few weeks." His eyes widened with that hopeful look in them she was coming to consider as indispensable to her own happiness. "I am a rapid healer, my heart."

She laughed and watched his face a moment, admiring the beautiful blue of his eyes, grateful, at least for the moment, to see the frown gone from between them. She thought of what Joseph had told her the night before and made up her mind.

Sarah held out her hand for the papers, wiggling her fingers when he seemed reluctant to part with them. He sighed and put the wad into her hand.

Sarah pulled the leather bag from the front of her habit and opened it. She removed the safe-conduct from General Clauzel and waved it in front of his eyes.

"These papers will fit in my boot as well as yours, dear sir, and I have this safe-conduct. I will ask these good folk to point me in the direction of Ciudad Rodrigo and be on my way."

"Oh."

"That's all you can say?"

He held out his hand to her, and she got off the end of the bed and came closer.

"Lean down, Sarah."

She did as he said, and he kissed her lips. "That's for luck," he said and then kissed her again, a kiss that belied his infirmity. "And that is for Colonel Sotomayor. In fact . . ." He stopped, winced, and sat up again. "I wish I could stand up. Sit down, will you? Right here."

He moved his legs, and she sat beside him. "I tried to tell you earlier, you know, back there on the trail."

He paused and chewed on the end of his mustache.

"It is hard to put into words, Sarah."

"Think of some," she said and twinkled her eyes back at him.

"I love you," he said simply. "Marry me."

Sarah smiled and kissed him. "Concise as always but so effective, Colonel Sotomayor. Yes."

"Even more concise. You will be a fine Spaniard, my love."

He kissed her again and several more times, to make up for his taciturnity.

"I'll be back, Luís," Sarah said a moment later, when she could speak again.

"I wouldn't chance it now, Sarah. Not until it is safer."

She rose quickly, even as he grabbed at her, and she stared at him, her hands on her hips. "I don't care what you think. I am coming back as soon as these papers are in British hands."

He smiled. "The answer I was hoping for. Very well, Sarah. Are you in charge now?"

"For a while. Until you are better. Someone must see that you arrive in Barcos at least in time for the Day of Three Kings, and we cannot always expect our Lord to provide."

Luís crossed himself. "He tries, my dear, He tries, but Spain has always been a difficult child." He took her hand. "Be careful, my heart."

She blew a kiss to him and went outside. Joseph stood by the front door, watching the French across the bridge as they doused their fires and mounted.

"I can offer you the loan of a donkey, my lady. It wouldn't be safe to take the colonel's horse," he said when the troops moved off down the road to Ciudad Rodrigo.

"I would welcome it, Joseph. Oh, what is your name? I do not know it."

He smiled. "It is better that way."

"I do not even know the name of this village, Joseph, where the pilgrims of Christ live," she said in her most elegant Spanish.

He bowed. "And I will not tell you that, either. Better sometimes that you know nothing, especially if the French ask you. And they will, my lady. You must go through them to reach Ciudad Rodrigo."

"Pray for me, Joseph," she said simply as she took off an earring and tried to hand it to the man.

Joseph stepped back and held up his hands to ward off her gift. "No, no, my lady. We did not do this for money."

She pressed the earring into his hand. "I know that. But can you use it to buy food for the village?"

He held up the earring, turning it this way and that in the morning light. "This is valuable." He handed it back with a wink. "Save it for when you fall among the English again, lady."

She laughed and put it back in her ear. "Happy Christmas, Joseph."

She did not encounter the French until far into the afternoon. The donkey acquitted itself admirably, picking a surefooted way on the rocky ground that gradually, almost imperceptibly, began to slope away toward a flatter, more gentle land. They were leaving behind the highest places of Spain.

By shading her eyes and squinting into the afternoon sun, Sarah was able to make out Ciudad Rodrigo.

"Merry Christmas to me," she said out loud.

And then the French were upon her. They rode leisurely toward her on the trail. Her heart in her mouth, Sarah dug her heels into the donkey and forced it to continue at a sedate pace toward the soldiers. Finally she dismounted and stood beside the donkey, saving them the trouble of ordering her to the ground. She held her head up and twined her fingers together so they would not shake.

They came close, wary at first, and then riding with confidence when they saw it was only a woman—and a small one at that.

As they looked her over, Sarah stared back and allowed a sigh of relief to escape her. They were not the same troops that had tracked them into the village last night. She looked until she found the man with the most gold braid and sighed again.

He had a rough face, a peasant face, and the hardened look of one who had spent all his adult years in the service of Bonaparte. His skin was coarse and lined from years in the outdoors, facing into the turbulent winds that blew all across Europe. He was a peasant, she was sure of it, one of the many who had risen from the ranks through a lifetime of soldiering. He probably could not read.

"You are the Englishwoman."

It was not a question but a statement, delivered in a flat, uncultured voice that further betrayed humble origins.

"I am," Sarah answered in French. "Lady Sarah Brill Comstock of Mansfield, Kent. I am on my way to the British lines in Lisbon, and I have a safe-conduct."

"Then produce it, *mademoiselle*."

Sarah pulled the safe-conduct from her pocket and handed it to the lieutenant, who looked at it a long time. Sarah came closer and pointed.

"See you there, sir, it says, 'General Bertrand Clauzel.'"

She had pointed to her own name. The lieutenant nodded and Sarah could barely contain herself. *So you cannot read, sir,* she thought. *I thought as much.*

He nodded finally and handed it back to her.

"Where is the colonel?"

She did not attempt to hedge about the issue. She raised her head as her eyes filled with tears. "He is dead, sir, killed last night from ambush."

The lieutenant held out his hand. "Give the papers to us then, my lady. That wily wolf we have tracked from Burgos would never permit them to be lost."

Sarah said nothing. The lieutenant came closer. She gritted her teeth as he drew his sword and calmly put the point at her neck and flicked at the leather string.

"*Mademoiselle,* I suggest that you present it to us before we are forced to strip you right here on the road."

And find the notes in my boot, she thought. *Never.*

With steady fingers, Sarah pulled out the pouch. The tears spilled onto her cheeks as she opened the bag for the last time and pulled out the Columbus papers.

She smoothed them out for one last look, remembering the long hours in the archives, James's great joy at finding Columbus' diary, and the feverish race to copy it all down as the French closed in. She handed them to the lieutenant with a great show of reluctance.

He snatched them from her as she sobbed.

"He told me never to let those fall into your hands," she cried, noting that the other soldiers backed away, uneasy with her tears.

"Ah, but here they are," said the lieutenant, looking at the words in old Spanish that told of Columbus's first voyage, with the exact readings of that first landfall. "The entire troop strength of every army we have in Spain." He bowed over Sarah's hand and kissed it. "How good to have this back again, *mademoiselle*. Such a Christmas present you have given me."

He turned and waved the Columbus papers to the others before folding them and tucking them into his tunic. "A promotion for the lieutenant, no?" he shouted, and his troops cheered.

Sarah dried her eyes. "May I go now, sir?" she asked. "I would remind you that I am an Englishwoman and not entirely friendless in the world."

"You may go." The lieutenant eyed her donkey for a moment and then waved her on. "Because it is Christmas and I am in a fine mood, we will not take your donkey."

"So good of you," she murmured. *And may I be far from here when your superiors in Burgos shout you out of the room for the Columbus papers and strip you down to private.*

The lieutenant helped her mount and handed her the reins. Sarah nodded in his direction and continued down the road to Ciudad Rodrigo.

When the troops were out of sight, she patted the donkey. "I should be sad, of course," she said. "All that James and I worked for is gone, but truly, Señor Burro, I have carried out Joseph's condition, have I not? I have returned a favor to a ... friend." She smiled. "And it would please the Three Kings."

Her voice lingered over the words, and Lady Sarah Comstock made another resolve.

She arrived in Ciudad Rodrigo at dark and was met at the city wall by a detachment of the 45th Foot. They looked scarcely better than the French troops, dirty and wearing uniforms long past repair or the efficacy of a scrubbing board. They smelled no better, either. Sarah wrinkled her nose and thanked the good Lord that it was winter.

She soon found herself in the middle of a group of officers, who hurried her into the stable that made up headquarters. She told them who she was, sat down, and calmly extended her right foot.

"If you would be so kind, sir, I have something that will interest you in that boot."

With a puzzled smile, the officer pulled off her boot.

Sarah thanked him prettily and reached inside, extracting the wad of paper.

"Colonel Luís Sotomayor sends Christmas greetings to the Marquess of Wellesley and apologizes that he could not carry these to Lisbon in person."

At the mention of Sotomayor's name, the major grabbed the papers and took them to the table, spreading them out and then uttering a low whistle. The others crowded around in silence that was broken by loud huzzahs and soldierly embraces.

Sarah smiled at their exuberance. "Little boys," she whispered. "Why must you go to war?"

The major remembered himself then and returned to Sarah. "The colonel?" he asked.

"He was wounded in ambush, but he is well enough. I told him that I would see the papers safely to Ciudad Rodrigo. Can I trust you to carry them to Lisbon?"

"Oh, most assuredly, Lady Sarah," the major replied. "And you too, of course. In no time, we'll have you safely home in England."

Sarah shook her head. "No, I think not."

The major stared at her, but he was too well-bred to say what he thought.

"No, sir, I will return to that little village. The colonel will need my help in getting to Barcos, where his children await him." She put up her hand when the major attempted argument. "I am over twenty-one, sir, and I know my own mind. I would ask the loan of another donkey, if you can spare one."

One of the subalterns spoke up, his voice eager, impulsive. "Lady Sarah, you may take my horse. Nothing is too good for such a heroine."

She smiled at his eagerness but shook her head. "I would not get very far on my way with such a steed, sir, before someone from some army or another relieved me of it. No, I prefer a donkey—and a modest one at that."

She looked at the major. "Sir, if you could spare a little food, it would not be wasted."

"Of course, Lady Sarah," he said, "but, really, I must protest."

Sarah touched his arm. "I know that you mean well, sir, and I thank you, but I will return to the village and go to Barcos and you cannot stop me. If you confiscate Joseph's donkey, I will walk."

The officers were silent then, the air tense. Then the major smiled and shook his head. "Very well, if you are sure."

"I have never been more sure."

Sarah looked about her at the other men. "There are two little girls in Barcos waiting for their father. There will be no visit from the Three Kings without a little help from you."

The major bowed. "I think we can find some candy about. You there, Monroe."

"Sir," said the eager man who would have given his horse away.

"That scarf about your neck is so colorful. Good enough for a Spanish lady of . . . of . . ."

"Four years, sir, I believe."

"Excellent. And I believe I have a doll I was saving for my own daughter. I can easily procure another."

"Capital," Sarah said.

"Two dolls, sir," said another officer. "For the other one who is . . ."

"Two."

"You will stay the night, won't you, Lady Sarah?"

"Oh, yes, and with pleasure," Sarah said, taking off her gloves. "I have several letters to write."

The letter to James's Oxford don would be difficult.

She would not even mention the Columbus papers. That scholarship would have to rest now until someone else in distant years came across the papers again, if anyone ever did. She sighed, clasped her hands together, and then put Columbus from her mind.

The letter to her father would be no easier. He would grieve for James and not understand what she was doing.

He might even disinherit me over this marriage, she thought as she watched the officers' cook bustle about over the simple meal. *A pity Papa's so high in the instep about deference due to English titles*, she thought. *He would only get all tight about the mouth if I told him that the Sotomayors were prominent in Spain at the time of Trajan, back when his Comstock ancestors were still painting themselves blue. Ah well. Father cannot tamper with that little legacy from my mother, and it will be enough to rebuild the estates and buy cattle. And perhaps if Papa has Sotomayor grandchildren with those beautiful blue eyes and blond hair . . .*

The major stood before her again, suspiciously blurry.

Sarah dabbed at her eyes and accepted the battered cup he held out to her. She raised it high.

"A toast to Christmas, Lady Sarah, and a prosperous new year for all of us."

"Hear, hear," she said and drank deep.

ABOUT THE AUTHOR

Photo by Marie Bryner-Bowles, Bryner Photography

Carla Kelly is a veteran of the New York and international publishing world. The author of more than thirty novels and novellas for Donald I. Fine Co., Signet, and Harlequin, Carla is the recipient of two Rita Awards (think Oscars for romance writing) from Romance Writers of America and two Spur Awards (think Oscars for western fiction) from Western Writers of America. She is also a recipient of Whitney Awards for *Borrowed Light* and *My Loving Vigil Keeping*.

Recently, she's been writing Regency romances (think *Pride and Prejudice*) set in the Royal Navy's Channel Fleet during the Napoleonic Wars between England and France. She comes by her love of the ocean from her childhood as a Navy brat.

Carla's history background makes her no stranger to footnote work, either. During her National Park Service days at the Fort Union Trading Post National Historic Site, Carla edited Friedrich Kurz's fur trade journal. She recently completed a short history of Fort Buford, where Sitting Bull surrendered in 1881.

Following the "dumb luck" principle that has guided their lives, the Kellys recently moved to Wellington, Utah, from North Dakota and couldn't be happier in their new location. In her spare time, Carla volunteers at the Western Mining and Railroad Museum in Helper, Utah. She likes to visit her five children, who live here and there around the United States. Her favorite place in Utah is Manti, located after a drive on the scenic byway through Huntington Canyon.

And why is she so happy these days? Carla doesn't have to write in laundry rooms and furnace rooms now, because she has an actual office.

31901055245791

0 26575 12272 5